Rosabelle's Way

WELCOME TO CHANCE
BOOK 2

Elsa Kurt

Rosabelle's Way

Limitless Publishing, LLC
Kailua, HI 96734
www.limitlesspublishing.com

Formatting: Limitless Publishing

ISBN-13: 978-1-64034-854-7
ISBN-10: 1-64034-854-9

Dedication

To my husband, always.

Chapter 1

Be of Good Cheer

Rosabelle checked her lipstick in the little sunshine-yellow Mini Cooper's rearview mirror. She caught sight of her red-tipped nose then met her eyes in the frost-rimmed glass. "Not too shabby, Rosie," she said under her breath.

"Rosie, babe. C'mon, I gotta roll." Miles rapped his knuckles hard against the passenger side window and widened his eyes at Rosabelle, stomping his feet in the packed snow and puffing into his red hands.

"I told you to let me pull in first. It's your own fault. And who taught you how to shovel a driveway? It'll be a sheet of ice when we get back tonight."

"What? Roll the window down, Rosie. I can't hear you."

Rosabelle sighed and cracked the window.

1

"Never mind. I'll see you tonight? Don't forget, my parents will be here, so please behave."

"Aw, c'mon, babe, you know I'll—"

"Behave, Miles. I mean it. And do me a favor?"

Miles stomped again and huffed into his cold hands. "Anything you want, if you promise to move it."

"Say it again."

"What?" asked Miles blankly. Then, dawning lit his face, and he beamed. "Fine. I…love…you. I LOVE you, Rosie. Happy now?"

"Completely. I love you too. And I love my necklace. It's perfect."

Miles gave his aw-shucks grin and blew her a kiss. "See you tonight, babe. Now please back out so I can get to work. Oh, and I need you to—"

Rosabelle closed the window as he spoke, laughing at his indignation. The old Rosabelle would've hung on his every word and jumped at his command. However, the *new* Rosabelle would not. The new Rosabelle Waterman was loved by and in love with the man of her dreams. She was confident, secure, and strong. That's what she told her reflection every morning in the bathroom mirror when she felt anxious, which she did as she backed out onto Dogwood Drive and drove toward Chance Public Library.

Today, Rosabelle Waterman would be finalizing the last details of her first ever solo art exhibit, happening in May. She'd done several shows where'd she'd been one of many, but this was all her. Fourteen paintings, various sizes, subjects, and mediums on display for everyone to see. And judge.

And criticize. And— "No, Rosie. A positive mind brings positive results. You've got this. You are as talented as anyone else. You deserve this. All will go well. Breathe."

Rosabelle inhaled sharply through her nose, counted to four, then exhaled slowly as she counted to eight. After doing this three times, she decided she felt much better and even managed a shaky smile.

The roads had been plowed overnight but a fine layer of fresh snow coated the macadam, making it slick and dangerous. Rosabelle was grateful she listened to Ricky Baker about putting on snow tires last week. Just in the nick of time too. The first snowfall of the season, two weeks before Christmas. It was far from her favorite time of the year—she missed her flower garden—but it *was* her favorite holiday. And her first one with a boyfriend. They'd yet to refer to each other as boyfriend or girlfriend in public or change their Facebook statuses to 'In a Relationship,' but they *had* said those three little words this morning. *That* told her everything she needed to know on the status of their relationship.

On the radio, a smooth baritone voice announced, "Good morning, you're listening to Allan, Mike, and Mary on Lite 100.5 WRCH. Hey, it is a Winter Wonderland out there, isn't it? Just in time for Christmas too. A time to be of good cheer and all that stuff. We've got holiday music playing for you all day long. Have a favorite song? Give us a call. Here's one of my favorites right now…"

The Little Drummer Boy—the Bing Crosby and

David Bowie version—began and Rosabelle looked at the dash to turn up the volume. The moment she did, the Mini Cooper began to slide. Her heart jumped, but her father's voice cautioned in her mind.

Pump the brakes, sweet pea. Just pump 'em, don't mash 'em. Atta girl.

When the car righted, Rosabelle released a small shuddering laugh and loosened her death grip from the steering wheel.

"All good. It's all good." That's what Miles would've said right then.

Her heart rate steadied, and she started to sing along in earnest with David Bowie. The light up ahead at the intersection of Elm and Old Maine gave her the green to go straight through. Everything seemed to be going her way. New hairstyle, a boyfriend, a new perspective. To top it off, her art hobby was becoming her art career. Yes, Rosabelle Waterman was finally living her dream life.

Rosabelle smiled and drummed the wheel with her fingertips to the beat of the music. She could see Mae in the window of the café, serving coffee to the Brightsiders. Across the street, Carla and Lewis were rehanging the garland over Lucky Loos that must have fallen overnight. She'd toot her horn and wave as she passed.

Rosabelle saw in her peripheral a dark mass moving toward her. There was a sound—high and screechy—that she couldn't place until it was too late. Fat Chris's protruding saucer eyes stared out at her from his pasty moon-face behind the windshield of his van, his knuckles white and his huge body leaned way back against his seat. His mouth was in an 'O' and Rosabelle knew he was saying one word, long and drawn out.

"Nooooo…"

Dumbly, Rosabelle thought, *You've got to pump the brakes, Fat—*

The thought cut off abruptly. A crunch, scrape, and glass bursting impact of metal to metal caused Rosabelle to think nothing more.

Chapter 2

Comfort and Joy

"Are you sure you're up to it, Mr. B.? One more week of rest?"

"I see my wife has gotten to you too, hasn't she?"

Mae looked from Mr. B. to Mrs. B.—who'd kept her nose to her menu during the whole exchange—and stammered, "I…she…I mean we never—"

"Oh, never mind, Mae. He's a stubborn old goat who doesn't listen. You have an arrhythmia, Charles. Nothing to play around with at your age. The doctor said so."

"Doctor-shmocter. Doogie Houster—"

"Howser," corrected both Mae and Mrs. Brightsider.

"Whatever. I told him, just as I'm telling you two—I had too much coffee and it set off my ticker.

6

I'm fine. Open Mic, tonight. I'll be here with my horn. You get your singing voice ready. Got it?"

"Yes, Mr. B.," grinned Mae. She gave him a wink then grimaced apologetically when she caught Mrs. Brightsider's raised eyebrow. "Sorry, Mrs. B. Look, decaf only from here on out."

Mae just finished pouring their coffees when Feather Anne exclaimed loudly, "Oh, shit!"

"Feath—" Mae paused mid-admonishment and followed her sister's shocked gaze. They all did.

Mae, Feather Anne, the Brightsiders, Bruce, the Mitchels, Joel and Charlotte Asheby, and Elise Martino watched in horror as Fat Chris's midnight blue van plowed into Rosabelle Waterman's bright yellow Cooper in the heart of the intersection, crumpling it like it was a Matchbox car.

Joel—with Bruce on his heels—was the first one out the door and running toward the gruesome scene.

"Call 911, dear," said Mr. B. solemnly.

"Oh, my God," whispered Mrs. B. against her shaking hands.

Feather Anne shook as well, tears brimming in her gray eyes. Mae ran past her and grabbed the phone off the cradle. Her own hand trembled as she pressed the keys. With her arm around Feather Anne's still too-bony shoulders, Mae spoke breathlessly into the phone when Lucy Hatch answered.

"911. Are you calling with an emergency?"

"Yes, Lucy, it's Mae. There's been a terrible accident. It's on the corner of Old Main and Elm. It's bad. They'll need ambulances and—"

7

"Slow down, Mae. How many vehicles are involved?"

"Two. Please, just send—"

"Are there any injuries?"

"I—Jesus, yes. I mean there must be. It's Rosabelle Waterman. Her tiny car got hit by Fat— by Chris O'Brien's van."

"Oh, shit. I mean, okay, we've got help on the way."

Mae hung up and joined the others at the windows. Lewis, along with Bart Sheffield, had joined Joel and Bruce in the middle of the road. The men circled the crushed car, trying to see around the airbags. Joel shouted orders and pushed Fat Chris— who was now out of his van and alternately gesturing and burying his head in his hands—away from the scene and onto the curb. He had on work boots, jeans, and a too-small t-shirt that exposed his bright pink belly, but he acted impervious to the cold.

Joey Mitchel said, "He's in shock. Mae, do you have any blankets?"

"I'll get one," sniffed Feather Anne.

In a flash, she was back with the thick wool blanket Mae kept in the storage room. Joey took it from her, tousled her hair, and jogged out past the wreckage to the large man. At the same time, Jillie Jacobson tottered out of the newly renamed Jillie J. Travel in her ruby heels and smart business suit. She had her hands pressed to her cheeks, and even through the glass, she could be heard shouting, "Oh, my God. Oh, my God, I saw the whole thing."

Mrs. B. glanced up at Mae in dismay.

8

"I'll get her," said Mae as she strode to the door. "Jillie! Get in here. You're no help to them out there, come on inside."

Jillie—resembling a soap opera actress in the scene of her life—turned from the accident to Mae, then back to the intersection. Mae sagged against the door and swore. Then she pushed the door completely open and went out to get Jillie.

"Come on, Jillie. Unless you're a doctor or a nurse, you'll only be in the way. Let them do what they can until help arrives."

Jillie let Mae guide her into the café and sit her at a table. Feather Anne needed to be distracted from what was happening outside as well.

"Feather Anne, bring Jillie a cup of tea and a scone, please."

"Peach, if you have it. And honey for the tea? Maybe a lemon wedge too," said Jillie.

Feather Anne opened her mouth, but Mae intervened. "Of course, Jillie. No problem. Go on, Feather Anne. *Please*."

In the meantime, two ambulances and four cruisers had pulled up to the scene. Lights and sirens filled the air and everyone in the café drew in closer to one another. The last time there was an accident of this magnitude in Chance was ten years prior. The Luscheks' only son, Dylan, had lost control of their SUV at the start of Chapman Bridge. They'd had flooding that week, and the Pathfinder had hydroplaned over a puddle, sending the inexperienced driver headlong into the concrete pylons. He was thrown through the windshield and died instantly.

"Do you think she's dead?" whispered Feather Anne.

"No, honey. Let's hope for the best," said Mrs. B. brightly. But the gaze that found and held Mae's showed no such hope.

"Say," said Krista Mitchel, "aren't her folks in town? Someone should call them."

And Miles, thought Mae with a start. She ran back to the phone and dialed Miles's office. On the third ring, he answered. "Hannaford Realty. Where your dreams—"

"Miles, it's Mae. You need to get here, now."

"Aw, that's sweet, baby Mae, but I—"

"Shut up, Miles. This is serious. Miles, it's…it's Rosabelle. She's been in an accident."

"Rosie? No, I just—I'm on my way."

Miles dropped the phone onto either his desk or the floor, and Mae could hear him shout to whoever else was there, "I've got an emergency. Cancel my appointments."

Mae hung up the phone, feeling relieved at his response. Rosabelle was *so* in love with him, but who knew with Miles? He was ever the showman, playing a role for an imaginary audience. Now Mae was unsure whether to hope his feelings for Rosabelle were real, or superficial. If she didn't make it…

"Mae, they got her out of the car. It doesn't look good." Bruce had come back inside, his face grim and pale.

"Babe, sit. You're white as a sheet," said Elise, coming up behind him.

"She's right. Go sit with Elise. I've called

Miles."

Normally, Bruce would've scoffed and spat something derisive at the mention of Miles Hannaford, but he let it go with merely a head shake. Mae left them and went outside. She heard Miles before she could see him.

"Rosie! Rosie!"

He'd run from his office two blocks away, either knowing that he'd get there faster or just in a blind panic. Regardless, he made it there as the EMTs carefully strapped Rosabelle's unmoving, bloodied body onto the gurney. He stopped beside Mae, panting and staring uncomprehendingly at the sight before them. The impact had spun Rosabelle's little car and the destroyed driver's side faced them.

Mae put a hand on Miles's arm and squeezed. He focused on her with wide, anguished eyes. "Jesus, Mae. I just told her I loved her for the first time this morning. I—"

"Get over there, Miles. Hurry."

He sprinted to the gurney, calling out his pet name for Rosabelle. The medics tried to keep him back, but when he shouted, "I'm her boyfriend and I'm not leaving her side," they let him climb into the back of the ambulance with them on the promise he'd let them do their job.

The ambulance carrying Rosabelle left with lights and sirens wailing. The second had Fat Chris sitting on the bumper, staring vacantly out at the snow-dusted road as the EMT assessed him and a police officer asked questions. Someone made the decision to take him in for further observation and that ambulance left with just its lights spinning, and no sirens.

All that was left was Ricky Baker's tow trucks and police, who—led by Joel—went around taking statements and recreating the accident. By the time the cars were gone, and the glass and debris swept away, it was afternoon. The lunch crowd came in as usual but in somber tones and hushed whispers. News of the accident had spread within an hour. As Mae traveled the room with plates and glasses, she caught snippets of conversations at each table.

"I heard she hit the windshield, and she's in a coma."

"And just before Christmas too."

"Fat Chris is going to go to jail."

"Poor thing has an art show coming up."

"Did you hear that Miles Hannaford rode in the ambulance with her? *Miles Hannaford*, can you imagine?"

Mae bit her tongue and said nothing. She was counting the hours until she could close the café and leave with anxious dread. Three more, she told herself, then she'd go to the hospital and see Rosabelle. She gave an involuntary shudder at the thought of that place. The last time she'd been there was when her father died, nearly six years ago.

The harsh fluorescent lighting, the scratchy, rough fabric of the office style waiting room chairs, the constant intercom chatter, and stethoscope draped white coats. The sound of the doctor's shoes tap-clapping against the speckled cream linoleum floor as he came down the hall. It came rushing back in a torrent.

"You can come back in the room, Miss Huxley.

It—it might be time to say your goodbyes. Do you have anyone coming to be with you?"

"I—yes, my aunt. She's on her way," Mae replied in a voice that sounded far away to her own ears. She'd known this moment was coming for months, and yet it felt surreal. *Time to say your goodbyes*. How? How was she supposed to let the best man and father in the world go?

A hand on her shoulder brought Mae back to the present. "Hello, sweetheart. "

Mae cried out, "William! You're home? But you weren't due back until next week. How—"

"I hoped to surprise you. Are you surprised, love?" William smiled at Mae but then saw that her face was wan. The café was unusually subdued for the number of people inside. "What is it? Has something happened?"

"Oh, William, it was awful. It *is* awful. Rosabelle's been in a car accident—it happened right outside at the intersection—and she's in the hospital in intensive care. We don't know if she's going to make it."

Mae's voice broke and William pulled her into his embrace. "I'm so sorry, Mae. What can I do to help?"

"Just having you home is enough. I've missed you."

Mae buried her face in his chest, curling her fingers around the lapels of his heavy coat and pressing them against her cheeks. She inhaled his reassuring, familiar scent, and suddenly everything was better.

"I've missed you more than words can say,

13

sweetheart." William pressed his lips to the top of her head, and just as Mae had done, he breathed in her fragrance. It filled him with a contentment he'd never known before her. But then a thought caused him to frown and pull back, so he could see her face again.

He asked, "But why are you still here? You and Rosabelle have grown so close. Surely Bruce was willing to stay so you could get over to the hospital?"

"I—he—yes, he would've. But I didn't—I couldn't…"

William's expression softened. "Say no more, love. I understand. The hospital, yes?"

Mae nodded, hot shame and guilt flushing her cheeks. "Am I a terrible person for not going right away?"

She gazed up at William with such mournful eyes that he had to kiss her. He took her face in his hands, caressed her soft cheek with his thumb, then pressed his lips to hers. "You could never be a terrible person. It isn't in your bones. We'll go together if you'd like."

Mae bobbed her head emphatically, knowing she was being childish, but unable to help herself. Yes, she could have gone on her own, but having William by her side, holding her hand and lending his strength, made it that much more bearable.

Chapter 3

Bells Will Be Ringing

Bruce flipped the OPEN sign to CLOSED with a long sigh. It had been a hell of a day. The image of Rosabelle Waterman's bloodied face and broken body being pulled from the wreckage of what used to be her car flashed in his mind repeatedly. The moments just before Feather Anne's exclamation and those that followed replayed as well.

He'd just stolen a kiss from Elise and was in the midst of telling her he'd pick up Chinese food on his way over later. *Do you want General*—the sentence hung unfinished on his lips—when his peripheral caught sight of the yellow mini Cooper and the advancing van. His mind made the rapid-fire synapses, connecting Feather Anne's words to what he saw happening. Amazingly, he even had time to think, "Shit, I don't want the kid to see this," and "Please don't let them slam into the building,"

15

along with maybe a dozen other thoughts.

"Hey, you doin' okay, Brat?"

"Yeah, I'm all right, I guess. You?"

Feather Anne threw a dish towel at Bruce's head and missed.

"Better work on your aim if you're gonna play softball next season."

"Who says I'm playing? I didn't agree. Yet," she added with a smirk.

Little shit, Bruce grinned. A year in and this kid had them wrapped around her finger like it was nothing. She used her kid powers to get him to teach her how to play basketball and football, now she was on to softball, and God knew what else. She got William to take her to not one, but three Broadway shows in the city, Joel Asheby to let her join the police explorers—even though she was technically not old enough—and Pedro Villeneuve allowed her to babysit all three of their kids. What she'd lacked in the way of father figures in the first half of her life, she was making up for in spades.

Mae busted their chops—said they were spoiling her—but she loved it. Sure, the kid gave Mae a run for her money nearly every day, but they'd bonded since Gina Byrd skipped town. Anger boiled up in his chest every time he thought of poor Feather Anne being abandoned by her shitty excuse of a mother, but Elise was quick to remind him if she hadn't, then the kid might not ever have had the life she deserved.

"Oh, you're playing, all right. You didn't get my ass out there the past month practicing your pitch for you to chicken out."

"I'm no chicken, buttface."

Bruce tucked his fists into his armpits and clucked loudly. "Chicken says what?"

Feather Anne threw another towel at him, this time hitting him square in the face. When he yanked it away, she was staring at him in that grave way that reminded him of Mae when she got so serious.

"I'm okay, Brat. Just—damn, huh?"

Feather Anne's brow crimped, and she nodded. "She gonna die, you think?"

"I dunno, kid. I hope not. Let's finish up here, and you can come with me to Elise's if you want. Okay?"

"Yeah, sure. I'll watch Gianna so you two can make out." She giggled and ducked as Bruce tossed the rag back at her, then ran into the kitchen for her book bag.

"Next snow day, I'm tellin' Mae to leave you and your fresh mouth at home," he called after her. Bruce shook his head. Kid still had Gina Byrd's genes, that was for sure. He grabbed his cell phone from his back pocket and dialed Elise's number.

"Hey, babe. Slight change of plans. I got Feather Anne with me. That okay?"

"Feather Anne? Why isn't she with Mae?"

There was an edge to her tone that Bruce tried to ignore. They'd been over this whole Mae/Feather Anne stuff already. Several times. He was always going to be friends with Mae and he was always going to watch out for Feather Anne. Period.

"Because Mae went to the hospital to see Rosabelle."

"Why isn't she with William, then? I heard he's

back in town."

"How did you hear—you know what, never mind that. He's with Mae. She didn't want to drive there by herself."

"Of course, she didn't," Elise sighed into the receiver. "Yeah, it's fine. Whatever." Then, softening her tone, "Gianna loves playing with her. Tell her she can stay over if she wants."

Bruce smiled into the phone. "Oh, yeah? And how about me? Can I stay over?"

A low chuckle, then, "Well, if you remember to ask for extra fortune cookies this time, then yes. You may."

They said goodbye, laughing amiably enough, but Bruce stuck the phone back in his pocket with a small frown. As much as he reassured Elise that his feelings for Mae were in the past, she still had 'reservations.' Which was just her way of saying-not-saying that his being around Mae caused her to feel insecure. Bruce understood and tried to ease the tension by suggesting the foursome get together back in the spring. It had been a disaster almost from the get-go.

Bruce and Elise had shown up at Mae's house at eight p.m., a bottle of red wine in hand. Mae had started martinis for everyone, something Elise didn't usually drink. But, for the sake of agreeableness, she accepted hers with a wary smile. William—who Bruce had nothing in common with aside from Mae—did his best to find topics of conversation they could join.

By the second round of drinks, everyone relaxed, and the story sharing began. William told them of the time he aided the rescue of an orphaned den of baby Bunyoro rabbits in Africa. Elise told about the time she'd taken Gianna to the mall and she became transfixed by the Easter bunny, so much so that when Elise tried to take her away, she screamed bloody murder until she brought her back.

This led to Bruce saying, "Oh, hey—Mae, do you remember the time that baby bunny got stuck in the fencing around the garden in back of the café?"

"Oh, my God," exclaimed Mae, slapping Bruce's knee, "yes! The poor little guy. I'd put deer netting over the snap peas and—"

Bruce picked up the story, "—you came running in, crying, 'Bunny! It's gonna die,' so I drop everything—"

"Like a madman! You ran out there so fast, I didn't even finish—"

"—your sentence and I get out there and see this little brown thing, all frantic and spazzy. I thought for sure it was gonna break its own leg. So—"

"So, Bruce goes in the garden and starts talking real soft. He's all like, 'It's okay, little bun-bun. Moose'll get you outta here,' and even with those giant hands of his, he managed to calm this wild animal, get it untangled, then carry it across the street to the little field, and set it free. Hero, am I right?"

"Aw, please. It was nothing."

Bruce and Mae turned to look at William and Elise. Both had gone quiet. William had a small, polite smile resting on his lips and wiped at an invisible spot on his pants. Elise made a slow display of setting her glass on the table and standing.

Without looking at anyone, she said, "Could I speak to you outside, Bruce?"

Bruce shrugged and stood, looking at Mae in puzzlement. Mae shrugged and mouthed 'sorry' for some reason. He hadn't known what was wrong, but Elise was swift to clue him in.

"Seriously," she hissed once he'd closed the French door to the backyard. "Do you not have any idea how I feel right now? The two of you, with your shared stories, and—and your shared *history*. Jesus, it was the Bruce and Mae Show in there."

"What? Aw, come on, Lissie. I told you, Mae and I are *friends*. Nothing more. Yeah, sure, we got a history, but that's *all* it is—history. Babe, I need you to find a way to be okay with this. Trust me. It's me and you. And not for nothin', William seemed cool with it."

"Oh, please. William is too classy and refined to make a fuss. I'll bet he's going to tell her to knock it off too."

"Oh, he's 'classy' and 'refined,' huh? Sounds like you got a little crush on him. You sure it's not me who has to worry?"

Elise punched him in the stomach—not lightly, either—and told him to shut up and kiss her, which he willingly did. They went back inside and carried on as if nothing was wrong, but the air in the room had thickened and everyone felt it. They made promises to do it again soon, but seven months after the first double date, there'd yet to be a second.

"Hit the lights, kid, will ya?"

Feather Anne thumbed down each switch,

sending the room into darkness starting from the farthest part of the restaurant to the kitchen, then pressed the power button on the iHome. Dean Martin stopped singing the chorus of *Amore* and she could hear Bruce out front finish the line.

"Don't quit your day job." She smirked.

He put her in a headlock and gave her a noogie. "You know what you need? Karate lessons. You gotta be able to get out of positions like this. We gotta sign you up."

He let her go and Feather Anne rolled her eyes as she smoothed her hair. Shyly, she said, "Hey, Bruce?"

Bruce caught the change in her tone. "What's up, sport?"

"When you—when you and Elise have your own kids, are you gonna still have time for me?"

A lump formed in Bruce's throat and he swallowed hard. "Always. I promise."

She threw her skinny arms around his waist and gave a quick, surprisingly strong squeeze, then shouted, "Last one in the truck is a rotten egg!"

"Yeah, yeah. Cheater! You know I gotta lock the door first." He shook his head, laughing. Feather Anne's words rang in his head, though. *When you and Elise have your own kids*. Right then, Bruce Grady realized how much he wanted exactly that. He wanted the whole thing—wife, kids, house. He wanted to put up the damn picket fence and buy the dog.

He and Elise got along great most of the time. Sure, she had a hot temper, but she was passionate in everything she did. It kept him on his toes, for sure. She was a great mom, kept herself in shape, and she was smart. Best of all, Bruce believed she truly loved him. So, what more could he ask for in a woman? He zipped his fleece, scanned the mottled, gray December sky, and thought, '*Maybe it's time to take the next step.*'

Bruce climbed into the cab of the truck and glanced over at Feather Anne. Laughing, he said, "You remind me of the Michelin Man in that coat."

Feather Anne scowled at him. "Who the hell is the Michigan Man?"

"Language, kid. And never mind. That's a hell of a coat you got there."

"Language, old man. And I like it, so there. Put on some music, will ya? *Not* Christmas music, either."

"Not Christmas music, huh? Okay, how about this?"

Bruce put on a station known for oldies. The sweet sounds of The Dixie Cups filled the truck. *Chapel of Love.* He looked at the stereo in the dash in disbelief. Talk about timing. How could he *not* think it was a sign? At that moment—in his truck with the Mini Michelin Man with a mouth beside him, behind the café, on the day that they saw a terrible accident hours earlier—Bruce Grady decided. He was going to propose to Elise on Christmas Eve. Which meant he needed to get a ring, fast.

Chapter 4

Tis The Season

"I imagine your Open Mic is canceled for tonight, Charles."

"Well, just in case, I want to be ready. Check her Facepage thing. Maybe's she's got an update?"

Georgie Brightsider tsked at her husband. "It's Facebook, dear. You know perfectly well what it's called. I've seen you checking my profile."

Charles gave a disgruntled grumble. "Facebook, Facepage, all the same difference. What do you people do on there all day but share pictures of food and gossip? I prefer to use the inter-web for more important things."

Georgie, who'd been sitting at her desk perusing the social media site in question, turned to her husband—who sat at his desk, on *his* computer— lowered her reading glasses, and said, "And what, pray tell, is it that you are doing on there that's so important?"

Without glancing up, he responded, "YouTube."

"YouTube," exclaimed Georgie, "what important things are you learning from that?"

"Well, I learned that I can watch entire performances by Itzhak Perlman, Andre Rieu, and just about anyone else I want. I even found a few of my own performances with the orchestra. Oh, and a tutorial on how to make a table from old pallets."

"And that's important to you right now? Making a table out of pallets?"

Charles batted a hand in her direction dismissively, then turned up the volume on his computer. Georgie lifted her eyes to the ceiling and went back to Facebook. They sat in companionable silence for another half hour, until Georgie exclaimed, "Oh, the Watermans have posted an update on poor Rosabelle!"

"Well, what does it say?" asked Charles.

"She's still in intensive care, but awake and alert. She has swelling on her spine, but the doctors are hopeful. Oh, dear, her leg is broken in three places, and her pelvis is fractured."

"It's a miracle she's alive," said Charles solemnly.

Georgie tutted her agreement and began tapping on the keys rapidly. "I've just told them that we are so glad to hear she's going to be all right and that we send our love."

"Well done, my dear. Now check the Mae's Café page and see if she's canceled or not."

"You check. Look, I made you your own account. Here's your login information. Don't lose it, now."

Georgie stood gingerly from her chair and walked the blue sticky note with her neat script over to Charles. He took it from her with a frown, read the words, then smiled.

"Username, Charles Brightsider. Password, georgiesman. Why, yes, I am. Yesterday, today, and always, my dear."

He rested his hands on Georgie's still slender hips and pulled her to him. Mabel and Rufus sprang from their dog beds and jumped and wagged at their feet, wanting in on the affection.

After they obliged the dogs with attention, Georgie said, "Sign in and look at your profile picture." She stayed beside him, her arm draped over his broad and only mildly stooped shoulder.

After a minute or two, they were staring at a square framed photograph of themselves on their wedding day, fifty years ago. Charles reached for his cheaters and peered again.

"Look at us, huh, Georgie? Weren't we something?"

"We still are, if you ask me." Georgie smiled. She dropped a kiss on the top of his silver hair, and he wrapped an arm around her waist.

"Indeed, my dear. We are. And you are as bewitching as the day we met."

"Oh, stop—"

"I mean it. No one has ever compared, Georgie. I'm the luckiest man alive."

"You sweet old fool, you. I'm the lucky one. We've had a good life, haven't we? Even with not ever—"

"I know, sweetheart. I know. You and me against the world. That's how it's always been, how it'll always be."

"And Rufus and Mabel, don't forget," added Georgie, dabbing at the corners of her eyes with her knuckle. "Speaking of which, I'd better get them outside to do their business."

"Would you like me to take them?"

"No, no. I could use some fresh air. You go on, play around on there." She waved at the screen. "I'm sure you'll get the hang of it in no time. Just don't leave your 'CAP LOCK' on when you type. People think you're shouting at them when you do that."

"Shouting? I don't—oh, I suppose that makes sense."

"Yes, the Watermans and Gloria Van Bergen do it all the time. It can be quite annoying. I mean, just wear your glasses, for heaven's sake."

Georgie tutted again and called for the dogs to go outside. They didn't need to be asked twice and were out of the office door before she even finished speaking. Charles went back to the computer screen and gazed at the photo of him and his bride. They'd been caught in a moment of laughter, and Georgie's hand was against Charles's cheek. If he recalled correctly, he'd just whispered something fresh in her ear, and she'd playfully pushed him away.

Nearly fifty years they'd been married, together fifty-one. They'd had more ups than downs, more laughter than tears, and more joy than sorrow. The Brightsiders were as fortunate as providence allowed. Children had not been a part of their story.

Georgie bore the brunt of that sorrow and regret more than Charles had. Sure, he'd wanted kids. Very much so, but he was pragmatic and deeply in love with his wife. He had everything he needed, anything more would be a bonus.

They'd met through her beloved daddy, a great jazz musician in a big band. Charles—a tall and amiable man of twenty-four years—had auditioned on a Sunday afternoon. In walked—no, sauntered— his Georgie at the very end.

"Daddy," she said, glancing archly at Charles, "I think you should hire him. I like the way he plays."

"Oh, you do, now? Hmm. All right then. Son, you got the spot if you want it. We rehearse Thursdays and Sundays. My wife makes a mean pot roast, and my Sunshine here makes a mean martini. Stay for dinner if you'd like."

"Thank you, sir. I'd be honored," Charles had grinned. He hadn't been able to take his eyes off the captivating woman with the pixie haircut and dancing eyes, nor she off him, and her father had taken notice. For whatever blessed reason, he was willing to give Charles a chance with both his band and his daughter. Charles made sure to never make him regret either. Or her.

As he reminisced, Charles scrolled through Georgie's friends list, sending each one he knew his own 'friend request.' He was proud of himself for figuring it out on his own. He paused the cursor over one face, puzzled. It was a man named Craig H. Davidson. His face looked so familiar, but Charles couldn't place him. His profile said he was fifty-three years old, lived in Washington,

Connecticut, married with three kids. He worked as an English teacher in a public school, and apparently liked *Star Wars*, based on the number of things he followed and liked. Nothing set off any bells of recognition, but Charles couldn't shake the sense of familiarity. Georgie had been retired nearly fifteen years from teaching, but he supposed they could be acquainted through the school system. At the last second, he clicked the 'add friend' icon, then moved on. He'd try to remember to ask Georgie about it later.

Rufus and Mabel charged back into the office smelling of winter and wet dog. The brisk air had invigorated them, restoring their puppy-like vigor, and they frolicked and play-barked at one another until Charles hushed them. Indignantly, they trotted to their respective beds and plopped down with doggy sighs.

"Well, what's the verdict? Am I putting on my nightgown or my Wellies?"

"I plumb forgot to look," exclaimed Charles. "Sidetracked again. Let's see. I type in the name up there, and—ahh, yes, there it is, Mae's Café—here we are. Ha! Open Mic is on. Get your Wellingtons, my dear, we've got ourselves a date."

Georgie suppressed a yawn, she'd been hoping for a quiet night. Even so, she'd never missed a single performance in their years together, and she wouldn't be starting now, either. The Brightsiders came as a set. Always had, always will.

"All right, then. I'll start getting ready," said Georgie with a forced smile.

As she turned to leave the room, Charles stopped

her. "Georgie, darling?"

"Yes," she replied, her eyebrows arched.

"Thank you. I'm sure you'd much prefer to put your jammies on and read."

Georgie's face softened. She went to her husband, giving him a tight hug and a kiss on his cheek. "There's no place I'd rather be than with you."

It was the truth. Charles Brightsider was the finest, most handsome man she'd ever known. She fell head over heels in love the moment he walked up to her daddy's garage on those long legs of his. That love had carried them through so many trials in life and never waned. Sure, they'd fought on occasion. But even then, it wasn't over anything important. Silly, trivial nonsense and jealousies— usually on her part, the women were always making eyes at her husband—that resolved quickly enough.

They knew they were viewed as patriarch and matriarch of the town, the two pillars, and an ideal example of a successful marriage and prided themselves on it. Best of all, it was genuine—*they* were genuine. They were honest but kind to one another and humor stood paramount in their day-to-day life. In their fifty-plus years, they kept no secrets from each other, either. Georgie's heart clenched at this thought. But there was one secret, wasn't there? One that had been buried for almost fifty-four years and must remain so.

Chapter 5

Voices Singing

Seconds after William and Mae exited the fifth-floor elevators, they found Steven and Ruth Waterman. They were a well-matched couple, similar in mannerisms and style. Both were average in height, had black and silver curly hair, and wore wire-rimmed glasses. Dressed in jeans, sneakers, and sweaters over polo shirts, the Watermans were unmistakably a long-married couple.

"Mae, honey. So sweet of you to come and see our Rosabelle," said Mrs. Waterman, pushing up her glasses by the bridge. "We're just beside ourselves. Although, Miles Hannaford has been helpful, strangely enough."

Mae cocked her head and stammered, "Oh—I—he"—she glanced at Miles, standing a few feet away, biting his thumbnail and darting anxious looks around the waiting room—"can I do anything for you two?"

Was it possible that the Watermans didn't know about Miles and Rosabelle's relationship? Surely, she told her parents? Mae decided to play it safe, then ask Miles after.

"We're all set for now, thank you. The doctors asked us to give them a few minutes with her, but you can go see her when they come out. It's Room 5905. Oh, hello. And you are?"

"Oh, I'm sorry, this is William, my—"

"Right, yes," Steven slapped his palm against his forehead. "Rosabelle told us about the famous writer in town. Very exciting." The effort it took to come out of his fog shown plainly. However, despite the fear and worry etched on their faces, the Watermans forced smiles and amiability for the sake of their visitors.

William shook the proffered hands and said, "Sorry to meet under such difficult circumstances. How is your daughter doing?"

Ruth and Steven Waterman exchanged glances, then Ruth spoke, "Well, there's trauma to her spine, which is their biggest concern. Her pelvis is fractured, and her right leg is broken in three places. She's conscious now but heavily sedated. She looks so frail—" Ruth's voice broke and she hid her face in her hands.

Steven put an arm around his wife. His chin quivered, and his eyes were red-rimmed. "Now, now. We're going to be optimistic. Right? She's going to recover fully. You'll see. My Rosabelle is a strong girl."

Mae, tearing up as well, nodded in hopeful

31

agreement. "Mr. and Mrs. Waterman, I'll go speak to Miles for a moment, okay? Oh, we brought you home-cooked—well, café cooked—food in case you're hungry."

Ruth dabbed her eyes and blew her nose with the handkerchief William had handed her, accepting the basket gratefully. "Sure, then after you're welcome to go in and see her. The doctor just said to keep the visits short." She leaned in conspiratorially and whispered, "The Hannaford boy has gone in three times. Is there something I should know? I do hope he's not interested in our Rosabelle. He has a reputation, you know."

William saved Mae from answering. "Ruth, Steven? What do you say I grab you some fresh coffees? How do you take it?" He gave Mae's hand a squeeze and tipped his chin in Miles's direction.

Mae squeezed back and mouthed, "Thank you," then went to Miles.

"Oh, hey, baby Mae," he said in a voice she barely recognized.

She realized with a start that he was on the verge of tears. "Hey, hey. It's okay, Miles. She's going to be okay," said Mae, rubbing his arm.

Miles nodded and sniffed, then came in for a hug. He had to bend low to put his head on Mae's shoulder and she awkwardly patted his back.

Mae cut her eyes over to where the Watermans stood eying them suspiciously. "Let's go over there, okay?" She led him by the wrist around the corner, over by the nurse's station. "Miles? Do the Watermans not know that you and Rosabelle are together?"

Miles gazed around, scratched the back of his head, then said, "I—I thought they did. But they seemed surprised to see me, now that I think about it. Mae, do you think she," he hesitated, "she's embarrassed to be dating me?"

Any other time, the typically asinine and conceited Miles Hannaford would follow up with a stupid comment, but the Miles of this moment was in a sincere state of devastation and confusion.

"Maybe she was planning on telling them in person," Mae suggested.

"Yeah, maybe," said Miles. Then, more firmly, "Yeah, that's got to be it. She wanted to surprise them."

Mae patted his arm and bobbed her head encouragingly. "See? You go sit down and have a bite to eat, okay? I brought chicken and salad and a few other things. You must be starving by now."

"Ah, I can't eat, Mae. Not while Rosie's hurting."

"You really do love her, don't you?" Despite everything going on, Mae smiled. It was plain as day, this unexpected and delightful news. Miles was in love with Rosabelle.

His smile came slowly, an expression of wonder erasing a few worry lines etched in his brow. He gave a short laugh and said, "I do. I love her. I love her like crazy. Hell, I want to marry her. Rosie's the best thing that's happened to me in my whole life. Even better than the Stillman house sale last year. And that was a million-dollar, one broker sale. So, I made—"

"I get it, Miles." Mae put her hand up and

clenched her teeth. There's the old Miles she knew and disliked. "Go. Eat. Stop talking. I'll handle the Watermans after I go in to see Rosabelle."

"Thanks, baby Mae. You're the best. Sorry you and I never worked out."

"I—we never—" Mae sighed. "Okay, Miles. No worries."

He reached out to give her a patronizing pat on the shoulder, but Mae walked away, rolling her eyes as she went. Taking a deep breath, she entered the darkened room. The curtain was drawn over the single window, and the only light came from over the bed and the beeping monitors arced around her. Rosabelle resembled a porcelain doll, so still and pale. Mae's breath caught in her throat at the sight of the cuts on her cheek and the bandage at her temple, all from the shattered glass fragments, no doubt.

As quietly as possible, Mae stepped bedside and whispered, "Hey Rosabelle. It's Mae," not expecting her to respond, but also not knowing what else to do.

"Mae?" Rosabelle's voice was sand-papery and strained.

"You don't have to speak. I just wanted to let you know we're all thinking of you, and we're here for whatever you need."

"Miles—does Miles know—"

"He's been with you the whole time. I called him from the café right as the ambulances showed up. Rosabelle, he ran from his office to get to you. Went in the ambulance and everything."

Rosabelle closed her lids and smiled. A single

tear slid from the corner of her eye. Mae grabbed a tissue from the box on the bedside table and dabbed it away.

She fixed her gaze on Mae again. "My—my parents. Are they—"

"They're here too." Tentatively, Mae asked, "Rosabelle? Do they not know about you and Miles?"

Rosabelle gave a small head shake. "I meant to tell them. Lots of times, but then—I don't know. Miles's reputation. My parents—"

"I get it, say no more. Should I—do you need me to break the ice or something?" Mae regretted the offer the moment it left her lips.

Rosabelle gazed up at her with such grateful, hopeful eyes and whispered, "Oh, would you? Thank you, Mae. Tell Miles I—"

"How about you tell me yourself, Rosie?" Miles stood in the doorway, looking almost shy.

Mae gave Rosabelle's hand a gentle squeeze and said, "I'll leave you two alone."

Back in the waiting room, William sat with the Watermans. They made polite, idle conversation in the way strangers do until Mae walked in.

Ruth stood and took Mae's hand. "Walk with me to the vending machines, will you?"

Mae looked at William questioningly, but he offered only a shrug. "Sure, of course." Ruth linked her arm through Mae's and together they strolled down the corridor.

"I didn't want to say anything in front of Steven. Fathers can be so irrational regarding their daughters, you know." Ruth stopped short, giving

Mae a repentant look. "Oh, Mae, sweetheart. I'm sorry. Of course, you know. You were the center of your father's universe. We adored that about Keith."

"Thank you, Mrs. Waterman. I am—I was very fortunate. So, what did you want to talk about?" As if she didn't know.

"Well, I'm glad you asked. It's the Hannaford boy. Please tell me my precious girl isn't with him. I couldn't stand it, really."

Mae was taken aback by her vehemence. It was true, Miles's reputation had long preceded him, and he was everything he was accused of—womanizer, narcissistic, egotistical, chauvinistic, obnoxious—but now, thanks to Rosabelle, he was something more. Something better. Mae suspected that it shocked no one more than it did him too.

In fact, Miles Hannaford and Rosabelle Waterman were everyone's new favorite 'not-secret' secret. Everyone except Brianna Baker, that is. But that was a whole other story and not Mae's most pressing concern. Right now, Mae had to figure out how to bridge the gap between Miles and Rosabelle's parents.

"Well," she began judiciously, "Miles has come a long way from the jer—boy he used to be. He's in fact very—" Here, Mae struggled for words that were truthful, "very…he's trying to be better."

Ruth pinched the bridge of her nose, forcing her glasses up and closed her eyes as if it pained her to hear Mae's words. She exhaled through her mouth and said, "I suppose it was his idea for Rosabelle to dye her hair?" Then, more to herself than to Mae,

"Her beautiful hair, ruined for that—that buffoon."

"Oh, Mrs. Waterman, no. I mean, not exactly. It was Rosabelle's idea. Miles wanted her to change it back."

Ruth Waterman harrumphed loudly. "Well, I don't trust him. Not for one minute, Mae. He caused enough grief in the Waterman home, thank you very much."

Mae was confused. "He did? How? I mean, I never knew they—"

"Rosabelle has been crazy over him since high school. No, middle school. He never once deserved her affection, believe me. And now look what happens. She dyes her hair and gets into this terrible accident."

"Mrs. Waterman, I don't think the two things—"

"Maybe if her thoughts weren't entirely about *him*," she sneered with disdain, "she'd have seen that van sooner and—"

"Excuse me, Mae? Mrs. Waterman? The, um, doctors want to speak to you."

It was Miles. He kept his head bowed and his eyes averted as Ruth brushed past him with barely an acknowledgment. Once she was out of hearing, he said, "Damn. She really doesn't like me, huh?"

Mae lightly punched his arm. "Give it time, Miles. You've grown on me, after all."

"Gee, thanks, baby Mae. Hey, Rosie looked good, right? I mean, you know, considering. Her, like, her color looked good. You think I should get her flowers or something? Or maybe those candies with the honey inside. She likes those a lot."

"I'm sure whatever you bring her will be fine,

Miles." It was bizarre to see Miles Hannaford behaving so—so *human*. She almost said as much, but her cell phone vibrated in her pocket.

"Hang on, Miles. Hello?"

An unfamiliar voice on the other end said, "Hi, is this Mae?"

"Yes. How can I help you?"

"My name is Jane. I saw that you have an open mic night at your café tonight, and we'd love to come down and play a few songs."

"Oh, I was going to cancel—" Mae caught Miles waving at her. 'Do it,' he mouthed, nodding vigorously. After a brief hesitation, she said, "but it's still on. Just so you know, it's an acoustic open mic. We don't have drums or anything—"

"No worries. I've got the whole band and then some with me. We had a wedding gig, but the bride ran off with the best man or some crazy shit."

"Oh, my. Well, that's too bad."

"Sure is. So, we'll see you at seven p.m. then? Oh, and my band is called Redhead."

"Okay, great. See you soon." Mae disconnected and said to Miles, "I don't know. It feels wrong to just carry on as if everything is fine when Rosabelle is in a hospital bed, not knowing if she'll ever walk—"

"She will, Mae. I'm positive. And I'm positive she'd want you to do whatever you normally do. You know it too."

William came up behind Mae, resting his hand at the small of her back. "Hello, love. Shall we get going and let Miles and the Watermans get back to Rosabelle?"

Gratefully, Mae leaned back against him. "Yes, that sounds good." To Miles, she said, "As long as you're sure you're okay to handle—"

"Okay as I'll ever be. Go on, now. I'll call you if there are any updates."

William and Mae said their goodbyes to the Watermans and headed toward the elevators. Once the doors had closed solidly, Mae wrapped her arms around William's waist, her head against his chest, and released a shaky breath.

"That was hard."

"I know it was." William tilted her chin to meet his gaze. "You did wonderfully. The amazing Mae, doing what she does best."

"Oh," she said grinning, "and what's that?"

"Everything."

"Good answer, Mr. Grant."

"Thank you, Mrs. Grant."

Chapter 6

Better Not Pout

"Sweetie, Mommy is on the phone. Go see Nanny." Brianna took her hand off the speaker as Cassidy toddled over to the waving arms of Mrs. Teccio. "Please take her outside to play, Nanny T. All right, what is it, Charlotte?"

Brianna had begun to preen in front of the foyer mirror, smoothing her salon perfect platinum blonde hair, carefully running one finger along the edge of her bottom lip, and checking for any possible hint of blemish. On the other end of the phone line, Charlotte Asheby—a woman she *used* to call her friend—prattled on about breakfast with her husband—the newly promoted police sergeant— and something to do with Fat Chris, an accident, and Rosabelle Waterman. Her ears perked.

"Wait, back up. Did you say Rosabelle Waterman was in an accident with Fat Chris?"

"No," stammered Charlotte, "well, yes. But—"

"Oh, now that's rich. Rosabelle and Fat Chris? Together?" Brianna started to laugh, then remembered they'd just been in an accident, and laughter wasn't appropriate until she knew they were both okay. "I—are they all right?"

Charlotte exhaled. "Chris and Rosabelle weren't—aren't—together. I saw the whole thing. Chris's van plowed into Rosabelle's little Cooper at the Mae's Café intersection. Chris has bumps and bruises, but he's fine. Rosabelle's in the hospital. She might not be able to walk again."

Brianna checked her teeth in the mirror, and said distractedly, "Terrible news," but then her eyes narrowed.

Why was Charlotte calling her with this? They'd hardly spoken since the whole Elise thing when Charlotte had been a traitor and sided with her over Brianna. She was willing to bet that Elise had put her up to the call. Give up a little gossip, squeeze her way back into Brianna's good graces. Yes, that was it, she knew it.

"Yes, it's just awful. I'm surprised you didn't know about it already. Ricky came out with his tow truck to take Rosabelle's car."

Was there smugness in her tone? Impossible. Charlotte Asheby wasn't capable. "He must've called while I was at the gym. I haven't checked my phone yet." Realizing she was on her phone, she added, "Until now. Now, don't take this the wrong way—I do appreciate you passing along the news— but why are you calling *me* with it? I mean, it's not as though Rosabelle or—God help me—Fat Chris

41

and me are friends."

Another annoying, delicate little sigh on Charlotte's end. "I thought you might be interested in who rushed to her side."

Silence. Then, unable to help herself, Brianna said in a voice more breathless than she'd intended, "Who?"

That damn Charlotte Asheby paused theatrically again, then said the name Brianna had dreaded and anticipated hearing. "Miles Hannaford."

At the same time, her side door—the one leading directly into the kitchen—opened and Ricky Baker walked in with a jangle of keys and thump of work boots. Brianna tensed, curling her manicured nails into the palms of her hands at the sound of his, "Yo, anyone home?"

Not bothering to cover the receiver this time, Brianna called out in a frosted singsong, "Gee, I don't know, Ricky. What does it usually mean when my car is in the driveway? That I'm not home or home?"

He matched her tone and cadence, "Gee, I don't know, babe. Maybe you could've taken the baby for a walk or something."

He never used to do that—talk back. He used to just apologize, then try to say or do something to make Brianna laugh. Sometimes it even worked. This was new, and she didn't care for it.

"Charlotte, I've got to go."

"Oh, sure. Me too, actually, I—" Brianna hung up on Charlotte's long-winded goodbye. She debated whether to go into the kitchen or upstairs for a nap. Ricky decided for her.

In his booming, too-loud for their elegant Victorian house voice, Ricky called, "Bri, where's the rye bread?"

Brianna threw her head back and shook her fists in his direction and strode on pointy-toed, pencil-thin heeled shoes into the kitchen to help her domestically challenged husband make a damn sandwich.

***

"Well, what'd she say?" Elise had one eyebrow arched at Charlotte from across Charlotte's kitchen island. She told her not to call, that it was a waste of time. But Charlotte, trained like one of Pavlov's dogs, still felt a need to call Brianna the moment any new gossip came down the line. This, even though their fivesome had fractured last year after Brianna spear-headed the Trash Elise campaign when she separated from Ethan. Old habits die hard, she supposed. Or maybe not at all, in some cases.

"Well, at first she acted totally disinterested. I think she even started laughing at one point. But I waited—just like you said—and then I dropped the Miles bomb on her. How does she not know about them after all this time? They're, like, the worst-kept secret since Mae's stuff with Gina and Feather Anne."

"Oh, please, she's known for as long as we have. Longer, I bet. She's just in denial. Plus, it's not as if she can say or do anything. Poor Ricky."

Elise shook her head. Talk about denial. He was married to a stone-cold bitch—one that cheated on him and had another man's baby and passed it off as his—and still acted like his wife was the greatest. She told Charlotte as much.

"Wait, you seriously think Ricky knows about—about…you know?"

"Charlotte, it's only you and I here. Even if Joel had the house bugged, it's nothing he doesn't know already."

"Joel would never. Anyhow, it just seems so, I don't know, like something out of *Days of Our Lives*. He can't possibly know, can he?"

"Truthfully? I don't know. But come on, Char. How could he not know?"

"Well," Charlotte cast her eyes away and blushed, "you didn't know about Ethan and Jack Jacobson until you walked in—"

"That was different," said Elise defensively. Then, resigned, "Okay, you got me there. I had no fricking idea. Fine, maybe he doesn't know."

"Listen, after everything Brianna started with you, I'm amazed you didn't rat her out to the whole world."

Elise shrugged. "For as much as she deserves that, Ricky doesn't. Her shit will catch up with her one day, you'll see. Eventually, we all get ours in the end."

"Well, that's bleak. I prefer to think of karma as, you know, a balancing of all things. Not just bad stuff, but good things too. Like the good you do will come back to you."

"Hmph. How's that working out for Rosabelle, huh? That girl's never done anything harmful to anyone and look where she's at."

Charlotte opened and closed her mouth like a trout, trying to come up with a reasonable retort and failing. Instead, she changed gears. "How are things going with Moose?"

At the mention of Bruce, Elise smiled. "We're good. Everything's going great. He's great with Gianna. Great with my folks. He's even great with the Ethan and Jack thing."

"Wow. That's a lot of 'greats' there. Well, I'm happy for you, Elise. You've had a crush on Moose since forever. It's about time he noticed."

"What—I—no, I haven't, Charlotte. Why would you even say that? And hurry up and open that wine, will you?"

Charlotte stared at Elise in disbelief. "You're kidding, right? You practically swooned whenever he walked by you in high school. You had that moose sticker on your—"

"Okay, shut up. Whatever. Just pour the damn wine." Elise tapped her empty glass with her nail and gave Charlotte a warning glare. Then, in a gentler tone, "Your hair looks fantastic, by the way."

It did. Charlotte Asheby—nee Charlotte Monroe—had worn her hair in the same boring, waist-long middle part since high school. Elise had convinced her to do something more stylish now that she was the wife of a police sergeant. Granted, she only cut off five inches and switched to a side part, but it was something.

"Why thank you. And fine, whatever you say. So, you and Moose are great. Now, how are you and Mae?"

"Me and Mae? Why do you ask?" The frost had returned to her voice.

Charlotte took her turn at raising an eyebrow. Sometimes Elise could be so…*un*forthcoming. She couldn't understand it. Charlotte shared everything. Virtually everything. She stuck by Elise's side instead of Brianna's. If she couldn't even open up about something so small, then— "I'm sorry," sighed Elise. "I guess I'm just used to being on the defensive. I swear I have Post-Traumatic Brianna Syndrome or something." She took a sip of her pinot noir, shrugged, and said, "Things with Mae are fine, I guess. It's just—"

"You like her, and you resent her?"

"Basically, yes. I know she and Bruce are just friends. But he's still at her beck and call all the time. I mean, why does he still help her all the time? He's got his own business to run. Do you know he ran out at midnight one night last week because the alarm went off at the café? I mean, it's her place, why didn't she go?"

Charlotte said nothing and topped off Elise's glass. There wasn't anything she could say. She was friends with both women and determined not to get in the middle. This was not to be a repeat of the Brianna years. Elise wasn't the only one with Post-Traumatic Brianna Syndrome.

"Well, if it helps, the only thing Mae ever says is how happy she is for the two of you," said Charlotte diplomatically.

Elise dropped her head onto the table and said a muffled, "That makes it worse. She's so *genuine*, and nice. It makes me look like Attila the Hun."

"No, it doesn't." Charlotte laughed. "You're just a woman in love, that's all. You want to protect what's yours. You should see me when those…those badge bunnies try hopping around Joel."

Elise snorted, "Badge bunnies? What the hell is that?"

"You know," sniffed Charlotte with disdain, "the trashy women who chase after men in uniform. Someone called them that on one of my police wife's groups." Her chin jutted defensively. "I'm trying it out."

Elise laughed and after a moment, Charlotte joined in.

"Oh, Charlotte," said Elise as their laughter faded, "I wish I could go with you to the open mic thing tonight, but Bruce is coming over with Feather Anne. Shit. What time is it?"

"Time for you to get going, I'm guessing," Charlotte chuckled, taking away Elise's wine glass.

"Ugh, this will be the only time you ever hear me agree with Brianna on something, but you seriously need to move to our side of town."

"I know, I know. Maybe someday."

They both knew she didn't mean it though. Being in walking distance of Brianna Baker was just too much stress. They said their goodbyes and Elise walked at a brisk pace to her car. The frigid air stung her eyes and made them water.

God, I hate winter.

A thin layer of frost coated her windshield, so she set her defroster on high and dialed Ethan's number while she waited.

"Hey, Ethan. Give me ten extra minutes before you drop Gigi off at the house, okay? I'm running behind."

They'd both come to terms with the divorce and decided the best thing for Gianna was for everyone to be as friendly as possible. At first, it was awkward and tense. But as the months rolled on it became easier. Now, a full year later, they could say with sincerity that they were friends. Ethan and Jack came over for dinner occasionally, they spent holidays together, and shared custody of Gianna. Unconventional, yes. Disapproved by her father and mother, definitely. But the only thing Elise cared about was making the best out of the circumstances for their daughter's sake. The brightest spot of it all had been Bruce.

He was so easy going with everything. He was even more unfazed by Ethan and Jack's relationship than Elise. In fact, their first dinner together came at the suggestion of Bruce. The man may look like a burly linebacker macho-man, but he was more a Grizzly Adams. A gentle giant. Elise smiled.

"Uh, you there, Elise? I said I'll bring her straightaway at seven, if that's okay with you?"

"Oh, sorry, yes, sure. That's even better. Gives me time to get settled."

"Terrific. Hey, I heard about poor Rosabelle Waterman. Dreadful, just dreadful news," said Ethan in his proper clipped English accent.

Elise murmured her agreement, and they spoke for a minute more before hanging up. Elise's thoughts went to Rosabelle. How crazy it was that she—that everyone—was just going on with their lives, griping over their little problems and inconveniences while a woman lies broken in a hospital bed. How petty was she, whining about her boyfriend's best friend? She tilted her rearview mirror and gave her reflection a dirty look. "Stop being a selfish bitch, Elise." And with that, she wound her way home through the snow-blanketed town.

Chapter 7

Wonderland

"Try to lie still, Miss Waterman. We're almost there."

Rosabelle could tell he was new, maybe fresh out of nursing school. His hands, red and almost raw looking from the constant hand washing, shook as he picked and peeled at the copious layers of tape on the crook of her arm.

"Can't you, I don't know, put Vaseline on her arm to make that come off easier?" Miles hovered over Rosabelle and scowled at the already anxious nurse.

Rosabelle put her free hand on his forearm and smiled gently up at him. "I'm fine, Miles," then to the nurse, "You're doing just fine, Freddy. This is the least of my pains in the past week."

Freddy grinned gratefully at Rosabelle, shot Miles a quick glance, then said, "Everyone's calling

50

you the Miracle Woman, you know. Nobody thought you'd be leaving here before Christmas. But here you are, one week after an accident that almost paralyzed you, ready to be discharged. It's a Christmas miracle, if you think of it."

"She's Jewish," said Miles wryly.

"Oh, I'm sorry, I—"

"Don't listen to him, Freddy. I'm not—well, technically I am Jewish, but my father converted for my mother. We celebrate Christmas." She turned a pointed look to Miles. "And you know that."

Miles didn't care for the way the young nurse was looking at Rosie. Like she was a—a Christmas angel or something. Everyone knows you have to just rip the tape off quickly, but no, Mr. Moon Eyes was taking his sweet time, just so he could talk to Rosie longer. He knew this guy's game, all right.

"Should I get one of the other nurses to help—"

Rosabelle dug her nails into Miles's forearm and gave him the look. The one every woman was born just knowing how to give. Bratty kids, husbands, and boyfriends alike shut up the second they were on the receiving end of that look. *If* they knew what was good for them. Before Rosie, Miles Hannaford had *never* known what was good for him. Everything was different now.

Freddy finished his task and explained the discharge procedure, shooting nervous but defiant glances in Miles's direction periodically as he did. Miles folded his arms and stared stonily at the man—not caring that he was behaving like a jealous high school boy—until he left them. Once the nurse walked out, Miles turned back to Rosie. Despite the stitches and bruising over her eye, she looked more stunning than ever to Miles. He'd missed seeing her face free of makeup, fresh and clean.

When she'd gotten her makeover, Miles had told her she looked hot, and he'd meant it. What he failed to say was that he liked the original Rosie more. The one with the no eyeshadow and no mascara, bright green eyes, the freckled nose and porcelain skin. He loved her natural beach-sand blonde hair and the way she tucked those long strands behind her ears. But the makeup and the hair color had made Rosie stand taller and act more confident. It made her see herself differently and Miles had no intentions of doing anything to take that away from her if he could help it.

"Why are you looking at me like that?" asked Rosabelle with an embarrassed chuckle. She bent her head, tucked her hair behind her ear, and flushed. She hated for him to see her looking so, so old Rosabelle. She needed her makeup bag. And her roots needed a touch-up. The shade was open, letting the bright winter sun cut a path across the hospital bed, catching Rosabelle in its path. Hyper aware of her plainness, she untucked her hair and let it fall over her face like a curtain. She felt the edge of the bed dip and Miles's cologne tickled her nose as he leaned in close. He re-tucked her hair and caressed her cheek with his thumb.

"Because you look so beautiful, Rosie." Before she could scoff or turn away, Miles kissed Rosabelle, quieting any protest she may have had.

"All right, Rosabelle," said the doctor brusquely as he entered the room, "looks like you're ready to blow this taco stand, hmm?" He gave a closed lip smile that crinkled the corners of his eyes.

Rosabelle giggled and nodded. "I am so ready, Dr. Matteson. Get me out of here."

"Young man, you'll be bringing her home, I take it?"

"Yes, sir, I—"

"Actually, we thought *we'd* bring Rosabelle home," said Steven Waterman from the doorway, his wife nodding authoritatively beside him and giving Miles a cool appraisal.

Ruth Waterman shifted her gaze to Rosabelle and at once softened. "Darling sunshine girl," she exclaimed, her arms outstretched. "Just look at you." Instead of going around to the other side of the bed, Ruth pushed past Miles and shooed him off the edge of the mattress as if he were the family dog. "Dr. Matteson, are you sure she should be going home so soon? She looks terrible. Her color is—"

"I assure you, Mrs. Waterman, we wouldn't let her leave if she wasn't ready. Now, she'll still need physical therapy for some time," he addressed Rosabelle, "but it looks as though you've got yourself a great support system. We'll see you in three weeks to check your casts. Good luck, my dear. I wish all my patients were as delightful as you."

The moment the doctor was out of the room, Ruth leaned in conspiratorially and said, "Did you hear that? He called you delightful. And I didn't see a ring on his finger, Rosabelle."

Rosabelle's eyes widened warningly at her

mother, then apologetically at Miles, who had moved to the corner and rubbed at his neck.

"Mother," she hissed.

Steven intervened, "Oh, now, your Mom's just making an observation. No need to get touchy, Buttercup." He didn't look back at Miles when he added, "We'll step out and let you girls get situated. I'm sure they'll be up with a wheelchair any time now."

He tapped the corner of Rosabelle's hospital bed and left the room, assuming—rightly—that Miles would follow. In the corridor, Steven paced back and forth, staring at his shoes. Miles leaned against the wall, perusing his emails on his phone. He felt Mr. Waterman's shadow fall across him and heard him snicker. He powered off the cell and studied Rosabelle's father in a way that was both respectful, and yet bold. He wanted these people to approve of him, but he wasn't going to beg.

"You young people, always on those smartphones these days," he sniffed and shook his head.

"Well, Mr. Waterman, I do most of my work from my phone. Answering emails, sending documents, looking up—"

"In my day, we used phones to call people. Not play games and take pictures of our lunch."

Miles bit his tongue. He made no comment on the fact that they didn't have the technology back then to do those things, or that Miles knew the Watermans both had cell phones and that Ruth was addicted to *Candy Crush* while Steven went on Facebook at least ten times a day. But he knew better than to say so. Silence was to be his best friend around Rosabelle's parents until she figured out how to get them to accept him.

Instead of saying what he wanted to say, Miles stated, "It'll be nice for Rosie—Rosabelle to be back home."

"Too inconvenient for you to come visit her at the hospital, is it?"

"No, sir. I just meant that—"

"She's got a long recovery ahead of her. She doesn't need any drama, I hope you know."

"Yes, sir. I'm aware."

"I don't know what kind of game you're playing at, Hannaford, or why you picked a girl like Rosabelle to play it on, but I've got my eye on you, son."

Steven 'V'-ed his pointer and middle fingers and jabbed them back and forth at eye level between them to illustrate his point.

Miles opened his mouth to utter another perfunctory 'yes, sir,' but something Steven Waterman said struck him. He cocked his head and said, "Sorry, sir, but…a 'girl like Rosabelle?' What do you mean by that?"

Steven squinted at Miles a moment, as if he'd said something unintelligible, or as if Miles was cracking a bad joke. "You know what I mean. A slick, GQ guy like you with a girl like her…it doesn't happen in real life. Only in those teenager movies she used to watch endlessly."

Miles seethed. "Sir, your daughter is one of the most beautiful women I've ever known. Inside and out."

Indignation flushed Steven Waterman's face. He straightened his back, trying to draw himself as close to Miles's height as possible and spoke with a caustic tone.

"*We* know that. Don't think for one second we don't know that, young man. It's you, people like you, that are the blind ones. Where were you in high school?" He put his hand up, warding off any reply, "Don't answer. I know where you were. You were dating the popular girls, the cheerleaders. Your type looks through girls like Rosabelle because they don't stand out, or you date them in secret. They're too plain. They don't—"

"I'm sorry you feel that way, Daddy." The nurse's aide had wheeled Rosabelle out of the room behind them. Ruth stared, stricken. Rosie had two bright splotches of pink on her otherwise pale face. Her eyes shone with unshed tears, but her jaw was set.

"No, honey, that wasn't what I—"

"Rosie, he didn't—"

"Miles, I'd rather you take me home, please." She stared over his shoulder as she spoke.

Miles's attention shifted from Mrs. Waterman—who still wore the panicked look of a bird caught in a net—to Mr. Waterman. Like his daughter, he sported two patches of red on his hollowed cheeks, and he seemed to have aged ten years in a matter of minutes. Despite his harsh, yet accurate words, Miles felt a stab of sympathy toward the man. He loved his daughter. That's all it was.

Steven glanced up at Miles, gave the shortest of nods, and turned away without sparing a look to his wife or daughter. With his long, thin hand cupped on the back of his neck and his head bowed, he walked desultorily along the corridor.

The nurse's aide volleyed her stares between Miles and Ruth, chewing her gum slowly. She took her hands off the wheelchair handles and put her hands up in a 'don't shoot me' gesture and backed away. "You all can figure this out while we walk to the parking garage. For now, I push. What floor you on?" She was looking at Miles for the answer.

"Oh—uh—I valeted?"

Nervousness made him pose it as a question though it was meant to be a statement. From behind Rosie, Ruth muttered something that sounded like, "Of course, he did." She'd regained her disdainful-of-anything-Miles-related composure, apparently.

"All right then," said the seemingly bored aide with a nametag that identified her as Theresa, "Momma, you're gonna walk right here alongside me. Boyfriend, you're gonna walk on my other side, you hear?" Both Miles and Ruth nodded and took their places. Rosabelle smirked up at Theresa, and Theresa winked at her. "That's right. Now when we get out of the elevator, you, Mr. Boyfriend Man, are going to run out and get your car brought up by the valet. Momma and I will wait right inside the doors for you where it's nice and dry and warm. Better button up that coat, temps have dropped."

Everything went as Theresa said, with the bonus of an awkward goodbye to Ruth Waterman thrown in for good measure. Miles had blasted the heat in the car, laid a blanket over Rosie's lap, then lowered the passenger window for Ruth, who stood stiffly on the curb, trying to look nonplussed by either the cold or her daughter's aloofness.

She bent down, sticking her salt and pepper colored, frizzy head partially through the passenger window of Miles's BMW. Her hazel eyes darted around, taking in the sleek black interior and pausing on the stack of NEW LISTING and FORECLOSURE signs on the back seat. "Well," sniffed Ruth, "I guess I'll go find where your father ran off to. Probably in that overpriced soup and bread restaurant, no doubt. We'll be over tomorrow morning, Rosabelle. Call me if you need anything."

"Thank you, Mother."

Rosabelle kept her eyes locked dead ahead. Her words came out calm and cool, but Miles saw her hand kneading the fabric of her skirt. She wasn't used to giving her parents the cold shoulder. He put his hand over hers and her hand stilled.

Ruth Waterman recoiled as if slapped. This was *his* influence, she was certain. He'd changed her into someone Ruth hardly recognized. Literally. Who was this defiant, stubborn girl sitting in a stranger's car? A BMW, no less. The absolute epitome of elitism and arrogance, in her opinion. She supposed their used Winnebago—with the tie-dye curtains on the windows and the PEACE and NO NUKES bumper stickers—embarrassed Rosabelle now. Maybe even *they* embarrassed her—with their non-designer clothes and simple minds—now that she was hanging around someone so materialistic and shallow.

"All right then. Well, goodbye," said Ruth with as much dignity as her red, running nose allowed her. Damn New England winters. They should have stayed in the Carolinas and flown Rosabelle down to visit *them*. Then none of this would've happened. But here they were, dealing with this—this person who'd infiltrated their daughter's life while they were gone. Maybe it was time they moved back. Clearly, Rosabelle needed—

"Okay, Mrs. Waterman. I promise I'll take good care of Rosie. See you tomorrow." Miles rolled the window up, effectively shutting out the stammered protestation she was surely ready to utter. Rosie stared at her lap, but a small smirk turned up the corner of her mouth. Miles silently breathed a sigh of relief. He had no idea what the hell he was doing, and as they pulled away from the curb, that fact hit him fully.

When was the last time Miles had ever taken care of anyone or anything but himself? He recalled his childhood dog, Randy. He really liked that dog, but it was always his dad's dog foremost. They'd supposedly bought it for him when he was nine—at least they said it was for him—an Old English Sheepdog that quickly became his father's pride and joy.

More so than Miles had been, despite his best efforts. Two State Champion awards, full ride to UCONN, a successful businessman before he turned thirty—with multiple awards, trophies, and certificates of excellence, mind you—and all Chet Hannaford could say were things along the lines of, "Team played well. Next time maybe you'll spot the guy who's open and you won't ground the damn ball in the fourth." Then, when he got the college scholarship, "Full ride, son. Let's hope you don't screw it up." When he'd gone for his real state license, "Kid gets a business degree, then becomes a real estate agent. I mean, isn't that a girl's job?"

Nothing he ever did was good enough for Chet. His mother, Jeannie, was the opposite. Maybe she tried to make up for his father's criticisms, Miles supposed. But she was forever bragging about his accomplishments to anyone who'd listen. "Jeannie Hannaford only raises winners, thank you very much," she was fond of saying to Miles. It was her pep talk before a game or a test.

She'd say, "Winners win, losers lose. Which one do you want to be?"

Miles gave the only answer there was to give, "A winner, Mom."

"That's what I want to hear." She'd smile, ruffle his hair, or pat his cheek.

Miles had spent his whole life trying to be the best at everything. His bookcase was lined with trophies and medals from football, tennis, and marathons. The awards and certificates sat proudly between them in black frames. Every accomplishment and milestone had a home on those shelves for anyone to see and admire. Only, the parade of women who'd come through his condo's front door had merely given a polite, cursory acknowledgment of the tastefully spotlighted bookcase.

When his parents first came to see the condo, Chet had scoffed and shook his head and said, "Let me guess, you got that thing at the IKEA store?" Then he walked to the kitchen and grabbed an IPA from the fridge. His mother studied each item on every shelf, then said, "Oh, sweetheart, why would you put the second-place medal in there? Just toss that one, no one will ever even know, right?" She smiled and patted his arm. After they left, Miles took the medal and dropped it into the garbage, feeling stupid and embarrassed that he'd ever put it up there. It was from his first marathon ever.

"Miles?"

Rosie's voice beside him startled him from his thoughts. He glanced over, worry etched across his face. Had he been driving too fast? Going over too many bumps? Was she in pain?

He frowned. "Everything okay?"

Rosabelle laughed and put her hand over his. "Everything is fine. I just wanted to say thank you."

Miles made a small *pshtt* sound and shrugged. "It's nothing, Rosie-Posie. We got this, no problemo, Senorita Rosa—"

"Miles. I know when you're anxious. You've only stopped tapping the steering wheel long enough to bite your thumbnail. I hope you don't play poker."

Miles laughed. "That obvious, huh?"

"To me, yes. Miles, I want you to know—you don't have to do this. You didn't sign on for—for taking care of an invalid."

Miles was quiet for a long moment. So long that Rosabelle had to turn away and look out the window so he couldn't see the tears in her eyes. He was going to break up with her. It was too much to ask or hope for that he could be the man she needed him to be. She should've known better. But at least

61

she got hurt now before things got too serious.

He said I love you, it's already serious.

Never mind that now. Her parents would be thrilled, at least. Just when Rosabelle was confident he would say nothing, his voice broke the silence.

"You want to know what I was just thinking, Rosie?"

She didn't but nodded, anyway.

"I was thinking about how I've never, ever had to take care of anyone but myself. I was thinking, 'how the hell am I going to do this,' and wondering who I could ask for guidance. But what I was *not* thinking—not for even one second—was that I didn't want to do it. Rosie, I'm in for the long haul. I'll be by your side the whole time. So much that you're gonna get sick of me, okay?"

They'd stopped at a red light and Miles had shifted to look her in the eye, but Rosabelle couldn't face him, her eyes flooded with fresh tears.

"Rosie, look at me. Please believe me when I say I am with you. No matter what. I love you."

She took a shaky breath, exhaled, and gazed back at him through the kaleidoscope of those unshed tears. "Okay, but I—"

A horn honked behind them. The light was now green and obviously had been for a few seconds too long for the other driver's liking. They both grimaced and chuckled and gave an apologetic wave to the driver behind them. Miles took her hand in his and they drove the rest of the way in contented silence.

Chapter 8

All Is Calm

If someone had held up a crystal ball two years ago and shown William what his life looked like today, he'd have laughed and said they were crazy. And not just because he didn't believe in fortune-telling. He'd have said, 'That ship has sailed, my friend,' because marriage—given the reclusive nature of his later years—was as unfathomable to him as moving to Mars.

Yet, here he was, sitting beside his *wife* before a roaring fire in their home, surrounded by friends and family on Christmas Eve. Soft music spilled from the speakers and laughter erupted from across the room, drawing their attention from the mesmerizing flames dancing in the fireplace.

"All right, you two, what's so funny?" asked Mae sleepily from the crook of William's arm. She had been so tired lately, William noted with concern.

"I was telling Jimmy here about the time your father decided to paint his room lavender and your grandfather nearly had a massive coronary stroke when he saw it."

Mae grinned. "I remember him telling me. But it wasn't just his room, right? It was the bathroom, and—"

"And the kitchen, and the doghouse," finished her aunt.

James McKenna, William's publisher and longtime friend, eyed Katrina with an interest that appeared more than professional curiosity. "Katrina, my dear, has anyone ever told you, you are a natural storyteller?"

"All the time, darlin'. I got plenty more too. Let's refill our glasses. You want anything, lovebirds?"

Both William and Mae shook their heads. When they were out of earshot, he whispered, "Looks like they're hitting it off, don't you think?"

Mae craned her head to watch them a moment, then giggled. "I think you're right. He's the first man I've seen around her that doesn't look slightly terrified."

"Well, they're both bulls in China shops, so it could either be perfect or a perfect disaster."

Mae elbowed him. He laughed and kissed her temple. "I suppose I should get up and be a dutiful hostess," she said.

"You're exhausted, and it's Christmas Eve. No one expects you to do anything, sweetheart. The food is out, the drinks are flowing, everyone is content. Relax."

Mae surveyed the room doubtfully. James and Katrina stood over the spiked punch bowl laughing and standing closer than necessary. Bruce and Feather Anne were having an intense game of Battleship as Elise and Gianna looked on.

"You're right, as usual. Don't you ever get tired of being right, Mr. Grant?"

"Well, I never get tired of hearing you *say* I'm right, Mrs. Grant." William grinned.

From beside the small bar in the far corner, a saccharine-sweet voice trilled, "Oh William, could you be a dear and mix a drink for me?" Charlene—previously Charlton—had come along with Katrina and had taken a shine to William, to his mild-but-amused dismay. William cleared his throat, raised an eyebrow at Mae, and stood wearily, affecting his best 'host voice' as he did.

"Of course, I can, Charl—Charlene."

Mae smirked into her hand and gave him a playful shove. Then she sat back, gazed into the fire, and let her mind drift. She was so peaceful and satisfied with her life. William, Feather Anne—they both had added such depth and breadth to her everyday existence. Laughter had returned to her house. It felt lived in again. She had two people to take care of, to love. A sudden, fierce sense of possessiveness flooded her entire body. They were *hers*. It took her a moment to place the reason for such a visceral reaction. Then it came to her like the remnants of a nightmare. Gina Byrd. *That* was what she'd tried to shove out of her mind, but like a bad penny, it kept turning up.

The day after Rosabelle's terrible accident, Joel Asheby stopped by the café with troubling news. They had reason to believe Gina might be back in town. They'd discovered that someone had been squatting in the newly built house on the old Jensen property. It was being used as a model home by the developer and had working electricity, making it an ideal hiding place.

"We don't know for sure it's her, Mae. Jason Marsdale—you know, the guy building the cul-de-sac over there—he came in this morning having a cow about beer bottles and cigarette butts in the kitchen. He found a sleeping bag and a radio in one of the rooms."

"So, what makes you think it's Gina? Could be anyone passing through," said Mae, crossing her arms and stepping back.

Bruce, who'd come out of the kitchen, came to stand in front of her as if Joel were threatening her with his service weapon. He said, "Could be teenagers, couldn't it?"

Joel's glance volleyed between them for a moment, then he said, "Yeah, we thought so too. It was the radio. Looks identical to the one that I'd seen back when she had the trailer on the lot. One of them old ones, from like the eighties or something. It even had a cassette player."

Mae crossed her arms and said nothing, and Bruce and Joel regarded one another silently, exchanging an unspoken conversation. Joel raised his pale eyebrows and Bruce nodded grimly. Out loud, he said, "Well, thanks for the head's up, Joel. 'Preciate it."

Mae spoke up suddenly, an octave higher than her normal voice, "She gave up her legal rights. She can't have her."

"I know, Mae. Try not to worry too much, okay? I got the guys doing extra patrol around the Jenson place and your street as well. We can't arrest her just for being here, but at least we'll be able to keep tabs…and keep her away from Feather Anne."

"Thanks, Joel. Let me know the second *you* know anything, please?"

That was more than a week ago, and Mae had been on pins and needles ever since, all the while pretending everything was normal for Feather Anne's sake. Her own too, she supposed. She imagined she saw Gina around every corner, lurking in alleys, or creeping around her backyard. Feather Anne was blissfully unaware, just as Mae had wanted—despite both Bruce and William's opinions differing from hers. The two former adversaries exchanged so many smug, knowing, mutually agreeing glances all week that she'd finally erupted at the both of them, offering an unladylike suggestion for what they could do with their judging stares. She wasn't wrong in protecting her kid sister, damn it.

Across the room, William subtly tried to catch Mae's eye for a rescue. She smiled benignly at him each time, blinking and feigning incomprehension. He stood straight-backed, one hand in his pocket, the other with his drink held high in front of his chest like a shield and wore an amused but polite expression.

Charlene was standing too close for comfort and

cupping her new breasts over the material of her low-cut, sequined sweater. Mae had to stifle the laughter that welled in her chest, her angst from a moment before set aside temporarily.

William could sense her mirth from across the way as he politely declined Charlene's third offer for William to 'touch them, they feel amazing.' He needed an out, and it was apparent his wife would not be any help. He glanced at the melting ice in his drink.

"Pardon me, Charlene. I think my drink needs—"

William stopped mid-sentence when the doorbell rang. He stiffened and locked eyes with Mae. Everyone stared expectantly, a palpable tension crackled in the air. Everyone except Feather Anne, who was concentrating on balancing her black checker piece on her finger as she waited for Bruce to take his turn. Bruce stood—resembling a protective bear shielding a cub from harm—and blocked her view of the door.

Mae had been so completely confident in her adamancy that Gina be kept away, and Feather Anne be kept unaware until that doorbell rang. Now, with only a wood door separating the past from the present, Mae felt suddenly less assured by her decision. She stood abruptly and glanced at Bruce, still in front of Feather Anne like a concrete wall. His expression was grim and resolute. Everything in it said he'd back Mae up whether he agreed or not. She gave him a small, grateful smile, and he nodded once in return.

Mae was not unaware of Elise's watchful eyes as

they traveled back and forth between them. She would have to talk to her, and soon. Before her jealousy ruined their fragile friendship. But for now, Mae could only contend with the problem—the *possible* problem—at her front door. It rang again, this time a double ring. One that said, 'Hello, hello, I know you're in there. Let me in.'

William saw Mae's frozen, stricken stance and strode to the door, giving her what he hoped was a reassuring smile before turning the knob. Although, if he were truthful—which he intended later—he was as anxious for the potential return of Gina Byrd as she was. With the slow deliberateness of someone opening a jam-packed closet and expecting a mountain of junk to fall on top of him, William cracked the door and peered out.

Mae, Bruce, and Katrina held their collective breaths and waited. William's tense shoulders dropped, and he swung the door wide to show the Villeneuves smiling apologetically, each with an adorable, black-eyed toddler in the crook of an arm and holding the hands of their little Ileana. The release of oxygen in the room was almost audible.

"Pedro, Marisol, come in," Mae exclaimed.

Her genuine surprise and pleasure at seeing them quelled the butterflies in her stomach and smoothed her worried brow. She'd invited the Villeneuves to join them for Christmas Eve as soon as she heard the forecasters warning of an impending storm. She knew they'd been planning to fly out to Miami on Christmas Eve to see Marisol's family for the holiday.

"We're so sorry to come unannounced," huffed

Marisol as she led Ileana in and jostled either Diego or Alejandro—no one could tell them apart yet—up higher on her hip.

Pedro added his apologies. "Yes, sorry to show up unannounced, but our flight was canceled last minute because of the storm, and we—"

"There's always room for more, please. Come in and get warm. We've got tons of food," Mae adopted a sing-song voice as she crouched near Ileana, "*and* Santa just might have left a few gifts for a special little girl."

Ileana grinned, then worriedly asked, "And my brothers too?"

A chorus of 'aww's rung out through the room and Mae beamed at the pretty four-year-old. "For Diego and Alejandro too. Don't worry."

Katrina bumped William with her hip. "That's our Mae, prepared for anything and everything."

William turned his cautionary gaze at Mae's aunt and said, "*Almost* everything."

A worry line etched a groove in his forehead as he watched his young wife sift through the mountain of gaily wrapped presents under the tree.

Katrina sighed beside him. "I suppose she is going to have to warn Feather Anne that her poor excuse of a mother might be back in town."

"She's *what*?"

They both turned and looked to see Feather Anne behind them, her small face pale and her eyes wide. Her exclamation cut through the room, causing everyone to stare curiously. Mae's stood abruptly, a box in her grips, and glared at Katrina, who mouthed, "Sorry," and put her hands up defensively as if Mae might hurl the package at her head. Mae considered it, but one look from William was enough to make her reconsider. She had crappy aim anyhow and would've probably missed.

Instead, she said, "Feather Anne, we don't know for—"

Feather Anne turned on her heel and stormed into the kitchen. Bruce patted Mae's shoulder and said, "I'll go talk to her, if that's okay?"

Mae answered apologetically, "She listens to you the best. If you don't mind?"

Bruce handed Elise his drink, not meeting her eye, and followed Feather Anne. The party had resumed as if nothing unusual had happened, but Mae's unease had yet to abate.

From behind her, Elise's tone was both ironic and sarcastic. "Thank God for Bruce, right? Always right there to clean up a mess or pick up the pieces when something goes wrong."

Mae's head drooped, and she inhaled. She knew she had to address the Elise issue, but this was just not the time. Too much was going on. "Elise? Can we get together next week? Just the two of us? I think we need to talk."

At first, it seemed Elise was going to shoot her down. Mae could almost hear her saying, '*Mae* wants to talk, so drop everything.' Then, Elise's face softened. Whatever she'd intended to say evaporated and turned into, "Sure. We can do that. Wednesday, maybe. Ethan will have Gianna."

Mae smiled gratefully. "Good. It's a date, then."

With that settled, or at least on its way to being settled, Mae took a gusty breath and set her sights on the kitchen where Bruce was undoubtedly doing his damnedest to calm Feather Anne. She feared this unwelcome news might set back Feather Anne's progress. She'd come *so* far over the past year in controlling her temper, getting along with the other kids—even making a couple of friends— and bringing up her grades. Could this undo everything they'd worked so hard at? Would she start getting into fights again? Or skip classes, showing up at the café when she was expected to be in school? So many meetings with teachers and Vice Principal McVicar. Mae couldn't let it happen. She *wouldn't*.

Chapter 9

Good Tidings

Christmas came and went in the blink of an eye for some, but for Miles Hannaford, it felt like it would never end. Christmas Eve was supposed to have been a quiet night. Just Rosie, Miles, and her ginormous Maine Coon cat, Ludo. However, the Watermans foiled that plan with a surprise visit.

Miles opened the door and stared, dumbstruck. From the couch, Rosabelle called out, "Mom? Dad? I thought we were going to see you tomorrow at the Hannafords'?"

"Well, your father didn't think we should drive all the way to Rocky Hill to see Cousin Odie and his new wife—what's her name again, Steven?"

"Karen. No, Corrine. Something with a K or a C."

"Corrine, that's right. Anyhow, your father said that RV is not good in this much snow. So, here we are." She shrugged and gave a laugh that sounded more like a bark. Ludo sauntered sleepily to the door, weaving through Miles's legs and giving him those aggressively affectionate, rough nudge-bumps with his forehead. Ruth frowned at the feline. "Oh, Rosabelle, aren't you afraid that cat is going to trip you? I hope you've got good help around when we can't be here."

Miles gritted his teeth. "No worries, Mrs. W. I'm staying here while she recovers."

Rosabelle shot a look at Miles. "Everything is fine, Mom. Ludo is a good boy. And—"

Steven's tone was a thunderous and his nostrils flared with indignation. "I'm sorry. Did you say you're staying…here? *Here*, as in Rosabelle's *house* here?"

"*Dad*-dy, please. I'm a grown woman. If you can't—"

"Now, now. No need for any hysterics, Rosabelle. Your father and I are just…surprised. Are you going to let us in, or—" She trailed off, gazing brightly at Rosabelle and ignoring Miles, even though *he* was the one at the door.

Miles looked from Rosie to the Watermans, then back again. He was unsure what to do. He'd never had to deal with parents before. Except that time Donna Hickey's father caught him in her bedroom and chased him all the way down Sycamore Lane. Oh, and the time Chelsea Kanowski's mother hit on him in their basement. Maybe that was Melissa What's-Her-Name mother. He couldn't remember. He found himself staring at Ruth Waterman. Her fall and winter attire—so far as he'd seen—

74

consisted of too-big sweaters with polo shirts underneath, faded jeans, and sneakers. Come to think of it that might be her year-round clothes. *His* mother didn't own jeans, except for her one pair of 'garden dungarees' that she donned ceremoniously to trim her rose bushes. Unlike Ruth Waterman, Jeannie Hannaford didn't use words like, 'groovy' and 'right-o.' Nor did she—a quietly staunch Republican—discuss politics, religion, or money in mixed company. These were some of Ruth and Steven's favorite topics.

"Miles? Mi-*les*. Let my parents in, please. It's freezing out there."

"Right," jumped Miles, opening the door wide and theatrically ushering them in, saying in his best French, "*Entre Vous, s'il vous plaît.*" The three blinked at him as if he'd grown a second head. "It just means—"

"We know what it means, Hannaford. We're not the simpletons you seem to think we are. So, why don't you—"

"Daddy, give Miles your coat and go into the kitchen. Mom, come sit with me," Rosie's tone was authoritative and confident. Miles beamed proudly at her. The Watermans gaped at their daughter, then exchanged 'you see, *this* is what I'm talking about' and 'mhmm, I *know*' looks.

As for Rosabelle and Miles, they too traded heavy, wordless conversations. Miles's wide eyes said, 'what am I supposed to do?' And Rosabelle's pursed lips said, 'I don't know, just figure it out.'

It would be on Miles to feed and entertain two people who couldn't stand him, because of course,

Rosie was unable to do much more than rest. The old Miles—the one who bolted at the first signs of attachment or the dreaded mention of commitment—hissed in his mind, "Dude, just say you've got an appointment you forgot about and flake out. Rosie'll get over it." But then Rosie's name in his head triggered another Miles voice—a Miles he barely recognized, a Miles whose heart did something weird when he looked at her and made him think dopey things such as, 'I want to be a better man' for her—and that voice said, "Come on, now. Don't be a dick, Miles. She needs you to do the right thing."

The old Miles's voice was strong enough to make him edge toward the door and pull his phone from his pants pocket, and mentally rehearse the, 'Aw crap, can you believe this?' he'd say as he grimaced at his phone. He even got the "Aw" part out when he looked up to see Rosie staring at him. The expression on her face—sad, forgiving, resolved in acceptance—she knew *exactly* what he was going to do. *How? How does she know me so well?*

The Watermans turned to look too. Annoyance showed plainly on their almost matching faces. He'd heard that people who are together for a long time start to look alike. He thought of his own parents and realized they *did* sort of match in their own way. Was it such a terrible thing to share so much life with someone that you grow alike?

He and Rosie could be their own little army of two. Them against the world, or something. When had anyone ever *really* been on Miles's side?

Never, until Rosabelle Waterman, who thought he was way better than he was. He held Rosie's gaze for a moment. They *were* their own little army of two, weren't they? All she had to do was say yes to his imminent marriage proposal, and it would be so for the rest of their lives. Miles made a small sound—a laugh that came through his nose—and pressed the button on the side of his phone, making the screen go dark again.

"Never mind, not important," he said and winked at Rosabelle.

"Are you—are you sure, Miles? If you have an important work call, I under—"

She was giving him his out, and it filled him with shame…and love. "Nope. You're the most important thing right now, and"—his watch beeped—"I believe you're ready for a pain pill, yes?"

"Oh, I hope you're not going to turn her into an addict. Those are very strong narcotics, you know. The opioid crisis is real," scolded Ruth.

"Not like the old days, when pot was just pot, and hash was just hash, and—"

"Okay, thank you, Dad. Mom, Miles has an alarm set on his watch for when it's time for me to take my meds. I plan to be weaned off them by New Year's Eve, so I can drink champagne."

"All right, all right. No need to get testy, Rosabelle. My, goodness, what's gotten into you these days?"

She darted a raised eyebrow at Miles to let them know exactly where she thought Rosabelle's testiness came from.

Miles, unable to bite his tongue, said acerbically, "I'm sure a fractured pelvis, a broken leg, a sprained wrist, four cracked ribs, nine stitches, and a totaled car have nothing to do with anything, right?"

Silence.

"Well," Steven coughed, then caught his daughter's eye, and changed his mind on whatever he was about to say, and instead supposed, "I guess that wine isn't going to open itself, is it?"

He set to opening the bottle, aware of the contrast of his wife's sour pout and his daughter's grateful smile. He was not prepared to accept the Hannaford boy into their lives—he tried to send the message to his wife telepathically—but he expected to get through the day for his daughter's sake. The plan had been to present a united front. He and Ruthie against Hannaford, but seeing his girl so...so *peaceful* made him waver. Maybe they were wrong about him. Maybe he— "Hey, Rosie, did you tell your parents about the gala?"

"Gala," said Ruth dryly, her unplucked eyebrows raised.

"Oh, right." Rosabelle blushed. She'd prefer he'd not mentioned it, but too late now. "Yes, um, Miles's parents host an annual gala at their place. It's for charity."

Just as Ruth began to ask, "What's the charity—" Rosabelle said, "It—oh, I think the lasagna is ready. Mom, could you check?"

Miles, oblivious of Rosabelle's wide eyes and small, rapid head shake, said, "It's for the TARS." Seeing the blank stares from the Watermans, he added, "You know, the National Teen Age Republicans," then popped a grape in his mouth.

Rosabelle dropped her head onto her hand. Steven coughed again. Ruth, who'd been on her way to the kitchen, slowly turned back, her face deceptively blank. "I'm sorry, the *what*?"

Ruth smiled politely, but Rosabelle recognized that horizontal line with no upturn at the corners. It was her, 'I'm *sure* that's not what you meant to say, so I'll give you a moment to rethink it,' smile. She nodded her head in the way you employed to coax a stubborn child. 'That's right, come over here now,' said that nod. Miles was walking into a trap, and she couldn't stop him.

"Yeah," Miles popped another grape in his mouth, "they, um, head the Connecticut chapter, so every February they hold the TARS Stars & Hearts Gala. It's a big deal. People from across the country come. I'm sure I could get you guys a special guest invite if you're going to be in town again."

Ruth and Steven blinked at him, then at each other. Ruth's mouth was twitching at the corners. Steven started to scratch the top of his head with his ring finger in long, slow tracks from the crown of his head to base of his neck, a habit Rosabelle recognized as his, 'I'm trying to stay calm, here,' go to.

"The young...*Republicans*?" Ruth squinted one eye at Miles.

"Close. It's the *Teenage* Republicans. Cool, right?"

"Cool? *Cool*? You think turning our youth into neo—"

"Mom! The lasagna. Please. Daddy?"

Rosabelle turned pleading eyes on Steven, then on Miles, who'd, at last, realized his faux pas. Ruth's face had gone red and her eyes blazed. Everyone stood silent for a long moment. Then, mercifully, the oven timer beeped.

"Ruthie, will you get the lasagna? Everyone's starving, so let's eat." Steven had stopped scratching his head and filled everyone except Rosabelle's wine glasses. She looked at him, then the glass. He paused, then nodded and poured a small amount in hers.

Dinner was eaten mostly in silence. Polite requests for more bread, or 'pass the pepper, please,' were the only utterances. Dessert was declined by each, and Rosie was helped back to the living room. They confirmed the time for Miles's parents' Christmas Day party—which they'd been invited to by Jeannie Hannaford herself, much to the dismay of both Miles and Rosabelle—and they said their goodbyes at the couch. Miles thanked them, then disappeared into the kitchen to clean up and discreetly remained there until the door clicked shut, placing the Watermans safely on the outside.

Miles took his time loading the dishwasher and wiping the counters. He didn't know what to say to Rosie. He screwed up, did the one thing he wasn't supposed to do—he touched on one of the three no-no's and further alienated Rosie's parents. Tonight was meant to be the night he won them over so that when he proposed to her at his parents', everyone could rejoice and cheer. He'd envisioned the whole thing, the tapping on the champagne glass, all eyes and warm, smiling faces on them. He'd make a great, moving speech—he was still working on it—and then pull out the ring with a flourish. Everyone would clap, and his mother would dab at the corner of her tear-filled eyes with her linen napkin. His dad would take one look at the ring and slap him on the back, and say, "Well, done, son." The Watermans would approach him with appreciative and, dare he say, loving expressions, and tell him, "We had our reservations in the beginning, but now we know you're the right man for our little girl. Welcome to the family, son."

Now he supposed that wasn't how it was going to go down. His big, Christmas Day proposal wasn't going to happen. Not with the way the Watermans were still looking at him. Maybe he should do it tonight, with just the two of them. He could tie the ring around Ludo's neck with a big bow and when Rosie saw it, he'd propose. Perfect. Miles dried his hands and ran quietly to Rosie's bedroom. She'd cleared a couple of drawers for him, and he'd tucked the robin's egg blue, white ribboned box in the far corner, under his boxer briefs.

Getting Ludo to cooperate proved a challenge. The fat beast was determined to bite and swipe at the bow—and Miles's hands—as he tried to tie it. Instead of walking to where Rosie was, as Miles tried to nudge him, he bee-lined for his litter box. The sixteen-thousand-dollar ring that Miles had bought at Tiffany's in Westfarms Mall was now in a cat's litter box.

At last, and with what Miles determined a derisive glance, Ludo sauntered into the living room. He followed closely behind, grinning in excitement and nervousness.

"Hey, look Rosie. Ludo's got something around his neck. Rosie?"

Rosabelle had fallen fast asleep on the couch, her head thrown back, mouth open. A soft, rhythmic snore escaped her parted lips.

Miles untied the bow and slipped the ring off the ribbon. He tucked a blanket over her and adjusted her pillow. When he kissed her forehead, she sighed and mumbled something unintelligible, but remained asleep.

"Goodnight, Rosie," said Miles. "I'll try again, don't worry."

He turned off the lamp and collapsed into the small loveseat across from her, pulled out his phone, and looked for the football highlights. Every so often he'd peek over at Rosie, still sound asleep. She had on the heart pendant necklace he'd given her the morning of her accident...

***

"You're up and ready early," she'd said as she walked into her kitchen.

Miles had showered and dressed and even made them breakfast. He paced the tile floor, waiting for her to join him. He had something he wanted to tell her, something he'd meant to say the night before, but he'd chickened out. But once the words were in his head, he couldn't *stop* thinking them. No matter what they were doing, what they were discussing, four little words repeated in his mind. *I love you,*

Rosie. I love you, Rosie. I love you, Rosie…

"I love you, Rosie," Miles blurted.

Rosie had just lifted her coffee cup to her lips. She blinked at him, cocked her head, and a slow smile crinkled her eyes. "Did you just say—"

"Yes. I did. I do. Rosabelle Waterman, I fricking love you. Here, I got you this. I was going to do this last night, but then you said your parents were coming to visit and I—"

"I love you too, Miles."

Miles exhaled as if he'd been holding his breath for a long time. "Good. That's good. That's really, really good."

They stood there in the middle of Rosabelle's human-sized dollhouse kitchen, grinning stupidly at each other. Miles's phone buzzed, and they jumped.

"The office." He shrugged and squinched his face up in a way he hoped to be endearing.

"Not until I've opened this," said Rosie, waving the long, rectangular, unmistakable Tiffany's box with its white bow.

"It's just a little something. If you don't like it, we can—"

She lifted the lid and said, "Oh, Miles. It's beautiful. I love it. Here, help me put it on."

Rosabelle handed him the delicate rose-gold chain with its dainty rose-gold heart and lifted her hair. Once the clasp was secured, Miles kissed the nape of her neck and whispered, "Now move it, Waterman. I gotta go."

Rosie had giggled and made him say, 'I love you, Rosie,' again before she promised to hurry. Then they'd rushed out the door—well, he'd rushed. Rosie had taken her time, teasing him all the while. They'd left in separate directions, blissfully oblivious of what was to transpire less than an hour later.

***

Time was a funny, tricky thing. Miles watched Rosie sleep, amazed at how much had happened in such a short while. A year ago, she was just Mae's cute, quirky friend at the café, who always seemed to be around but melted into the background. He was a serial bachelor with no intentions of settling down. Love 'em and leave 'em, that was his style. No woman could lasso Miles Hannaford. No way. Now look at him, folded up on a flowery loveseat, waiting on the wants and needs of a chick that wasn't able to do the deed for a couple of months. And he was completely fine with it. *That* was the shocker.

Nora—his part-time agent and full-time pain in his ass—always said that the right woman was going to come along and turn his world upside down. Damn, she loved telling him she was right. Rosabelle Waterman had upended his world, all right. And he wouldn't trade it for anything.

Chapter 10

Oh, Christmas Tree

As soon as she came back into the kitchen, she noticed it. Everyone was acting weird still. Feather Anne squinted at Mae, William, Aunt Tree, and Bruce. She could tell they were having a 'this is serious, but let's try to make it look casual for the kid's sake' conversation. She'd seen it enough times outside the principal's office last year. They'd ask Feather Anne to 'wait here,' and go out into the hall. She did, grudgingly, but could see them through the slats in the blinds. Their voices were too muffled to make out their words. So, Feather Anne watched their body language and made up her own dialogue.

"Well, Miss Huxley, your sister is an evil street urchin and you should do better at controlling her."

"Vice Principal McVicar, I just don't know what to do with her, she's wild. I'm so sorry she smashed the beakers in the science lab. I'll pay for the damages, of course. Just please don't suspend her again."

"Well, she should be locked up. She'll probably end up in jail one day, anyhow."

"You're so right, Vice Principal McVicar."

"Yes, Mae and I couldn't agree more, Vice Principal McVicar."

Then they'd walk back in with fake, tight smiles and Mae would say, "Let's go, Feather Anne." And they'd leave.

William and Mae later had hushed conversations when they got home that looked just similar to this one, only this time Bruce and Aunt Tree were in on it too. They had their 'tells.' That's what Aunt Tree called it when someone tried to bluff at poker. Mae always put her hands on her hips when she was serious, William always crossed his arms and put his hand on his chin. Bruce and Tree were even less subtle. They both kept darting glances at Feather Anne and giving her dorky smiles. She smiled back, then rolled her eyes.

Four sets of eyes shined brightly—too brightly— at her. Everyone was smiling that stupid—what was that word William used the other day—*patronizing* smile. Like she was five, not eleven. She wanted to tell them to stop acting like freaks, damn it. But it was Christmas morning, and there were presents. A lot of presents. Like more than she'd ever gotten in her whole life.

Gina's idea of celebrating Christmas was to only get buzzed instead of blackout drunk on Christmas Eve. Feather Anne sometimes woke up to a box of

Entenmann's chocolate chip cookies wrapped in newspaper—or tinfoil if she had any in the trailer—a sweater from the Goodwill, also wrapped in newspaper or foil, and either a pack of Bubblicious bubble gum or a jumbo Reese's. Depending on how buzzed Gina was the night before, there might be other stuff wrapped up to make it seem like there was more. Once she'd wrapped a fork, her toothbrush, and half of a dinette chair.

Now, boxes of various shapes and sizes, wrapped in real wrapping paper and tied with lovely, shiny bows at the corners waited underneath a real Christmas tree for her. There were twelve gifts—she'd counted them after everyone had gone to bed—from Mae and William alone. Earlier, when Bruce had rung the doorbell—waking everyone up at seven in the morning—he had a tower of boxes balanced precariously in his hands.

Aunt Tree had yawned and swore as she brought out six more from the spare bedroom. Charlene had pulled a hot pink and white polka-dot box from her leopard print overnight bag.

Mae had scolded Bruce as she swung open the door. "For the love of God, why are you here so early? You guys should've just stayed over."

Bruce just laughed at her and said, "Get over it, Huxley. This is the brat's day, and I'm not missing it. Now go brush your hair. Geesh, you're a mess."

Feather Anne had stood in the center of the room, watching everyone. A strange sensation, akin to watching a movie of someone else's life, overwhelmed her. This couldn't be *her* life. She was the ratty girl no one ever noticed other than to make fun of her. Trailer trash Gina Byrd's trailer trash kid, in this charming house that always had music playing, people laughing and singing, and being n*ice.*

A stab of guilt pierced her ribs and poked her heart. Gina didn't deserve a second of her thoughts, but she *was* still her mother and she couldn't help herself. Happiness and guilt wrestled in her head. Feather Anne's eyes began to sting, and she swiped hard at them with the heels of her hand. There were too many feelings at once. She loved her new life, but sometimes she felt guilty for loving it. She hated Gina…and she *didn't* hate her.

William appeared beside her as if by magic. He said nothing and put his arm around Feather Anne, tucking her gently to his side. He kissed the top of her head and whispered, "I understand."

That was all Feather Anne needed—someone to understand—and William always did. She wrapped both arms around him and squeezed tight enough for him to 'oof' and then chuckle. They stayed that way while everyone bustled around. Mae flipped on the Christmas music—a new singer named Lauren Daigle she was obsessed with, enough so that she had forgone her Elvis Presley Christmas album— and began making breakfast for everyone. Tree and Charlene were looking at Charlene's phone and laughing. Bruce poured himself a cup of coffee and sang loudly off-key in Mae's ear.

The smell of bacon and waffles drifted through the house, making Feather Anne's mouth water. She released poor William from her death grip.

He'd smiled at her and said, "Mae told me once

that her father, Keith, used to call this," he waved his arm to encompass the house and everyone in it, "the 'good stuff.' I understand now what he meant. Feather Anne, *this* is the good stuff. Let's you and I just enjoy every moment of it, yes? These are the things to hold on to. The good stuff, not the bad."

Mae called out, "Breakfast is served, and it's buffet style, so make your own plate."

Breakfast, like the dinner the night before, was a feast and everyone had dived in as if they'd not just eaten a similarly extravagant spread less than twenty-four hours ago. Once they'd finished, Feather Anne had dashed to her room to get the presents she'd made for everyone and hurried back out to the kitchen with her arms full. *That* was when she found them huddled up and whispering. For a second, she thought maybe they had a big surprise—like the pygmy pig she'd been dropping not-so-subtle hints about for the past two months—but they weren't acting excited. They were acting nervous. Feather Anne knew why, of course.

She had enough. She dropped the gifts on the kitchen island and huffed, "I'm *fine*, weirdos. God. Can you guys stop talking about me and relax? I told you last night, I don't *care* if Gina's back. I'm not gonna see her, so whatever."

Mae, using her new mom-voice that Feather Anne found both hysterical *and* kind of sweet, said, "I know, sweetie. But—" Mae took a deep breath, gave a quick shake of her head, and plastered a big smile on her face. "Never mind all that. And anyhow, we were just discussing when you should get to open your presents."

"Mhmm," said Feather Anne.

"For real," said Bruce. "Your sister thinks you guys should have a tradition. I think you should just go crazy and open everything now. Tree's with me. William here is whipped, so he's going along with whatever Mae says."

Through slanted eyes, she glared suspiciously at each of them. It was Charlene who broke the tension.

"Girl, you all have, like, the best amenities at this here Huxley-Grant House. I think I'm going to give you a five-star rating."

They turned. Charlene continued to towel dry her hair, her head tipped as she squeezed out the excess water. When no one spoke, she glanced up through a curtain of damp amber curls, taking in their various expressions. She put her hand on her hip, clacked her tongue, and wagged one long, red fingernail at them.

"Oh, I *know* none of you are having drama on this here Christmas Day. It's the *Lord's* day, child, not yours. Or yours, or yours. Git going with all that sour face nonsense, you hear?"

She snapped her fingers at them and clucked her tongue before walking off, muttering under her breath something in the vein of, 'Buncha drama queens in there,' then she began singing along with *Jingle Bells*. She actually sang really well. The tension left the room, and the adults smiled sheepishly. Feather Anne still wore an apprehensive look until Bruce caught her eye. With deliberate slowness he stuck his finger up his nose, keeping his face impassive. Feather Anne laughed, just as he hoped.

Somehow, they managed to put thoughts of Gina Byrd in the farthest back corners of their minds and had a very merry Christmas. Bruce stayed long enough for Feather Anne to open all her presents. Then he hurried off to go to Elise's. Aunt Tree and Charlene decided to stay one more night, thanks to Mae's spiked eggnog. William played the piano, and everyone sang, even Feather Anne. That was a first. She sang softly, not wanting anyone to hear her, but she sang nonetheless.

She didn't get the pygmy pig, but Mae and William surprised her with horseback riding lessons in the spring. They said if she liked it, they'd consider getting her a horse—big emphasis on consider. Of all the gifts Feather Anne received—and there were a lot—her favorite of all was the pendant necklace from Mae. She had two specially made, one for Mae and one for Feather Anne. They were white gold circles with a dangling silhouette of two girls holding hands. On one figure it read, 'Sisters' and on the other, 'Forever.'

Feather Anne had jumped up and hugged Mae, then pushed away just as quickly. She teased, "Oh, my God, Mae. Are you crying? You're such a dork."

"I am not a dork, I'm emotional. Brat." Mae nudged Feather Anne with her toe.

Feather Anne considered saying something obnoxious, then changed her mind. "I love it, Mae. Thank you."

William winked and nodded his approval. Feather Anne stuck her tongue out, then laughed.

Can't give them too much sensitivity, the saps.

Much too soon, the best Christmas ever reached its end with Mae declaring with a yawn at ten-thirty, "All right, I'm afraid I need to call it a night."

"Party pooper," said Aunt Tree, her head lolling onto Charlene's shoulder.

Feather Anne was the only one still wide awake. William helped Mae from the couch like a prince handing a princess from a carriage and Mae smiled up at him adoringly. They were the most romantic couple Feather Anne had ever seen. Not that she'd tell them that, of course. Aunt Tree and Charlene staggered off to their rooms, mumbling goodnights and Merry Christmases to all. Feather Anne stayed seated on the carpet by the tall evergreen, gazing up at the twinkling white lights and sparkly ornaments.

William looked over his shoulder and said, "Aren't you going to bed too?"

Feather Anne shrugged. "Can I stay up a little while longer and look at the tree?"

William looked at his watch, then said, "Not too much later, okay? See you in the morning."

"Goodnight, William. Oh, and Merry Christmas."

"Merry Christmas to you as well, sweetheart. Goodnight."

Once she heard the soft click of their bedroom door, Feather Anne sprang up and grabbed a pillow and blanket off one of the couches and went back to the tree. For a while she just sat there, huddled underneath the blanket, staring up at the twinkling lights. This time last year she'd done the very same, only back then, it was so different.

Last Christmas, Feather Anne had studied the heavily ornamented evergreen intensely, her neck craned and eyes wide as she scrutinized each ornament, committing them to memory. It was the first one she'd ever had, making it by far the most magnificent and special. She guessed it might be her *only* Huxley house Christmas. There was no way Mae could want to keep her. Now that William was back, and they were in love, Feather Anne would be an intrusion. Any day now, Feather Anne expected to be shipped off to a foster home. She refused to care though. *Whatever. I can take care of myself, screw them. As soon as they drop me off at… wherever, I'll run away, and they'll never find me.*

She had a secret stash hidden under the bed in a spare room. Cash, candy bars, clothes, all zipped up in a One Direction backpack Gina had 'found' the year before and tossed at her on the third day of school.

"They're not even a band anymore," Feather Anne had scoffed.

Gina had shrugged. "That or nothin', kid. Suit yourself."

Their first Christmas together came and went, as did New Year's Eve and Day, and still, Mae acted as if Feather Anne were staying with her. She said things like, "We'll have to go shopping for some better winter clothes over the school break," and, "I think in the spring, you should try out for the track team."

Feather Anne shrugged and said 'whatever' to each suggestion. New clothes? Playing sports? It was too much to hope for, so she refused to let herself. Indifference was her shield. Attitude was her armor.

The first Christmas break of her new life had ended, and it was time to go back to school. *Now she'll see how bad I am. Now she'll get rid of me.* It wasn't like she *tried* to get into trouble, it just…happened. When Jessica Fignola got everyone to call her 'Garbage Girl,' she did her best to ignore them. But then Carlos put a bunch of trash from lunch in her backpack—she *knew* it had to be him—and she lost it. It was worth the in-school suspension to see him holding his nose and crying, "It's broken. She broke my nose," in the hallway. It's nothing like in the movies, by the way. No one cheered and patted Feather Anne on the back for defending herself against a bully. Instead, they stared and snickered at her as Mr. D'Mateo marched her down to Vice Principal McVicar's office. Somehow, *she* was the bully, and Carlos was the victim.

Everyone still called her Garbage Girl. No one sat with her at lunch. Well, no one except Brandon Bourdreau. For some reason, he liked Feather Anne, even when she was mean to him. She had a feeling, if his family ever found out they were friends, he'd be totally grounded for life. Or at least forbidden to hang out with Garbage Girl. Kids like Brandon Bourdreau probably never got grounded. They got awards and stuff. Ponies on their birthdays and shiny new cars when they turn sixteen. Not stolen backpacks and newspaper wrapped stale cookies.

Mae spent a good deal of time in Vice Principal

McVicar's office well into those first months. She never got mad though. Well, she never *acted* mad. Feather Anne waited for it each time she came out of the office. When it didn't happen, she figured, 'Ah, she's waiting till we get in the car. *Then* she'll let 'er rip. But nope, Mae just kind of sighed, gave her a funny look, and said, 'C'mon brat. Let's blow this joint,' or something along those lines.

It wasn't until the last week of school that Feather Anne started to believe that she was really going to stay with Mae and now William as well. That day was etched in her mind forever. A Wednesday, eleven-forty-two a.m. Brandon was out sick that day, so Feather Anne had the table all to herself. Someone had thrown a crushed chocolate milk carton onto her tray and the last drops of mud-brown liquid splattered the front of her shirt. They wouldn't have done that if Brandon was there. They never bothered her when he was near. Her ears burned, and she could taste blood in her mouth from biting her inner cheek.

A shadow fell over her, too immense to be a kid. That meant a lunch aide, who would yell at her for the spray of milk on the table. Instead, another voice spoke.

"Hey, brat. What do you say we get McDonald's instead of this crap?"

Feather Anne looked up at her sister. She half wanted to cry with relief, and half wanted to duck under the table in embarrassment. She'd bet Mae Huxley never sat alone at lunch. Or got called Garbage Girl. She flushed with mortification. Around them not-so-quiet whispers of, 'Who's that?' and 'Probably her social worker,' and 'she's too pretty to be related to Garbage Girl.'

Mae heard them. Feather Anne could tell because her nostrils flared, and her eyes got this hard look in them that Feather Anne had never seen. Only, she wasn't giving Feather Anne the look, but the kid who'd just said, 'Garbage Girl.' He was the same one who'd thrown the milk carton. Mae held up one finger to Feather Anne, sauntered around the table to where the boy and his friends sat, her eyes burning a hole through him. Feather Anne had to twist in her seat to see what she was doing. Mae smiled at all of them, and they smiled back. Nervously.

She stooped and whispered something to the boy. As she did, she reached out and grabbed one of the milk cartons—chocolate, coincidentally or not—and slowly poured the contents into the boy's lap. He stayed stock still, his eyes squinched shut and his lips a thin white line. When it was empty, Mae set the carton back in front of the slack-jawed boy, reached in her purse, and pulled out a dollar.

"You can buy a new milk. Have a lovely day, boys. And you," her voice hardened, "remember what I said." To Feather Anne, in a light airy voice, she said, "C'mon, sis. We're out of here."

They walked to the car in silence, both grinning Cheshire cat smiles. At the drive-thru, Mae ordered Feather Anne's favorites—two cheeseburgers, extra pickles, a large fry, soda—and even got herself a milkshake. Mae hated fast-food joints, but for some reason, she'd made an exception.

"Hey, this isn't the way home. Where we

going?"

Mae had turned onto the highway. She wore a small, secretive smile. "Somewhere. You'll see." Then, seeing Feather Anne's worried expression, added, "It's good. I promise."

Feather Anne relaxed in her seat and dug into her bag. The one thing she'd learned of Mae so far was that she never lied. Or tried to trick her. If Mae said it was something good, then it was. Plus, she'd just dumped a carton of milk on a kid for her. In front of everyone too. Mae must've been reading her mind.

She said, "That kid was an asshole. Don't repeat that, please. How—how long has that been going on? What else has been happening?"

Feather Anne shrugged. "I don't know since, like, forever. Don't worry about it. It's cool."

"No, not cool. It's awful. Why didn't you tell me that they call you—that they call you names? Is that why you punched that little creep—what was his name, Brandon?"

"No," Feather Anne exclaimed sharply. "Not Brandon Bourdreau. He's nice. That was Carlos. Just—don't worry, Mae. I'm used to it."

With a vehemence Feather Anne never imagined her capable of, Mae said, "Listen to me. No one treats my kid sister like that and gets away with it." Then, after a few minutes, she added, a waver to her voice, "I'm so sorry that I had no idea what was going on. I should've known. I should've been paying more attention. I—"

"Chill, Mae. You're already doing a *way* better job than Gina ever did. It's cool, really."

She could tell Mae was trying not to cry, and that

made Feather Anne love her more, even though tears were super embarrassing and she hated emotional stuff. So, she did something she'd never have done before. She offered Mae a French fry. One of the good ones too. Not the hard little burned up ones from the bottom, but a long squishy one.

Mae stared at it as if it was a worm instead of a fry, but she took it, perceiving it was kind of a significant gesture on Feather Anne's part. She took a tiny rabbit bite and said, "Salty. Hmm. Hey, it's good." And they both laughed.

By then, they'd pulled in the lot of a brick building. Mae hurried her inside, hissing, "Go faster, we're going to be late."

They followed a sign that said, 'Probate Hearings' with an arrow pointing down a long corridor and then they were suddenly in a large room with a handful of people in suits and smart looking dresses. It was then that Feather Anne noticed that Mae wasn't wearing her trademark Converse with her dress, but patent leather Mary-Janes. She kept smoothing her hair and taking these slow breaths through her nose and exhaling through her mouth like she did when she meditated in the backyard.

There were a few rows of chairs, but only three people took up the front row. When Mae and Feather Anne walked in, they all turned. It was William, Aunt Tree—she was still getting used to calling her that—and Bruce. They were smiling.

"Mae, what's going on?"

"Well, brat, today's the day I become your official, legal guardian. If that's still okay with you, of course?"

Mae bit her bottom lip and her eyebrows went up. Feather Anne pretended to think hard, then she said "Um, duh. Of course, it is," and suppressed a smile.

Secretly, she loved that Mae made such a big fuss out of everything. Ever since she'd gone to the trailer that first time, she'd been trying to 'make up for lost time,' and apologizing for being 'such a crappy sister.' Those were Mae's words, not Feather Anne's. She understood it. Who the hell wanted to claim Gina Byrd as their mother? And as for Feather Anne, she was just a reminder of a crappy mother for Mae. Couldn't blame her for not wanting *that* around.

Anyhow, the next thing she knew, the judge lady was telling her she was under the permanent legal guardianship of Miss Mae Scarlet Huxley, and if she wanted to change her name legally from Byrd to Huxley, they could begin the paperwork for adoption.

They went out that night for pizza and Mae had them bring out a cake at the end. It was cool. Like, *really* cool. After that, things calmed down. Feather Anne stopped getting into so much trouble, and the other kids didn't pick on her as much as they used to. Not to her face, at least. The teachers were even nicer and Vice Principal McVicar actually smiled and said good morning to her when he passed her in the hall. She suspected it all had something to do with Mae's visit to the school. Feather Anne wouldn't have even known about it if not for Brandon.

"Hey, your sister is here again," he said on the Monday after the guardianship hearing.

"Oh yeah? Where?"

"She's in the office with McVicar, a bunch of teachers, and even Principal Cassavella is in there. I couldn't hear what she said to them, but they all look scared. Your sister's badass, Feather Anne."

Feather Anne had choked back a laugh—Mae was literally the nicest, most gentle person on the planet as far as Feather Anne could tell—but then it hit her, '*Yeah. You know what? My sister is a badass, she's taken me on.*' So, Feather Anne said, "Yup, she is. Hey Brandon?"

"Yeah," said Brandon, shoveling creamed corn into his mouth, making Feather Anne want to gag.

"How come you're nice to me?" She'd always wanted to ask him that, but up till that moment, she'd been too shy.

Brandon looked up at the ceiling and frowned. Then he shrugged and said, "I dunno. I think you're cool, Feather Anne. You're not like everyone else, you know?"

"Oh, I know," said Feather Anne, stabbing a tater tot with her spork.

Brandon leaned in. "Different is good, Feather Anne. Trust me."

Right then Feather Anne got a glimpse of the future, grown-up Brandon Boudreau. He'd be a good man someday, she just knew it. Though she'd never in a million years tell him or anyone, she loved him right then. Of course, he had to ruin it and open his mouth to show her the chewed up creamed corn, making her want to vomit.

She never found out what Mae said to the principals and teachers in the office that day—or what Mae had said to the jerk with the milk carton, for that matter—all she knew is that things started to get better.

Now it was a full year later, and she was under a similar Christmas tree, with the same ornaments—plus the new ones that Feather Anne had made—and everything was so different, so…good. Only one dark cloud could overshadow this newfound peace. Gina. What might happen if Gina was back? What did it *mean*? If Gina wanted her back, how could she say no? What if, deep down, Mae was relieved, and let Gina take her? Why did part of her hope that she was back?

It was more than she could think about. Feather Anne covered her ears as if the words were coming from around her instead of inside her head. There was dampness on her cheeks. She pulled the blanket over her head and flopped down, her face into the pillow so no one heard her crying. She still hated for anyone to see her cry. Her best days had slipped into one of her worst nights, and all she could do was hope that Mae fixed it for her. Feather Anne's sleep that night, and the next nights after, were to be restless and worry-filled.

Chapter 11

Peace On Earth

If Miles had any illusions of what Christmas Day might be like, the senior Hannafords and Watermans obliterated them within the first twenty-five minutes of the afternoon. The first inkling came when Jeannie opened the door to the over-enthusiastic Ruth and Steven.

"Jeannie Schwartz, it's been forever," said Ruth.

She said it so quickly and robotically that Rosabelle suspected she'd rehearsed the line the entire car ride over, trying to get the inflection just right. Jeannie's hand rose to her chest, her polite smile faltered just long enough for it to be noticed.

"Ruth, Steven. So delightful to see you both. Come in, won't you?"

"Nice place you got here, Chet. Very…spacious," said Steven as Chet thrust an amber-colored drink in a cut crystal glass in his hand.

"Thanks, Steve. We enjoy it well enough. Rosie here tells us you've been traveling the country in your recreational van."

"It's just called an RV, Dad." Miles chuckled nervously.

"Recreational vehicle, technically. She's a 2005 Winnebago—we call her Winnie—thirty-nine-footer, class A, diesel pusher with all the toys, three slide outs, auto levelers. Got her at a decent price too. Yep, just me, the wife, and the open road. We're taking a real slice of Americana, I like to say."

"Yes, that's very—" began Chet. His mind said, 'very…pedestrian,' as he struggled for an appropriate adjective.

"Intriguing," finished Jeannie smoothly.

Miles and Rosabelle let go the breath they'd both been holding. So many minefields to navigate. They could only hope none exploded in their faces.

Steven frowned at the glass in his hand, sniffed the contents, and jerked his head back in disgust.

"Whatcha got in here, Chet? Rocket fuel?" Steven laughed at his own joke.

"That, my good man, is a sixteen-year-old small batch, Black Maple Hill bourbon. One-hundred-and-fifty dollars a bottle. I have twelve of them. Go on, try it. Put hair on your chest." Chet laughed as he clapped Steven hard on the back.

Rosabelle winced. Miles grimaced. They looked at one another and offered weak, 'let's just get through this' smiles. Meanwhile, Jeannie took Ruth down the long hall to the kitchen.

"Ruth, dear, you didn't have to bring anything. The caterer's prepared a scrumptious lamb, along with a beautiful—oh, now what was it they said— oh, yes, a roasted garlic and clementine carrots dish, and a spinach salad. What was it you said you brought?"

Ruth looked at her green bean and French-fried onion casserole in its white Corningware dish. The beans had lost their crisp, verdant green hue and now appeared limp and almost gray. Jeannie's beige heels clipped and clacked across the marble floor, while Ruth's sneakers made small squeaks that reminded her of quiet middle school corridors and students staring out classroom doors as she passed by.

"It's just a casserole. Don't feel you have to put it out," she said in a voice reminiscent of the one she had used those long past middle school days when the popular girls—like Jeannie Schwartz, now Hannaford—ruled the school and girls like Ruth Bogar got called Ruth Booger.

"Don't be silly. Of course, we'll put it out. Set it here with the rest of the food." She turned to a shockingly tall woman with a severe bun knotted at her nape. "Helga, be sure to bring out Ruth's casserole with our meal. We'll dine at four, yes?"

"Yes, Mrs. Hannaford," said Helga with a curt bow. She shot a glance at Ruth's sad dish, her face impassive. Whatever she thought of Ruth Waterman's casserole, she hid expertly.

"This is quite a kitchen, Jeannie. I never imagined you'd be a—a gourmet."

Jeannie laughed as if Ruth had said something

hilarious. "Oh, God—no, honey, I don't cook. We have someone for that." When Ruth didn't laugh along with her, she said, "Come on, let's go find the rest of them. Chet's probably showing your husband the game room."

Ruth followed behind and hoped that the 'game room' meant a pool table and such, and not stuffed animal carcasses staring blindly from walls.

As for Jeannie, she only hoped they could get through the evening without mention of the president, climate change, or animal rights. How her son connected himself to such a liberal family was beyond her. The girl seemed sweet enough, at least. Artsy, but relatively quiet. She painted animals, landscapes, and people, nothing controversial. None of that ridiculous abstract nonsense that a five-year-old could paint.

"There you two are. I was just showing Steven the game room. Says he used to play a pretty good pool game back in college—" Chet turned back to Steven. "What college did you go to, pal?"

Steven stood taller and said, "Mount Holyoke College."

Chet said, "Course you did. I'm a Texas A&M University fella, myself."

Wryly, Steven said, "Of course, you are."

Before the sudden chill in the room had time to settle, Miles jumped in and said, "Wonder what's taking those appetizers so long. Mother?"

"Hors d'oeuvres," corrected Jeannie. "They'll be out any moment now, I'm sure."

As if she'd been hovering around the corner, awaiting her cue, Helga appeared with a silver tray laden with fancy, bite-sized food. Everyone selected from the proffered dish, took a napkin and busied themselves with eating. The lapse in conversation was magnified by the lack of distraction.

"Music," declared Miles, too loudly.

Rosabelle looked up at him and nodded encouragingly. "Oh, that's a wonderful idea, Miles. What's Christmas without holiday music, right?"

The Watermans shrugged and nodded agreeably. The Hannafords exchanged perplexed looks as if they didn't understand the question.

"Dad, the Bose I bought for you last Christmas, remember? You connect it to the Bluetooth on your phone and—never mind, I'll set it up."

Within minutes, Miles had classical Christmas music playing in the background low enough to not be a nuisance, and loud enough to fill in the gaps in conversation. He anticipated many of them...unless they started arguing, which Rosie and Miles were most fearful of. Most of their evening was spent on guard, ready and waiting to redirect any time a topic veered toward the unspeakable. The Waterman and Hannaford seniors kept them busy.

They'd almost made it through dessert when the conversation train derailed. Miles excused himself and dashed out to the car under the guise of searching for his wallet, but really getting the ring from the glove box. They'd managed to keep everyone civil, which had to be good enough. He couldn't keep letting that proposal burn a hole in his head much longer. Tonight was the night.

Inside the foyer, as he shook off the cold, he picked up the sound of raised voices from the dining room. Shit. He'd left them alone for only a minute, but it was a minute too long, apparently. Miles hurried down the hall and burst into the dining room. The first eyes he met were Rosie's. Helplessly, she put her hands up to say, 'I tried,' then gestured to the two men having a heated debate. Words like, 'snowflakes' and 'neo-nazis' were volleyed back and forth, as were 'socialists,' 'tree huggers,' 'capitalists,' and 'planet destroyers.'

Ruth bowed her head and massaged a spot between her eyebrows. Jeannie filled her wineglass to the brim, raised it to no one in particular, and took a long sip. Miles slipped the ring box into his back pocket and pulled his sweater over it. Tonight would not be the night after all.

Chapter 12

Silver And Gold

Bruce watched Miles as he spoke animatedly to the Watermans over Rosabelle's head. She gazed lovingly up at him, the Watermans less so. In fact, they looked to be barely tolerating him. Even *he* wanted to tell the guy to stop trying so hard, and Bruce couldn't stand Miles.

Rosabelle caught Bruce's eye, and she shrugged, shaking her head at the trio talking above her, forgetting she was there. The skin around her stitches had turned a mottled green and yellow. It would still be weeks before she could walk more than a few steps unassisted, but the doctors had been encouraged by her progress.

Meanwhile, in the dining room, Charles Brightsider appeared beside Mae with Mrs. Brightsider trailing behind. "Mae, dear, you've thrown a wonderful New Year's Eve party. To think, we were going to stay home tonight! Your father would be so very proud."

Georgie Brightsider batted her husband's arm in that impatient, 'Out of my way, you old coot,' way that long-married wives do with their husbands. "Charles is right—don't let it go to your head, Charles—this *is* a wonderful party. When on earth did you find time to decorate?"

"William helped." Mae smiled.

"You look tired," said Charles somewhat abruptly.

"Charles," admonished Georgie, "you look lovely as always, dear. But…you do look peaked. Are you feeling all right?"

"Yes, yes." Mae brushed off their concern. "Perfectly fine. 'Tis the season, I suppose. I'm just a bit wiped out by the holidays, that's all. Once January starts, I'll be able to relax again."

Charles asked, "Still going to do your open mic nights, though, right? Invite that band back again too. That fella—you know, the one who played all the Beatles' songs—I liked him."

"Oh, yes. Beatle Al, they called him, right? Yes, they said they'd love to come back," said Mae.

Georgie gave Charles the 'Wife Glare' and said, "*Really*, Charles. Never mind him. You should take the winter to just slow everything down. Save the open mic thing for the spring!"

Mae took Georgie's hand in hers and put the other one on Charles's sleeve. "Thank you both. Actually, the lead singer offered to run the open mic for me. I'll have the best of both worlds, music and relaxing."

"Wonderful!" Charles clapped. His mind began to spin with the musical possibilities. He may be seventy-three, but he had the spirit of a much younger man. He could keep time with the best of them, and then some. "You know, I even pulled my clarinet out of storage. Been practicing at home for a while, but I might be ready to try it out live."

"Please, just don't take up the drums again, dear. All that banging sets the dogs wild," declared Georgie.

"I've heard you when William and I walk by on our way to the beach. Sounding great to me," said Mae earnestly. Was there an instrument Charles Brightsider *couldn't* play?

Mae left them at the buffet table and leaned against the wide doorframe. She scanned the room, making sure all was well, everyone had what they needed. Bruce and Elise were in the corner by the tree with the Ashebys. Charlene, Katrina, and James smiled over an old photo album. In the farthest corner of the room, by the towering tree, Miles caught Mae's eye, took a gulp of air, and tapped the side of his wine glass. The sharp *plink, plink, plink* caught everyone's attention, just as he'd intended.

"If I could have your attention, everyone? Thank you, thank you. As most—if not all of you know—" he dared a glance at Mr. and Mrs. Waterman, who he still had not been offered to call Steven and Ruth— "Rosie and I have been dating. What you may not know, is that we've been together for over a year now."

Several not-so-hushed whispers erupted. Phrases of, 'No, duh,' were coughed into hands, and James

McKenna called out, "Hell, even I knew, and I live in New York, son," causing a ripple of laughter to spread around the room. The only ones who were not amused were Steven and Ruth Waterman. They looked as if their glasses held lemon juice instead of white wine.

"Anyhow," said Miles pointedly, "I'd love to take this opportunity, in front of our nearest and dearest family and friends, to—"

"Oh, for hell's sake," muttered Steven Waterman loud enough to be heard.

Miles paused, forced a placid smile, and continued, "To show my love for Rosie." He turned to an enraptured and stunned Rosabelle and kneeled beside her. From his pocket, with a trembling hand, he pulled out a small robin's egg blue box.

"Rosabelle Waterman, I kneel here before you, in front of our friends and your parents, to ask...will you marry me?"

Rosabelle's shaking hand fluttered to her throat, then covered her mouth. Her eyes were wide and tear-filled, and she was too overcome to speak, but she nodded her head emphatically.

From behind her, her mother gasped, "Oh, no," and dropped her head against her husband's arm. Steven Waterman looked as if he had a mouthful of barbed wire.

Miles pretended not to notice their reactions as he slipped the three and one-half carat, princess cut diamond and platinum engagement ring—a ring Ruth Waterman would later sniff and call ostentatious—onto Rosie's trembling finger. Around them, applause and surprised exclamations broke out, followed by back-claps and congratulations, toasts, and laughter. It was almost perfect, save the Watermans' less than warm rejoinder.

The only person besides the Watermans to look displeased was Bruce. He scowled, grabbed his beer, and slipped out back.

"Mae, is there any more cheese for this fondue thing?" Joel Asheby held up a metal skewer with a square of French bread perched on the point.

"Oh, there you are, Mae. Can you believe this? I mean, a *proposal*? We can't have this." Ruth Waterman was speaking so close to Mae's face, she could smell the wine on her breath.

"Mae, I've been wanting to talk to you about having my book club meeting at the café next month," said Georgie.

At once, Mae felt hot. Voices were coming at her from all directions, loudly and yet sounding far away. Her vision blurred, then cleared. She tried to step back from Ruth Waterman and her wine breath, but Ruth matched her step back with a step forward.

More harshly than she'd intended, she said, "Excuse me," and Ruth blinked at her, surprised. "I—sorry, excuse me for just a moment. I have to get more ice from out back."

She abruptly turned and bee-lined for the French doors to the patio. Her mouth flooded with saliva and her throat constricted as she closed the door between her and the noise and odor-filled house. With hands on her knees, she forced herself to draw the icy air slowly in through her nose, into her lungs, willing the wave of nausea to dissipate.

"Too much eggnog, Huxley?"

She stood, still measuring her breaths carefully. "It was only one glass, Grady. What are you doing out here?"

Bruce shrugged, took a swig of beer, and said, "Eh, needed fresh air."

Mae's legs felt wobbly as she sat beside him on the bench swing. He stepped a heel back to make the bench swing and Mae grabbed his knee in a vise-like grip.

"Don't you dare make this thing swing."

"Whoa." Bruce laughed. "You're really not feeling too good there, are you, sport? If it wasn't the eggnog, then what's got you all queasy, Miss 'I've-Got-An-Iron-Stomach?' If you've got a stomach bug, get away from me." He laughed again and pushed her to the farther side of the swing.

Mae didn't say a word.

"Huxley?" Bruce's expression changed. "Huxley, are you...*pregnant*?"

Mae grinned sheepishly at him, then nodded. "Yes, but you can't say a word, Bruce. You hear me? Not a word. I haven't even told William yet. I can't even believe it myself."

"Holy shit, Huxley. A baby. Wow, that's—that's great news." Bruce shook his head ruefully. "Geez, you guys are all a bunch of thunder stealers, you know."

"What? What do you mean?" Mae was perplexed.

"Huxley, I was planning to propose to Elise tonight. But Hannaford beat me to it with *his* big proposal. The dick."

"Oh, my God, Bruce. That's wonderful." Mae clapped excitedly, instantly forgetting her nausea. "Can I see the ring?" She slid back next to Bruce and tugged on his sleeve. "Come on, come on, hurry. Before someone comes out."

"Okay, okay. Geesh." Bruce stretched and twisted to pull the square velvet box from the back pocket of his jeans. With a flourish, he flipped open the lid to reveal a stunning round diamond in a vintage floral halo style platinum setting.

"Bruce, it's perfect. Elise will love it. I'm so, *so* happy for you."

Bruce put his arm around Mae and pulled her in for a side hug. "I'm happy for you too, Huxley."

"There you two are. It's almost midnight," Elise stood in the doorway shivering. Her expression was as icy as the winter air.

"Hey, babe. We were just—"

"Just talking. Yeah, I know."

Elise shook her head and went back inside. Bruce swore under his breath and Mae stood.

"I'm sorry, Bruce," she said guiltily.

"No, stop. It's fine. It'll be fine, honest. She's just—well, it'll all be okay." Bruce tried to sound confident, but Mae knew him too well and for too long to not recognize the uncertainty in his voice.

She gently punched his arm and said, "Of course, it will. Let's get back inside."

"Yeah, it's fricking cold out here. Hey, and you—hurry up and tell your husband about the future rug rat so we can celebrate, will ya?"

"Tonight, I promise."

Inside, Mae found William with a beaming Miles

and Rosabelle...and a less than cheery Ruth and Steven Waterman.

"There she is." William smiled, then, in her ear, he whispered, "everything all right?"

She squeezed his hand and nodded. "Congratulations, you two. Miles, you sneaky devil, I can't believe you kept this a secret."

"Sorry, baby Mae, I knew you wouldn't mind my hijacking your party for such an important announcement, though.

"Well, you *assumed* she wouldn't mind," inserted Ruth.

"No, I—" sputtered Miles.

"All right everyone," called Katrina over the music and conversations, "get your champagne glasses. The countdown starts in five minutes."

Mae sent William for their champagne and dashed down the hall to get Feather Anne, who had babysitting duty to Gianna and Benjamin Asheby.

"Thank God. They're all leaving after this, right?" Both toddlers were sound asleep in their pack-n-plays, toys strewn everywhere. Her bedroom resembled a daycare center.

"Yes." Mae laughed. "You can leave them alone for the countdown, come on."

They joined William by the fireplace as Charlene gave the one-minute warning. Everyone—even the Watermans—wore matching expressions of anticipation. A new year was ready to be rung in, the old said goodbye to.

"Everyone has their glasses?"

A chorus of yesses answered.

"All right then, you get ready now," sang

Charlene.

The countdown began at ten. Mae's heart thumped. When everyone shouted 'three,' she gazed up at William and motioned for him to give her his ear. At 'two,' she whispered, "We're going to have a baby."

At 'one,' William stared at her in disbelief, a slow smile of comprehension spreading across his face. At the collective shouts of 'Happy New Year,' he said, "A baby? A *baby*. We're going to have a baby," with such wonderment and joy that tears sprang to both of their eyes.

At one minute after twelve, Mae said, "Happy New Year, William."

"Happy New Year, my love," said William.

Two minutes after twelve, the doorbell rang.

Chapter 13

A Cup Of Kindness

Brianna jabbed her fork at the roast chicken lying artlessly on Kasey Baker's circa nineteen-eighty-four Corelle plate. It bore a striking resemblance to the roasted turkey from Thanksgiving and the pork roast from Christmas Eve. At her parents' house, they were feasting on a rack of lamb or petite filets. Maybe even jumbo stuffed shrimp, pending Gordon's mood. Mother probably had to go to the store at least three times to accommodate his ever-changing moods.

"Brianna, dear?"

"What?" Brianna looked up to see Kasey and Robby Baker, Great Grandmother Baker, and Ricky all staring at her.

"Mom asked if you want mashed potatoes," said Ricky.

"Oh, God no," she said before she could censor

117

herself. "I mean, thank you, but no. I'm Paleo, so no carbs. I'm sure it's…delicious, though."

She was sure of no such thing. It would have a gallon of salt, a pound of butter, and sour cream as well. It amazed her that Ricky wasn't a big fat butterball growing up. Brianna shot a glance at his stomach. It strained at the buttons around his mid-section. She'd pointed it out to him before they left for his mother's. He tried telling her he was rocking the 'dad bod,' or something equally stupid. She told him he'd better get back in the gym. If she took care of herself, then it was only obvious he should do the same. Ridiculous that she even had to tell him this.

Ricky gave a small cough and said, "Ma, I'd love more of your famous mashed potatoes," giving Brianna one of his, 'please just be nice,' looks. She ignored him.

While she tried to figure out how she could discreetly get rid of the slab of dry meat on her plate, Ricky and his father embarked an overly animated conversation about—God help her—football. His older sister, Bethany—Bethy, as they insisted on calling her—gushed to their mother about the green bean casserole as if the woman hadn't made it for the past three holidays in a row.

"Well, Bethy, I love that you love your momma's casserole," enthused Kasey.

"And I love how you take care of all of us, Momma Bear," gruffed Robby, taking a pause in his diatribe on why the Patriots were the greatest team in the history of football.

They were all oozing sentiments and sweetness at one another. Even Cassidy—the little traitor—

enjoyed all the Baker family sappiness. Brianna was in absolute hell. She considered the places she'd rather be. In Aruba. Home. At Katie's party. Anywhere. Hell, she'd rather be at her own parents' house. At least she'd see Brandon. Anything was more favorable than being bored. To. Death.

Brianna used the wooden tongs to pick through the matching wood bowl of salad. Iceberg. Of course. God forbid these people ever bought a spring mix. She fished out three cherry tomatoes— cherry, not grape—and dodged the five thousand croutons. Her glance over the table for oil and vinegar was cursory, only Kasey Baker's ever-present bottle of Italian Seasonings dressing ever graced their table. Just perfect.

"So, the expansion on the shop is going all right, son?"

"Yeah, Pop, so far. I think it'll be ready by May. April, if we're lucky."

"You'll be lucky if Skinny Chris doesn't completely rob you blind," muttered Brianna under her breath.

"What was that, Brianna dear?" Kasey blinked and smiled with that annoying dimpled cheeked, doe-eyed face of hers. She was too old to look doe-eyed.

"Mom, can you pass the pepper," asked Ricky before Brianna could respond.

He gave her 'the look,' the one that begged, 'please not in front of my parents, Bri.' It was the holidays, so she smiled and said, "Everything is delicious—" then dropped the sentence. Eleven years and she still didn't know what to call Robby and Kasey Baker. Mom? Pop? No, impossible. Robby and Kasey? Absurd. Those were children's names, not middle-aged adults. So, she just avoided calling them anything. Unless she could use Cassidy as her go-between.

For example, "Cassidy, would you prefer to give Grandpop a hug or a fist bump?" It was a perfectly reasonable method of name avoidance.

Brianna didn't believe children should be forced to hug or kiss anyone, ever. Cassidy would be raised with a strong sense of autonomy. She would be allowed to decide whom she showed affection to, thank you very much. Ricky agreed as he should.

"Does Cassy want some tay-toes," cooed Bethany to Cassidy.

"Cassidy," said Brianna through her teeth.

"Sorry, it's just that 'Cassy' rolls off the tongue so easily, don't you think? And it fits right in with all our names too. You know, Robby, Kasey, Ricky, Bethy—"

"I'm aware," said Brianna, her smile tight.

How could she not be aware? It was the Baker family badge of honor, their absurd, stupid two-syllable, ends in 'y' names. It was more than enough that she'd given in to a 'y' ending name. That was as far as she'd bend.

Ricky stiffened and Brianna saw them exchange glances. She pretended not to notice, or care that her cheeks suddenly felt hot. Why did he insist on making her suffer through these abominable dinners? If Brianna had her way—which she usually did—then Ricky would've taken Cassidy to his parents, and she could've gone straight to Katie

O'Brien's house under the guise of 'helping out.' Katie didn't *need* any help, of course. It was a catered event. One that Brianna and Ricky should've been hosting. But no, Ricky didn't want to spend any extra right now because of the stupid auto body shop expansion.

Then again, that stupid expansion was likely going to bring in more money to the Baker household, so she supposed she could suck it up for one more year. Next year, she intended on hosting the mother of all parties. And she would not invite Elise or Charlotte. They could go to one of their boring Huxley parties and stew in their jealousy at missing out on the party of the century. A smirk pulled at the edges of her mouth as she pictured them.

In the car, after their twentieth goodbye to the Baker clan and a cheery, fat little hand waving Cassidy, they were at last on their way to Katie and Billy's house.

"Holy shit," exclaimed Ricky with a chortle.

"What? Damn it. You startled me," said Brianna, running her finger over the small smear of lipstick below her lip line. "Don't do that, you made me smudge." She punched his arm for good measure.

Unfazed, he said, "I just got a text from Bruce. Says Hannaford and Rosabelle Waterman got engaged. Wow. Never saw that coming. Did you know they were a thing?"

Brianna's voice was shrill. "No—I—yes, of course, I knew." As of two weeks ago. "And what is this, you and Bruce are now the gossip queens of Chance?"

"No," said Ricky defensively. "I texted to tell him my dad's thinking of selling his Mustang, in case he was still looking for one. And, you know, I asked how the party was going."

Brianna spun in her seat. "You did what?"

"I said, I asked him—"

"Oh, my God. Tell me you did not ask after Mae Huxley's—or Grant's, whatever, party. Are you trying to kill me? Do you want me to die? Is that what you're doing?"

"Bri—I didn't think—"

"Exactly. You didn't think, Ricky. Have you forgotten he's dating my archenemy? If he tells her that you asked about the party, she'll believe *I* wanted to know and told you to ask."

"What?"

Jesus, he could be so thick sometimes. How was it not obvious? "*Elise*, Ricky. Your buddy Moose is going to tell Elise that *I* wanted to know what was going on at their stupid party."

"But…I asked. Not you." Ricky put his palms up and shrugged his beefy shoulders. "Babe, I don't understand what the big deal is. You girls should just—I don't know—have one of your girls' nights and, like, talk shit out. You been carrying this on for too long now. I mean, how long you all been friends? Twenty years?"

Brianna jerked her body away from him and toward the window while he was mid-sentence. Ricky could never understand. He was a guy.

Talk it out. Please. There was nothing to say. If Elise couldn't see how this was any of her fault, and not Brianna's, then what was she to do? It certainly was not Brianna's problem that Elise failed to disclose her husband's tawdry gay affair and thereby let Brianna believe Elise was cheating on Ethan with Bruce Grady. Which—not for nothing— became a real thing, anyhow. And really, how could Brianna not then tell Brittany her suspicions?

Obviously, she told her not to say anything to anyone. It wasn't as if she could control Brittany's big, gossipy mouth. She remembered the conversation as if it were yesterday, and not last year. She was in Brittany's too yellow kitchen, drinking a God-awful concoction she'd blended up post-yoga session.

"I still can't believe Elise and Charlotte didn't show up for the seven a.m. class. I think that's extremely rude."

"You know what I think? I think Elise is hiding something from us, don't you?"

"Totally," agreed Brittany with a hungry look in her eyes.

"She's spending a lot more time at the café. Haven't you noticed?"

Brittany clapped her hands and rapidly tapped her fingers together, causing her to look like the Cookie Monster anticipating a cookie. "Ooh, do you think she's going to make a move on Mae's old man crush?"

"Are you an idiot? Seriously, where is your head? She's not into William Grant." Then, to herself, "Although he is hot."

"Wait, you think she's got something going on with Moose? But he's in love with Mae. Everybody knows that."

"Yes, but only me, you, and Katie know of Elise's long-time infatuation with Moose."

"And Charlotte," added Brittany.

"Yes, whatever. Her too. My point is—don't you think it's interesting that Katie found them at Elise's house alone and reeking of alcohol?"

Brittany scrunched up her face and said, "Well, I don't think she said they *reeked* of—"

"She smelled alcohol. They were acting funny. And Elise couldn't get Katie away from the house fast enough. They are having an affair, I just know it."

"Poor Ethan," pouted Brittany.

Brianna rolled her eyes. "Oh, please. You and I both know he's a total weenie."

"True." Brittany shrugged indifferently. "Too bad, because European guys are usually so hot."

"Stay focused, Brittany. And by the way, this stuff is disgusting. Get it away from me." Brianna shoved the tall glass of chunky, pea-green muck away and took a swig from her water bottle. "What I'm saying here is that my best friend since third grade is keeping secrets from me, and it's awful."

"You mean, like, *our* best friend, because we're all best friends, right?"

Brianna blinked at her. "Right, yes. Totally. So, what are we going to do?"

Brittany scrunched up her face again and pulled back as if afraid Brianna might strike her if she gave the wrong answer, and said, "We're going to...ask her what's going on?"

For a moment, Brianna did want to slap the stupid out of her. Instead, she took a cleansing breath and calmly announced, "No, Brittany. We are going to force her hand. She needs to confront this little problem of hers. And we're just the ones to help her. But don't say anything to anyone. You hear?" Brianna stood, grabbed her purse, and winked. "We'll fix her wagon, won't we?"

Now, looking back, she supposed Brittany had taken that wink wrong. It was the timing of it that had been off. Brittany thought that wink meant, 'I don't mean that you shouldn't tell anyone.' And Brianna hadn't corrected her. Too late now. What's done is done. Now the fivesome was divided, sharing Katie as if she were a child caught in the middle of a custody battle. Sure, she'd been miffed that Brianna—well, Brittany, technically—had spread the Elise and Moose story, but she got over it. Katie never could bear to have anyone not like her.

Brianna smirked. It was probably driving her crazy that Elise and mamby-pamby Charlotte weren't going to her party. Maybe that would be enough to push her over the edge and finally declare herself as Team Brianna, instead of Team Switzerland. Was Switzerland even a neutral country still? Surely, they had to have taken sides with someone by now?

"We should go to Switzerland one day," said Brianna.

Ricky took his eyes off the road briefly and stared at her as if she'd just had a sudden onset of Tourette's. "Uh, Switzerland? What made you think of that?"

"I don't know. Nothing. Never mind. We do

need a vacation though. Let's go somewhere. Somewhere warm, like Aruba."

"Babe, you know I've got the big expansion in the works. We can't go anywhere until at least spring. Once we start selling cars from the lot, there'll be more money. Then we can go on a trip."

Brianna pouted. "*You* can't go anywhere. Who says I can't?" Then, she had a flash of brilliance. "Maybe I should plan a girls' weekend. Brittany keeps saying she needs a break from the yoga studio. And Katie definitely needs a break from those horrible children of hers."

Ricky stayed quiet. He always got quiet when Brianna's thoughts turned to spending money. It was like he went into a spontaneous coma. She stared at his profile, waiting. Studying him. Grudgingly, she acknowledged he was still very handsome. His jawline was a bit fleshier. He had faint lines at the corners of his eyes now. At his temples, a few silvery strands mixed in with the brown. His hairline had receded, but not by much. Maybe it was the cheap wine from dinner, but a wave of uncharacteristic tenderness swept over her.

Brianna suddenly remembered, as she often did at odd times, that she loved him still. He was tall and strong, a good provider and father. He was a better husband than she was a wife, that was for sure. In the quiet of her own thoughts, she recognized that Ricky was kinder and better than she'd ever deserved. Above all else, he was tolerant. Somehow, for all these years, Ricky Baker had managed to abide Brianna's mercurial moods, her fixation on money and status, her vanity. Why?

How?

At the same time as Ricky said, "I could manage it if you want to get away," Brianna asked, "Why do you love me?"

Ricky shot a quick side glance at her, his brow creased. She'd just as quickly turned her head away.

"What kind of question is that? I've loved you since we were kids, Bri. You know that."

"Yes, but why?"

"What's going on here, babe? You all right?"

Brianna shrugged and twisted her ring. She felt ridiculous now. Childish. What had come over her? Ricky's love was the same as breathing, she just expected it to occur. She didn't need to think about it. Yet, she was. Often lately. Especially when she looked at Cassidy. If he ever— "I'm fine. Never mind. I'm just being sappy. New Year's Eve, all that *Auld Lang Syne* crap. Just forget it."

Ricky didn't say anything. He reached over the console and found her hand, covering it with his large, warm, callused one. Brianna kept her head turned to the window, pretending to watch the houses and other cars as they drove through the night. Pretending. It was the one word that summed up her entire existence.

Chapter 14

Merry And Bright

"Never a dull moment, huh?" Bruce's chuckle came out hollow.

"Nope, never is," agreed Elise. She did not laugh.

Silence ensued. Bruce turned up the radio. Elise turned it off.

"How about that proposal? You see, the Watermans' faces?"

"Yup. Sure did."

Another long, ominously silent gap. Elise looked out the car window. Bruce studied the road ahead.

"Crazy that Gina Byrd—"

"Don't. Just—I don't want to hear another word about Mae Huxley's latest drama, okay?"

"Lissie, come on, babe. It's not like—"

"I know, Bruce. I know she didn't plan to take on the responsibility of her sister. I know she didn't make the café's alarm go off while we were out for dinner last month. I know she didn't mean to call while we were in bed the other night. And of course, I know she didn't ask for Gina Byrd to show up at the stroke of midnight on New Year's Eve. I get it, Mae is the perpetual victim of life."

Worst of all, Elise knew she was being a jerk. She liked Mae, she genuinely did. But she loved Bruce. Probably always had. Sure, he claimed to love her as well. Yet Mae was always around every corner, sneaking into nearly every conversation, always needing him for something. When was she ever going to come first?

"Babe, come on, now. That's not fair—"

"I know, Bruce. Jesus. It's just—how do I even compete with all of that? With her? Mae calls, you run. I call, you get there when you can. Unless Mae needs you for something."

What was wrong with her? She knew that wasn't entirely true. Bruce was always there for Elise. Their whole relationship started with him being the one who came to help her with her new washing machine last year—the same day she discovered her husband in bed with another man. Bruce stayed for that drama too. Pragmatism couldn't contend with Elise's champagne-fueled pity party. She'd immersed herself in the narrative and couldn't back out. So, she dug her heels in deeper.

"You're still in love with her, and you're just too nice of a guy to say so. I'm just a poor substitute for the one you really want, admit it. I'll bet you—"

Bruce jerked the wheel and pulled the truck to the side of the road, unlatched his seatbelt, and

129

faced her. His eyes blazed with intensity. Damn it. He was going to dump her, right here on Cardinal Lane, on New Year's Eve. Well, New Year's Day, technically. She pushed him too far, and now he was done.

"Elise, listen to me. Yes, I love Mae...*as a friend*. But I am *in love* with you. Understand? You, Elise. No one else. I love you so much that I was gonna propose tonight, except that asshole Hannaford beat me to it. I don't want anyone else. I want a life with you and Gianna, and your crazy weird relationship with your gay ex-husband and his boyfriend. I—"

"Did you just say...you were going to propose?" A slow grin spread across Elise's face.

"Yeah, but—"

"Yes." Elise's smile spread wider.

"I—wait. Yes? Are you saying yes, you'll marry me?"

"Well, you still have to ask me properly."

Bruce's dumbfounded expression cleared, as did their argument. "Elise Marie Martino, will you marry me?"

Elise clapped and laughed. "Yes, you big dope, I will."

"Oh, shit. Wait." Bruce patted each of his coat pockets, his front right pocket and lastly, his back pockets. He stretched and twisted until he could fish the ring out. He popped open the box, blew the tiny fluff of lint off the diamond solitaire, and held it up to Elise with a rueful smile. "I know it's not as big as your last diamond, but—"

"It's perfect. I love it, and I love you."

Sure, it wasn't the most conventional or even romantic proposal story to tell, but it was *their* story, and that made it good enough for her.

"I was worried maybe you'd think it was too soon after—you know, Ethan and everything."

"You know better than anyone that my marriage was over long before we officially ended it. I'm sure certain people will talk, but they'll talk no matter what. So, screw 'em."

She was referring to Brianna and Brittany, of course. Once they got wind of this, they'd have a field day. Elise pushed the thought of her former best friends out of her mind and smiled at the dainty, princess cut diamond. She guessed it to be near two carats, but not more. A size Brianna Baker would call 'cute,' and 'adorable' if they were still friends.

The ring Ethan had bought post-elopement had been a four carat, Asscher cut, halo diamond in a platinum setting. He'd picked it out himself and the only thing she'd loved more than the ring itself, was the way Brianna coveted it. Less than a month after she'd shown it to her, Brianna made Ricky upgrade her three-and-a-half carat emerald cut to a five-carat round brilliant, which she was quick to point out that, 'her jeweler said a round cut brilliant is the absolute best for sparkle and shine,' and she'd considered the Asscher cut, but he said it wasn't nearly as remarkable. Typical Brianna.

Elise shook her head, clearing Brianna from it and refocusing her attention on Bruce and the fact that they were engaged. *Engaged.*

"Oh my God. We have to set a date. I have to

call my parents. And Charlotte, and—"

"Slow down, it's two o'clock in the morning. You'll scare the shit out of everyone if you start calling now. We'll tell everyone at brunch tomorrow." He looked at the time on the dashboard. "I mean today."

"Brunch?"

"Yeah, at Mae's. It's—" Bruce stopped.

He didn't want to start that argument up again, not right after getting engaged.

"It's tradition. I know. Listen, it's fine. Honest. But are you sure it's still on? After the Gina thing?"

"Oh, it'll be on. You'll see. You check if your parents can come, and I'll get my dad there too. Sound good?"

Bruce held his breath. He couldn't miss the annual New Year's Day brunch, but he couldn't piss off his fiancée either. *Holy shit. I have a fiancée.* The realization floored him. Bruce Grady was going to get married.

Chapter 15

Mother And Child

Gina looked around the room. All those faces, staring at her like she was an alien or something. It was a stupid idea, going to Mae's house. She couldn't stop herself though. Her feet had their own mind or something. One minute she was dumpster diving in the back of Lucky Loo's, the next, standing at the bottom of Mae's front steps. She could hear them inside, counting down. They sounded happy, excited. As if the new year was gonna magically bring everyone, like, health, wealth, and happiness. Or some shit like that.

Gina Byrd knew better. The new year didn't mean shit. Not to her at least. Not that she hadn't tried though. Sure as hell, she tried. Got up to New Hampshire last year, dried out, even got a job. Crappy job washing hair in a Podunk town. The old lady—Zuzu, she called herself—let her sleep in the back room when it was too chilly to stay in the van. Said she'd been homeless herself once upon a time, so she knew how it felt to need a hand up.

She was all right, that Zuzu. She had one stipulation though. No booze, no drugs, no exceptions. Zuzu was a twelve-stepper. Gina had gotten as far as step five—admitting to God, herself, and another person her wrongs—before she stalled out. Thing was, in Gina's mind, she'd had more wrongs done to her than the other way around. How come she had to apologize when no one else ever did? It wasn't fair, damn it. Gina Byrd was a victim of circumstance. Of society.

She told old Zuzu she'd pray on it, sent her home with a promise to clean up and lock up. Gina left Zulu's Hair Palace that same night. Not before dying her hair and clearing out the safe though. She left a note, apologizing, which she thought was mighty big of her considering how lousy the pay had been. She took what was her due, so no big deal.

Anyhow, the only person she needed to apologize to was Feather Anne. Maybe Mae too. Not for giving her over to Keith Huxley to raise. Hell, she made out all right in that bargain, didn't she? Gina figured she only owed Mae an apology for showing up at Keith's funeral way back when. Looking back, she couldn't recall what made her think it was a good idea to do that.

Yeah, you do, Gina. You thought she'd welcome you with open arms. Admit it. It was true. There was a part of her that thought, maybe since her dad was gone, she'd want a mom around. Sure, Gina maybe wasn't the best choice, but she was her blood. They were family whether Mae accepted it or not. Besides, Feather Anne was outright obsessed with her. She knew that girl was sneaking over to Mae's house and the café any chance she got. If she could just do one thing right by that kid, she'd get her under Mae Huxley's roof.

Ta-da. It worked. There they were, cozy and warm, snuggled up tight like a little family. She could see the two of them beside the tall older man. Smiling at each other. The countdown continued. Five. Four. Three. Mae lifted herself on her toes and whispered something to the guy. Feather Anne grinned up at the both of them. Two. One. Cheers, party horns, laughter.

Suddenly, she was ringing the doorbell. She didn't even remember going up the steps. But there she was. The door swung open and another tall man looked down at her. She recognized him as the boy who'd always hung around the café. Moose, they called him. Such a nice, handsome kid. She never understood why Mae didn't hook up with him. Although, he didn't look so nice right then.

He stared at her with frosty disdain, like she'd done something personally to affront him. Someone came up behind him and pushed the door open wider. It was Feather Anne, looking so different, yet the same. Her hair was longer but styled and shiny. Her face had filled out and her legs seemed too long for her body. She was dressed in leggings, tall boots and a loose gray sweater that matched her eyes. It was like looking at a miniature, black-haired version of Mae. As if *she'd* given birth to the kid, and not Gina.

"Hey, girl," said Gina shakily.

Feather Anne said nothing. She just stared at her, like she was a stranger. Gina was so shocked by the blankness of her expression that she stumbled back. Bruce, on instinct, grabbed her arm and steadied her before she toppled down the stairs. He could smell peppermint Schnapps—or a bottom shelf version of it—on her ragged breath.

"Bring her inside, Bruce. To the kitchen, please."

Gina looked around the mountain that was Bruce and saw Mae, her arm draped protectively over Feather Anne's shoulders. Her expression wasn't precisely warm, but it also wasn't hateful. Bruce walked her inside past Mae and Feather Anne. She felt all the eyes on her but couldn't meet any of them.

"Mae's got a pot of coffee brewing. How do you drink it?"

"B-black, please." Gina's whole body shook.

Bruce glanced over at her, pursed his lips, and shook his head. Then he took off his thick fisherman's sweater and walked it over to her.

"Put it on before you catch your death."

"That's real nice of you. Thank you—Bruce. It is Bruce, right?" Bruce nodded, his back to her as he poured the steaming black liquid into a white mug. "I used to come to the football games back when you were all kids. You were real good, I remember."

Bruce set the mug before her and gave a terse smile. She could tell he had a great deal to say, that he *wanted* to say, but maybe he figured it wasn't his place to say them. From the other room, she could hear the strained, murmured goodbyes of the guests. They were all leaving because of her. She'd ruined the party for everyone.

The front door closed audibly, not quite a slam, but close. Someone turned off the music. Several voices carried—a man's, a woman's, a girl's—then silence. Bruce crossed his arms and looked everywhere but at Gina. Katrina Huxley leaned in through the doorframe and gave Gina a glare but addressed Bruce.

"Moosie boy. You got this for a minute?"

"Yeah. Just, uh, ask Elise to give me a few?"

"All good. She's rounding up her kid and getting your coats."

Gina stared into her cup. Her ears, fingers, and toes were burning, and her lips felt dry and cracked, but thanks to the sweater Bruce had handed her, she'd begun to thaw.

"You don't have to stand here with me. I ain't gonna steal anything," said Gina.

"Just keeping you company until Mae comes in," said Bruce evenly.

Minutes ticked by, and the sounds of a house shutting down for the evening filled the rooms. Lights dimmed. A toilet flushed. Water ran in a sink, doors clicked shut as floorboards creaked. Hushed voices. A call of goodnight. Then, Mae walked into the kitchen. Alone.

"Bruce, thank you. Elise is in the car with Gianna. Go on, and I'll see you tomorrow for brunch."

"You sure you're—"

"I'm sure." She put a hand on his arm and smiled up at him. It was a weary smile.

He gave her a quick hug and nodded briskly to Gina.

"Wait, your sweater," stammered Gina. She stood to pull it off.

He waved her away. "Just keep it until tomorrow."

Once Bruce had left, Mae busied herself with filling a floral teapot with cold water at the sink. She set it on the stove and lit the burner. She pulled out a teacup, tea bag, honey, and a spoon all with such slow precision that Gina suspected she was stalling. Or maybe just collecting her thoughts. Or getting ready to let loose on her. Anything was possible.

Gina's eyes darted repeatedly from her coffee to the doorway.

"She's not coming. I offered. She wanted to go to bed."

Mae had turned back around and studied her with unreadable storm-cloud eyes.

"Oh," said Gina.

"She doesn't know how to act. Or feel, for that matter. Neither do I, to be honest. What the hell are you doing here, Gina? What do you want from us? You know I have legal guardianship over her, right? You can't just show up out of the blue a year—*a year* after you abandoned your daughter and expect everything to be cool."

"I know, but—"

"No, Gina. There is no 'but' here. You have no right to do this to her."

Barely above a whisper, Gina said, "Her, or you?"

"Either one of us. You—you *sold* me to my father without batting an eye. You walked away from Feather Anne—you abandoned a nine-year-old girl in a trailer—and now you just show up with no warning. You should be in jail, you know."

"I—I can't undo any of it, Mae. I know that. And I know I'm a shitty mother, okay? Don't you see, though? That's why I did what I did all those years ago. I knew I could never give you the kind of life Keith could. I couldn't even take care of myself, let alone a baby. When Feather Anne came along—I don't know—I guess I thought she was maybe my last chance at doing something right. At having something good in my life."

Gina's voice broke, and she stopped. Mae said nothing. After a long silence, she went on.

"Anyhow, I just—I just could never catch a break, you know? I tried to get clean. Lots of times. It's a disease, they say."

"Bullshit, Gina. It's a choice. You chose drugs and alcohol over your kids."

"You say that because you've never had a moment of adversity in your life. I'm glad for that, though. I wouldn't *want* you to know what it's like. Look at me, Mae. I'm a fifty-year-old woman who looks like she's pushing sixty. My hands shake all the time. I got no money, no home, and no family. At least none that'll claim me. You think this is a *choice*?"

Despite herself, Mae felt a tremor of self-doubt. Was she being too hard on Gina? Maybe it was the

139

pregnancy hormones, maybe it was exhaustion, but suddenly Mae heard her own voice saying, "There are clean towels in the linen closet and spare toothbrushes in the third drawer in the bathroom. The spare bedrooms are taken, so you'll have to sleep on one of the sofas."

Gina brought her head up to look at her eldest daughter, her eyes shining with unshed tears. "You're—I can stay?"

"Do you have better plans?" Mae cleared her throat and softened her tone. "It's 20 degrees outside, and it's two o'clock in the morning on New Year's Day. What kind of person am I if I let my— if I let someone leave with nowhere to go?"

Gina heard the near slip. She'd almost said, 'my mother.' Maybe there was hope for them after all. She mustered as much dignity as she could and said, "Thank you, Mae. I'll—I promise, I won't be any trouble."

"Too late for that, Gina," Mae muttered and flicked her hair over her shoulder, barely glancing at her biological mother. "Listen, I'm beat. I—I can't do this," she waved her hand between them, "tonight. Maybe not ever. I don't know. I'll, uh, put some fresh clothes outside the bathroom door. We're close enough to the same size."

"Thank you," said Gina, barely above a whisper.

"You don't have to thank me. Just don't—"

There was a list of 'don'ts' on the tip of her Mae's tongue. Don't make me regret this. Don't take Feather Anne. Don't let her down. Don't let *me* down. None of them came out.

"I won't," said Gina, as if she'd heard every

single one.

Chapter 16

Faithful Friends

Pedro stuffed a mini quiche into his mouth, then elbowed Miles. "So, the parents don't care for you, huh?"

"Understatement of the year, my friend," said Miles.

"Marisol's parents didn't like me in the beginning, either." Pedro shrugged.

"And now they love you, right?"

Pedro barked a dry laugh. "Nope. I'm the *ladrón* that stole their only daughter away from them."

"Damn, they call you a thief, huh?"

"Hang on, hang on. You speak Spanish, *carbrón?*"

"*Si, un poco, no mucho,*" said Miles, shrugging ruefully.

"Shady bastard. I knew I shouldn't have trusted you when we bought the house. I told Marisol—oh, you knew what I said to Marisol. Yikes. Sorry, man."

Miles laughed good-naturedly. He'd been called plenty worse over the years. "All good, man. Just make sure you come to me when the in-laws decide to move to town."

"Oh, hell no. Over my dead body are Marisol's parents—"

"Marisol's parents *what*, Pedro?"

Marisol had snuck up behind Pedro and gazed up at him expectantly. Miles took it as his cue to walk away. He excused himself, ignoring the 'save me' look in Pedro's eyes and found Mae by the buffet.

"Hey, baby Mae. Great spread, as usual. You know, any time you want to expand this café into a full-blown restaurant, I can get you a great deal on some property."

"Thanks, Miles, but this is just right for me. Hey, sorry I didn't get a chance to congratulate you and Rosabelle properly last night. Things got hectic, as you know."

"You can say that again. Gina Byrd, back in town. Wow. She was looking hella—"

"Miles," Mae interrupted abruptly. She motioned to the woman beside her. "Gina, meet Miles Hannaford. Miles, Gina Byrd."

Miles face clouded with confusion, then surprise, to at last comprehension. "I—you—ah, nice to meet you, Gina. I've heard so—you look—excuse me, Rosie needs me."

After Miles had hurried away, Gina scoffed and said, "That one's got a way with the ladies, huh?"

Mae surprised herself—and Gina—by laughing.

"Believe it or not, he had quite a reputation for *exactly* that over the years. He's just surprised to see you looking—"

"Like a regular person, and not a street rat?"

Mae fidgeted uncomfortably. That was what she'd meant. She, along with everyone else, couldn't stop giving Gina sidelong appraisals. Her hair was clean and styled, her clothes—borrowed from Mae—fit loose and tastefully, and she even had a subtle hint of makeup. She bore all the appearances of a regular mom. A very uncomfortable, fidgety, nervous mom, but a mom nonetheless.

"Listen, I've got to make the rounds. Just, uh, help yourself to whatever. William and Bruce are floating around too, if you need anything."

"Mae, I can't thank you enough for—"

"Don't mention it," said Mae breezily. Too breezily. She was still unsure of this new development.

She spotted Rosabelle across the room and wove her way through the restaurant to her side. She sank heavily and dropped her head on Rosabelle's shoulder.

Rosabelle laughed and patted her head. "Oh, stop. You're acting as if throwing a New Year's Eve party, having your biological mother crash it, then hosting a New Year's Day brunch for sixty is a big deal. Toughen up."

Mae giggled and popped her head back up. "Don't forget a surprise engagement proposal. Let me see that gorgeous ring again."

Rosabelle fluttered her fingers at Mae. "Don't let

the glare blind you, darling."

"Damn, girl. I need shades for that thing. Your boy Miles done good. Speaking of, where is your Prince Charming? I thought he was on his way over to you after he stuck his foot in his mouth in front of my—in front of Gina."

"You *can* call her your mother, you know. Uh-uh, don't make that face at me. You and I are going to sit and talk this one out. Soon. Oh, and Miles is over there, talking your husband's ear off about my parents. In fact, he has made his way around the room to ask everyone their advice on how to win over Ruth and Steven. He's driving me nuts, Mae."

"Aww, it's sweet though, isn't it?"

Rosabelle smiled. "It is, totally. But I just don't think it's going to happen. You should've seen Christmas Eve. And don't get me started on Christmas Day. It's like, the harder he tries, the more they resist. Honestly, Mae, I don't know if I can marry him without their approval. Even if they are wrong, they're still my parents, you know?"

Rosabelle looked so forlorn that Mae instinctively hugged her and said, "It'll all work out, Rosabelle. It *has* to, right?"

"I hope you're right. Mae? Can I confess something to you? It's—well, it's the real reason my parents despise Miles, and it's all my fault."

She hadn't even planned on telling anyone her embarrassing secret. But it was eating a hole in her. She *had* to tell someone, and who better than Mae?

"Rosabelle, of course, you can talk to me. Whatever it is, we can make it right, I'm sure."

"Well, I'm not so sure. You see, in high school, I

sort of had a crush on Miles." Her face reddened as she added, "Okay, truthfully, I was pretty obsessed with him. As in, I had pictures of him in my room—perks of being on the yearbook editing committee—and I kept a journal of made-up stories about him and I—" She covered her face and spoke against her palms. "I can't believe I'm telling you this. So embarrassing."

"Don't be embarrassed, we all did that kind of stuff. For me, it was Lance Bass. Yes, I get the irony. Keep talking."

"Lance Bass, huh? That does make me feel better. All right, anyhow, in that journal, I'd made up this whole pretend relationship. Like, a secret one that no one knew about, just me and Miles. My mother found it one day and went ballistic. She believed I was secretly dating *Miles Hannaford.* The thing is, for as mad as she was that I had such a big secret, I could tell she was kind of excited for me. That her mousy, dorky daughter was dating one of the popular boys."

Mae had an idea of where this was going. "Oh, boy. Go on."

"Mae, I was so mortified. I couldn't tell them it was all made up. That their daughter was a weirdo stalker in a make-believe relationship with the captain of the football team. They wanted to *meet* him, Mae."

"So how did—"

"Mae, sweetheart, are we out of rolls? Sorry to interrupt," said William apologetically.

"No, there's more in the pantry. They're—hang on. Sorry, Rosabelle, I'd better get them myself. I'll be back."

William shrugged good-naturedly at Rosabelle. "I could've handled getting rolls from the pantry."

"You know Mae." Rosabelle laughed.

Together, they deadpanned, "Control freak."

The rest of Rosabelle's mortifying story had to wait. Miles brought her a plate of food and regaled her with the multitude of contradicting advice he'd collected. Elise brought Gianna over and sat with her for a while, as did Charlotte Asheby. She was still shy around them. It took getting used to, having the popular girls from high school—girls who'd never given her a second glance—treat her like a friend. She only wished her parents were here to see.

Steven and Ruth had claimed headaches that morning and declined the invitation to the café for brunch. Rosabelle was too hurt and disappointed to ask them to reconsider. Miles, though relieved for himself, made a good show of acting disappointed as well. She'd seen right through him though.

"Miles," she'd said solemnly, "we have to get my parents onboard for this engagement. I can't marry you until they do."

Miles false gravity suddenly became real. "Wait, seriously? Rosie, what if they never accept me?"

Rosabelle's eyes filled with sadness. "I don't know what to tell you, Miles. I guess we just have to find a way."

One that didn't involve her confessing her humiliating fake romance with him in high school.

Rosabelle knew the only thing stopping Ruth and Steven from tearing into Miles for what they believed to be his horrendous treatment of their daughter, was their fear of upsetting her. After their pseudo breakup, Steven had wanted to confront Miles, and Ruth had wanted to call his mother. Apparently, she'd played her role of jilted secret girlfriend a little 'too well. Her only recourse—aside from confessing the truth—was to dig her heels in harder and threaten them with running away and never speaking to them again if they confronted him.

The Watermans had never seen their normally gentle and sweet daughter behave so hysterically. Beside themselves, they argued late into the night on what they should do. Ultimately, they abided her vehement wishes and said nothing. But now, more than fifteen years later, they were pots on a stove ready to boil over.

Chapter 17

Mix And Mingle

Feather Anne watched everyone from the café's kitchen. Her eyes landed on Gina often, then slid off toward someone, anyone, anything on the opposite side of the room as quickly. Mae compulsively checked on her every five minutes, Bruce and William in between those times.

She told them on Christmas that she didn't want to see or talk to Gina Byrd. Not now, not ever. Why Mae let her stay overnight was beyond her. Gina probably stole a bunch of stuff while everyone slept. Now she was here, at New Year's Day brunch, wearing Mae's clothes and acting like she belonged. Well, she didn't. No matter what she did or what she wore, she'd always be the same old Gina.

"Hey, brat. You're missing the fun out there. Wanna come hang out with me and Elise?"

149

Bruce leaned his back against the doorframe, a plate in one hand, a croissant in the other. He didn't look at Feather Anne, but out at their friends and family. Someone—likely Charles Brightsider—had started a sing-along over by the dessert table. Elise and Charlotte Asheby sat with Rosabelle, and Mae flitted around from one cluster of people to the next. William chatted with Pedro and Marisol, Joel Asheby handed out books on a police family to the kids at the children's table—something Charlotte had written and illustrated, called My Blue Family—and Georgie Brightsider sat with the Colonel and Mrs. Van Bergen.

Gina Byrd stood alone in the corner closest to the patio, a plate of food held high and close. Her eyes darted around the room, then back at her plate. One of the Petrova twins approached her with a linen napkin and a kind smile, both of which she accepted gratefully. Mr. and Mrs. Petrova joined their daughter and introduced themselves. Just as Gina reached out to shake the offered hand of Mikael Petrova, her eyes met Feather Anne's from across the room. Feather Anne ducked back into the kitchen, behind Bruce.

"No thanks," said Feather Anne. "I'm fine right here."

Bruce shrugged and said, "Suit yourself, kid. My opinion? It's best just to rip off the Band-Aid."

"Huh?"

"It means, get it done and over with instead of prolonging it. Just, you know, talk to her. Tell her how you feel. Let her—I don't know—explain herself."

Feather Anne made a sound somewhere between a snort and a laugh. What could Gina have to say? 'Gee, sorry I abandoned you in a trailer home that was about to taken to a junkyard?' Or, 'Sorry I didn't leave you so much as a donut when I took off in our van.' Oh, and don't forget, 'Sorry I couldn't even be bothered to show up for your guardianship hearing.'

"Nah," said Feather Anne as flippantly as she could. "I'm good."

Bruce took a deep breath and exhaled slowly before answering. "All right, kiddo. It's your call. If you need to talk or anything, I'm around. Elise is leaving soon to visit her friend Katie, so I can—"

"Yeah, yeah. I know."

He ruffled her hair and went back to the party. Feather Anne's stomach was grumbling, but she was afraid if she went out there, then Gina might try to talk to her. Suddenly, a heaping dish appeared before her face. She looked up to see the twinkling faded blue of Georgie Brightsiders' eyes.

"Thought you might be getting hungry back here. I took the liberty of putting some of everything."

"Thanks, Mrs. B. You're the best." Then, suspicion crept in. "Wait, there's a catch isn't there?"

Georgie feigned surprise. "Not at all, sweetheart. What would this catch even be?"

Feather Anne's narrow shoulders rose then dropped. "I dunno. I'll have to talk to Gina if I want to eat, or something?"

Georgie Brightsider chuckled and patted Feather

Anne's cheek affectionately with her soft, creped hand. "Now, now. I wouldn't dream of giving such an unfair ultimatum. You should—as a matter of course—be allowed to choose when or if, or even how you talk to Gina Byrd. After all, she's given up her right to have expectations of you, hasn't she?"

Feather Anne straightened and thrust her chin out. "Yeah, exactly."

It was a surprise that Mrs. B. saw things her way and it made her love the woman—who was the closest thing to a grandmother that she'd ever known—even more.

"I mean," continued Georgie, "even if we suppose that she knew—in her heart—that Mae would've stepped up to the occasion and taken you in, it *still* does not excuse her actions." She saw a flicker of doubt and confusion cross Feather Anne's countenance and continued. "Just because Gina knew that Mae could give you the best life—a much better one than she could, certainly—it doesn't mean she should've just left you the way she did."

Feather Anne chewed the inside of her cheek and frowned. "You think she knew Mae would take me in?"

"I do, yes." Georgie nodded. "For what it's worth." She shrugged casually as if it were of no relevance whatsoever.

"Yeah, but *how* could she know that? Mae wouldn't even admit we were sisters before Gina left."

Georgie smiled kindly. "Tell me, Feather Anne, what kind of person do you think Mae is, now that you really know her?"

Quickly, easily, Feather Anne said, "Mae? She's the best. She's, like, the nicest, mushiest person ever. She's the way a mom is supposed to act. She—" Feather Anne gave Georgie a 'you got me' look. "Oh, I get it. You're saying that Gina did what she did cuz she thought I'd have a better life with Mae."

Georgie Brightsider looked taken aback, but she wore a small smile too. "I've said nothing of the sort, dear." Her smile grew. "*You* did. Now, get some meat on those skinny bones. Talk to Gina, don't talk to Gina…the choice is yours. If you need me, you know where to find me."

She left Feather Anne to ponder this new perspective and rejoined her husband by the dessert table. As she passed Gina Byrd, she dipped her head in a quick acknowledgment. There was nothing she had to say to the woman, but their eyes had met while she'd been speaking with Feather Anne, and she'd appeared so hopeful, as if she knew or suspected that Georgie was trying to build a bridge between mother and daughter.

Feather Anne took a few bites and shot furtive glances in Gina's direction. She was alone again, the Petrovas having moved on to more stimulating conversationalists. An unexpected wave of empathy flooded Feather Anne's heart. It wasn't so long ago that she felt the same way Gina was likely feeling. Insignificant. Inferior. Dirty. Stupid. Alone. It was a terrible way to feel, to live. No one, not even Gina, deserved to feel so awful.

Setting her plate on the kitchen counter, then wiping her damp palms on her jeans, Feather Anne slowly walked out and around the counter. Rather than taking the direct path across the room to Gina, she weaved through the crowd in a wide, zig-zagging arc until she was almost suddenly beside Gina. They didn't say anything, not at first. Side glances, mouths opened and closed with no sound, Gina picking at the food on her plate with her fork, Feather Anne picking at her cuticle.

"I'll take the pickle. You hate pickles," said Feather Anne at last, jerking her chin at the lone dill spear pushed off to the edge of the dish.

Gina looked at it as if just noticing its existence. "Oh, yeah. Cool. Thanks." Her tone sounded nonchalant, but the way her hand shook as she stabbed her fork into the pickle and reached it out to Feather Anne told otherwise.

Mae stood beside the table holding coffee carafes, teas, and mugs, watching the pair covertly. They resembled any other mother and daughter, ones that could at any moment walk out to their SUV, hop in, and head over to tennis lessons or ballet class, or a mother-daughter trip to the mall. Unlike the Gina and Feather Anne of a year ago, they looked as though they *belonged*. It was almost shocking how transformative clean clothes and grooming could be. *If only it were that easy to change a person's insides as it was their outsides.*

Mae frowned at the uncharitable thought. Everyone deserved a chance, no matter their past, right? But what if Mae was betting on a losing horse at the expense of her sister's well-being? What if Gina was just conning them all with her repentant demeanor and grateful platitudes, all the while biding her time and pocketing valuables? She still hadn't said why she came back, or if she intended on staying. Regardless, Mae had made it clear that Feather Anne would be staying with Mae, and Gina hadn't argued.

"Now, what did that coffee stirrer ever do to you?" asked William.

Mae looked at the little plastic straw, now twisted and bent at knotted angles. "Do you see? Over there." She tipped her head toward her sister and biological mother. "Should I go over?"

William gently took the mangled straw from her hands and cupped her face. "No, love. You should stay right here with me. If Feather Anne needs you, you'll know."

Mae held his wrists and bowed her head to his chin. "Fine," she relented. "I'll butt out. For now," she added petulantly.

Mae tucked herself under William's arm and together they observed their guests, trying not to let their eyes linger too long on Feather Anne and Gina. Instead, they discussed Bruce and Elise's announcement, mutually noted Miles's irritation at the declaration, and mused over when and where the two weddings would occur, and if they'd entertain the idea of a double wedding. They laughed heartily at that unlikelihood.

By three, the group of sixty had dropped to fifteen. When the grandfather clock by the bookcases struck four, they were saying goodbye to the last of the stragglers and cleaning. Bruce tapped Mae's shoulder and gave her a rueful look.

Mae, bewildered, said, "What's that face for?"

"I just wanted to apologize for, you know, the way Elise announced our engagement earlier. I meant to kinda tell you—and William—first, then everyone else."

"Oh, you. Please, it's totally fine. I'm so happy for you. I really am."

She'd never admit to the sharp sting of realizing her best friend was beginning a new life that put her on the peripheral. She rationalized that she had no right to feel that way. Still, she couldn't help but wonder if this was how Bruce had felt when she'd accepted William's proposal. And besides, she *was* genuinely happy for both Bruce and Elise. They adored each other, clearly. Once Mae and Elise cleared the air, then everything would be perfect.

"Thanks, Mae. Hey, Feather Anne and Gina seem to be doing okay, huh?"

"Yeah, looks that way," agreed Mae. She frowned and looked around. "Speaking of, where are those two?"

Bruce and Mae turned in opposite slow circles. William dragged a long table toward the back wall. Joel Asheby was dumping paper plates and napkins into a black garbage bag. Charlotte was reading to Gianna and Benjamin.

"You check the kitchen. I'll check the ladies' room," said Mae, a quaver to her voice.

Bruce nodded and strode to the kitchen, only to find it empty. He met Mae at the counter, his eyes questioning. She shook her head grimly.

"Son of a bitch," hissed Bruce.

Chapter 18

Old Acquaintances

Ricky kicked off one heavy black boot, then the other. Then he pulled each shade up to let the weak afternoon sunlight into the bedroom.

"What the hell, Ricky," moaned Brianna. She blindly groped for one of his pillows and pulled it over her head, simultaneously wriggling further under the covers.

"It's one-thirty in the afternoon, Bri. I've already unloaded and stacked half a cord for the fireplace. *And* picked up Cass from my Mom's place."

Brianna dragged the pillow away from her face. "Did you say one-thirty?"

"Yes. One-thirty in the afternoon."

"Well, obviously it's not one-thirty in the morning, genius. Shit," said Brianna, sitting upright. "I'm supposed to meet Brittany and Katie for a late lunch at two."

"You just spent New Year's Eve with them. I hoped we were going to stay in today and just hang out."

"Oh, my God, Ricky. I'll only be gone a couple of hours. You and Cassidy can have some Daddy-daughter quality time. Now move. I have to get ready."

Ricky said nothing. He considered a few sentences, tasting them in his mouth before forcefully swallowing them. Sentences like, 'You move pretty fast when it's for something *you* want to do,' and, 'Glad your friends take priority over your family, Bri.' However, Ricky knew that *those* sentences could lead to arguments, and arguments led to tears, and inevitably ended with Ricky spending money on apology gifts that Brianna picked out herself and charged to their account.

Not for the first time, Ricky wondered about that post-partum thing that some women got after they had babies. Ever since Cassidy was born, Brianna had been tenser and more snappish than usual. Particularly with Ricky. He couldn't say or do anything right. Ricky had even suspected her of having an affair with that jackass Miles Hannaford last year. Well, not an affair. Maybe just an attraction or something. Which was bad enough.

Brianna had always sworn how much she couldn't stand him. He'd been crazy to even think it for a second. Too bad he'd gone to Hannaford's office *before* that understanding hit him. He still got a laugh remembering Hannaford's scared face and his stammering. Fricking coward. Ricky still couldn't believe that prick got cute, quiet Rosabelle to agree to marry him. She was totally not his type.

Then the whole thing with Elise and Charlotte happened. Sure, Brianna should've stayed out of Elise's business, but Elise shouldn't have cheated on her husband. Wait, *she* didn't cheat. It was that husband of hers who had an affair. With a *dude*. She and Bruce hooked up after that. It was all coming back to him although he still didn't get why the girls hadn't made up yet. Guys handled shit much more plainly. Throw a few punches, drink a couple beers, shake hands and let it go. No marathon conversations, or crying, or grudges the way chicks do it.

"Jesus. Why are you still standing there? And get those filthy, nasty boots out of the bedroom. What is *wrong* with you?"

Brianna pushed past Ricky in disgust, adjusting her earring and appraising her appearance in the full-length mirror by the door.

"You look perfect, babe," said Ricky earnestly.

He could see Brianna roll her eyes in the mirror, but he could also see her try to suppress a smile too. It was enough for him to see that stifled smile. Enough for Ricky to know she loved him. Enough to make him willing to put up with the mood swings and the spending. Enough for him to forgive almost anything, really. He loved her that much. Always had, always would.

Their eyes met in the mirror. Whatever she'd opened her mouth to say, died on her lips and her face softened. Brianna walked briskly up to Ricky and lifted her face to his. Their lips met, and he inhaled the scent of Chanel. He moved in to pull her in close, but she'd already stepped back.

"That's enough of that. I'll be back in a couple hours."

Brianna left Ricky standing in the bedroom doorway, a noticeable bulge pressing against his jeans, and hurried down the stairs with the snappy click of her heels echoing behind her.

Ricky had blocked her car in with the truck, and now she had to pick her way over the icy driveway and walk over to Katie's, two houses down, carefully. She debated texting him to come move the truck, then heaved an agitated groan.

"Damn, it, Ricky," she muttered, "great job shoveling. If I break my fucking neck, I swear to— oh."

Brianna looked up mid-oath to see that she'd come face to face with Elise. Mutual expressions of surprise, then discomfiture crossed their faces until a practiced detachment settled.

"What brings you this way?" asked Brianna coolly.

"The plow is going down Cardinal. Scares Gianna, so we're taking the long way to Katie's house," answered Elise, matching Brianna's tone.

"Oh? Well, *I'm* meeting Katie for lunch, so—"

"Hang on. You're meeting Katie for lunch? Uh-uh. *I'm* meeting her. Obviously, there's been a misunderstanding on *your* part."

Both of their phones chirped simultaneously, displaying the same message.

Katie: Yes, both of you.

Katie stood leaning against one of the tall pillars flanking her front porch steps. She watched them with her arms crossed and a stern, 'I mean business' set to her mouth.

"You've got to be fucking kidding," said Elise.

Brianna gave Elise a furtive glance. "Now what?"

She'd never admit it, especially not to Elise Martino, but she missed their little group. There was only so much of Brittany she could take, and Katie was no fun at all anymore since she became a politician's wife. Not to mention those four psychotic rug rats of hers always underfoot.

Elise bit her lip, thinking, *This is totally unlike her. What if something's wrong?*

"Shit. *Cancer.* I'll bet she's going to tell us she has breast cancer or something."

"Jesus, you think?"

"Well, it runs in her family. Oh, God. What if she wants us to be the children's guardians? Like in *Beaches*, or something."

"What—no, she's got Billy to take care of the kids. And any one of her five sisters, for that matter."

Brianna's eyebrows twitched up, and she cocked her head to one side. "True, but—"

Their phones chirped again.

Katie: Hurry up. Freezing out here.

To emphasize, Katie hugged her arms around her waist and shuddered theatrically from her porch. She texted a row of exclamation points.

"Well, I do need to get Gianna out of the cold, so—"

"Ricky's watching Cassidy for a couple hours, so I suppose I might as well take advantage of it."

They began walking together. As if by unspoken agreement that it was too weird to be walking together, Elise slowed, and Brianna picked up her pace, nearly slipping on a patch of ice. Elise smirked and said nothing.

Brianna took rapid, choppy steps up Katie's front steps, greeting her caustically as she did. "Well, isn't this a fun little surprise you've planned for us? I hope you've got wine in there."

"Uh, hello? A little help here, thank you?"

Elise remained at the bottom of the stairs waving her hand impatiently back and forth between the steps and the cumbersome stroller. Brianna huffed and clomped down the stairs less gracefully than she'd gone up and hooked her hand under the front of the stroller.

Elise whisper-hissed, "Play it cool until we know for sure she's not dying."

"Shit, right." Brianna winced.

Inside, Katie said, "Elise, you can bring Gianna in the playroom with Maggie and Nanny Marta, then meet us in the sitting room."

"Yep, sure thing. Where are the boys?"

"Oh, Billy took them out for a hike. Maggie wanted to stay home with me, so…" she trailed off.

"Wine, Katie. Wine," stated Brianna. Her civil expression was a façade on the verge of crumbling.

"Yes, right. Of course," said Katie.

Ten minutes later, the onetime best friends sat

across one another, separated by an antique rosewood coffee table laden with petite sandwiches, fruited iced teas, and a bottle of crisp white wine, while Katie sat between them on the sofa. Brianna would've preferred a red, but the white served her needs well enough. She glanced around at the authentic Victorian décor—Katie had hired an interior designer, of course—and felt a pang of envy.

It should have felt austere and uninviting with its dainty floral-patterned chairs and lace trimmed window treatments, but it was the opposite. Burgundies married rose-petal pinks and powdered blues charmingly. Curved, etched mahogany met flowery upholstery with crocheted throw pillows artfully. Heavy looking wallpaper paused at ivory wainscoting warmly.

Her Victorian now rivaled Katie's in square footage, but Katie's still bore a warmth and welcome that Brianna had thus far found unobtainable in her own home, even with authentic décor.

Elise broke the tense silence. "You still manage to keep them out of your sitting room, huh?"

"So far, at least. I caught Liam trying to sneak in the other day. I told him he'd have to do an hour of knitting with me if he came in here, so that changed his mind." Katie laughed.

Brianna smiled politely, and Elise bobbed her head and made a small sound that might have been, 'Oh,' or 'Ah.'

The heavily ornate bronze clock on the small fireplace mantle ticked loudly in the too quiet room.

The muffled sounds of Maggie and Gianna playing drifted into the room. The three women picked at their food and sipped their wine. Katie's eyes volleyed between her two friends as they studiously avoided looking at each other. The room was like a tea kettle ready to boil.

As if a starting gun had been fired, they all spoke.

"All right, what the hell is—" started Brianna.

"Listen, whatever you're—" began Elise.

"I'm pregnant," blurted Katie.

Elise and Brianna blinked and snapped their mouths shut like twin trout. They looked at each other, perplexed. Katie flushed and sat at the edge of her sofa, clasping her hands under her chin and waiting.

Brianna put her wine glass on the table and gave her full attention on Katie. "Pregnant? Did you just say…you're *pregnant*?"

"*Again*," added Elise before she could stop herself.

"You *guys*—"

"I'm sorry, but—" Brianna stretched her arm out toward Elise, "are we supposed to congratulate you right now, or offer our sympathies?"

"Yeah, I mean, you just had Ian only—"

"He's fourteen months, thank you. And you should be congratulating me, you jerks."

Katie's chin quivered, and Brianna and Elise's faces fell in mutual shame. They jumped up and hurriedly book ended their friend on the sofa, patting her back and offering a jumble of apologies and congratulations.

"We're just surprised, is all," pacified Elise.

"That's right," said Brianna, still trying to wrap her head around anyone wanting *five* children. She was exhausted by the one, not that she didn't adore Cassidy, of course. Still, one was plenty for her.

Brianna continued to pat Katie's back and Elise put her hand on Katie's knee as she sniffled. Brianna looked to the coffee table for a napkin to give Katie, and that's when she saw it.

"Elise?"

Elise took her sympathetic gaze off Katie and looked at Brianna, who was staring at Elise's hand. She slid her hand back, but it was too late. Brianna had noticed the engagement ring. Quick as a bolt of lightning, Brianna grabbed Elise's wrist.

"Oh, no, you don't," she said with mad glee.

"It just happened last night. Or this morning, technically. Bruce proposed, and well, I said yes."

There was a sudden stinging in Brianna's eyes. She blinked rapidly. Then, before she could think about it, she sprang up, pulling Katie and Elise with her, and pulled them both into a fierce hug.

"I'm so happy for you. For *both* of you." And she meant it.

Elise had tensed at first, the past year still fresh and bitter, but there was no denying she had missed her friend. God help her, but she had *missed* Brianna Baker. The three women squealed and giggled just as they'd done when they were teenagers. Only now, instead of shrieking over boyfriends and gossip, their excitement revolved around babies and engagements.

"Hey, what'd I miss?"

Brianna, Elise, and Katie looked to the doorway to see a pouty Brittany scowling at them. The trio laughed and beckoned Brittany to come in.

"See what happens when you're late?" said Brianna archly, "You miss everything. Elise is engaged to Bruce. Katie's having another baby—congratulate her—and I...well, I'm thinking about going back to work."

They all peered at her as if she'd grown a second head, then exchanged glances between each other.

Katie was the first to speak. She chose her words carefully, tentatively. "Well, that's...great, hon. So, what—I mean, where—"

Elise interrupted. "What she's trying to say is, you've never worked a day in your life. What type of job are you getting?"

It was just like old times, the way they fell into their roles in the group. Only, this time, a subtle shift in power had occurred. Brianna had lost her superior, dominating edge and Elise slipped into position as smoothly as if she were born for it. Maybe the others hadn't noticed yet, but Elise and Brianna did. They exchanged a look that could only be understood by them and could only be described as a passing of a torch.

"You have room for one more?" asked a shy voice from the doorway.

"Charlotte! You made it," exclaimed Katie.

"Looks as though I've got catching up to do." She smiled tremulously.

"Get in here, you," said Brianna as warmly as she knew how.

Brittany said, "You didn't miss much. Just that

166

Katie's having another kid, Brianna's getting a job—we don't know what it is yet—and Elise is engaged." She nibbled on the corner of a sandwich, then added with a shrug, "just an ordinary day in the lives of The Real Housewives of Chance."

"No," said Brianna.

"Uh-uh," said Elise.

"Oh, God, no, Brittany," said Katie disdainfully.

"What?" blustered Brittany, "Like, the show. You know—*The Real Housewives of*—"

"We know *exactly* what you mean, Britski," said Elise dryly. "Stop trying to make Real Housewives happen. It's never going to happen, Brit."

After a pause, they all fell about laughing. Referencing *Mean Girls* quotes never got old. Brittany laughed too. Just not as heartily. Brianna and Elise had taken back their original chairs and Charlotte and Brittany took up their spots on either side of Katie. More wine was poured. Elise and Charlotte traded secret smiles—she'd already known of the engagement, of course—which Brianna caught, but chose to ignore.

Instead, she said, "So, Katie. When are you due?"

"Early August," said Katie.

Brittany grimaced. "Ugh, you're gonna be all big and preggo for the sum—"

"It'll be great," interrupted Brianna with a pointed, icy glare at Brittany. "And we'll all be here for you, naturally."

"Joel and I have decided to try for baby number two, so maybe we'll be pregnant at the same time," added Charlotte shyly.

"Oh, Charlotte, that will be so fun," squealed Katie, clapping her hands.

"Well, *this* factory is closed, I can tell you that much," said Brittany, motioning to her abdomen. "Multiple sets of twins run on Bart's side. Devon and Dylan are plenty, thank you very much. Besides, I'm not ruining this figure, damn it."

"What's up with you, Elise? Does Bruce want a kid of his own?"

"Oh, well, we haven't talked about it, to tell you the truth. I mean, I think so. Yeah, no. Definitely. I'm sure he does."

The others swapped glances. Katie leaned forward and half-whispered, "You maybe want to have that talk before you two get married, right? I mean, you always said you wanted at least two. If he's—"

"Of course. Yeah, totally," said Elise. It was obvious that she wasn't as confident as she tried to sound.

Whether sensing her discomfort or just wanting her turn in the spotlight, Brianna cleared her throat and said, "Well, doesn't anyone want to hear about my new career?"

"Yes, please," said Katie with genuine enthusiasm.

"Duh, yeah," said Brittany with her usual elegance.

"All right then. I, Brianna Bourdreau-Baker," she paused theatrically, relishing the attention, "am starting an event planning company." She took in their polite, blank stares, fluttered her lashes, and said, "You know, like Jennifer Lopez in *The*

Wedding Planner? Except I'll do all sorts of parties. Except children's parties. Those are a hard pass. Unless it's a quinceanera or a sweet sixteen."

"Well," said Charlotte thoughtfully, "you *do* throw killer parties."

Katie agreed, "That's true. You single-handedly saved my New Year's party last night." To the others, she lamented, "worst event planner ever screwed everything up. But Brianna just swooped right in and started ordering everyone about, and suddenly it was perfect."

"That's right," said Elise, pointing at Brianna. "You planned all of our birthday parties in high school. You know, Bri? I think this really is your calling."

Brianna beamed. If she were to be honest, the idea wasn't hers initially, but the flustered caterer from last night. She'd come right out and said, 'You should be getting paid for this,' and those words had sparked an excitement in her that she hadn't felt since—well, she couldn't remember.

"So, what does Ricky think?"

"I haven't told him yet, Brittany. But I will. Later."

Ricky had always been notoriously possessive of Brianna. He wasn't a Neanderthal, nor was he a chauvinist. He merely had Brianna on a very high pedestal, one that made him blind to her faults and an enabler of her self-centeredness. Between the four women, they felt Brianna used her shitty upbringing as an excuse and means to guilt him into doing whatever she wanted him to do. Not that Gordon and Martha Bourdreau's parenting was anything to make light of, they were easily the cause of her many issues. What they'd put her through could fill a book.

Chapter 19

Better Be Good

"It's fine, don't worry. Mae will understand," said Feather Anne, leading Gina up the street.

"You sure? The last thing I need is to piss her off," sniffed Gina.

They were half a block from home, trudging past the high mounds of dirty snow. The sanding trucks had come through again yesterday morning, obliterating the last trace of white alongside the roads. It befits the start of January, the longest, most boring month of the year in Feather Anne's opinion.

"Nah, it's fine." Although, for a moment, Feather Anne doubted herself. She should've told someone they were going back to the house, but Gina looked so uncomfortable and out of place—maybe even ready to cry—that Feather Anne just wanted to get her out of there before she embarrassed anyone. She'd call the café the minute they walked through

171

the door.

Only, when they'd reached the house, Feather Anne realized she'd forgotten her house key. Fortunately, Mae kept a spare in the backyard under a planter by the goat pen.

"Holy shit, you've got goats?" Gina laughed her raspy smoker's laugh and grinned.

"Yep. Chickens too. I'm trying to convince Mae we need a pig. I think I've almost got her."

Feather Anne turned her smiling, rosy-cheeked face to her mother. Gina was smiling too, but it was a sad smile and didn't reach her eyes.

"Come on, I'll introduce you," said Feather Anne, before Gina could say anything sentimental.

Feather Anne coaxed Fred, Ginger, Georgie, and Gracie out from their cozy goat house and fed them their snacks. Gina was afraid to at first, but Feather Anne showed her how to do it properly.

"They have four stomachs, you know. But you can only feed them little bits at a time. And it's got to be small pieces, otherwise, they'll choke."

Gina stretched her hand out to Gracie, halting and jerking back every time the goat craned her neck toward the offered food and making nervous sounds. This cracked Feather Anne up.

"Stop laughing at me. They have big teeth, geez," said Gina mildly defensive, but laughing too.

"They can sense your fear, Mom. Just relax."

Feather Anne's armpits tingled with cold sweat and her ears grew suddenly hot. She hadn't called Gina 'Mom' since she was six years old.

"Feather Anne, I—"

"Come see the chickens. There's ten now. Mae

said in the spring we can get a rooster and hatch eggs. Cool, right?"

"Sure, kid. Show me your chickens," said Gina instead of what she'd wanted to say.

Gina, for all that she lacked in parenting skills, at least knew when to back off. Feather Anne didn't want to have a heart to heart with her, and she couldn't blame the kid. Maybe in time, she could tell her things, apologize. Now was obviously not the time.

By the time they'd gotten inside the house, they were both shivering, frozen to the bone. They'd been mutually wary of the prospect of trying to find things to say to one another, so they'd prolonged their time outside despite the numbing cold. When at last they could no longer bear the risk of frostbite or hypothermia, Feather Anne suggested they make hot chocolate and start a fire, to which Gina gratefully agreed.

"You go start the fire, and I'll make the hot chocolate, okay? Wait, you know how to make a fire, right?"

Gina raised a dark eyebrow. "Uh, yeah. Been doing it since before you were born, sport."

"Well," said Feather Anne smugly, "a fire in an old tire rim is different from one in a fireplace, so I was just making sure."

"They both take wood, don't they?"

They'd fallen into their old way of bantering, like two cantankerous sisters rather than mother and daughter. The realization struck them simultaneously.

Feather Anne stammered, "Well—I—I'll go

make the hot chocolate," and disappeared into the kitchen.

As she pulled out the cocoa, milk, and mugs and set a pot on the stove, the sounds of the fireplace cover being moved, newspaper crumpling, and wood being clunked together came from the living room.

"Did you remember to open the flue?" hollered Feather Anna.

"No duh," yelled Gina back.

A second later there was the scrape of the flue being opened. Feather Anne smirked. It wasn't until she'd set the carton of milk back on its shelf in the refrigerator that she realized she'd never called the café to let Mae know they'd gone home.

"Shit," said Feather Anne just as the front door opened.

Mae, red-eyed and pale, stopped in the doorway, looking from Gina to Feather Anne—coming out from the kitchen—in disbelief. Joel Asheby and a uniformed police officer trailed her, making the same track between mother and daughter.

"I—you—" stammered Mae. Then her eyes fluttered, and her knees buckled. Fortunately, Joel was quick to grab her before she fell. He half walked, half carried her to the couch as he called instructions to his officer.

"Call dispatch. Let them know we've got her, and the kid is safe." To Feather Anne, he said, "Sweetie, can you get your sister a glass of water?" Once she rounded the corner, he spoke to Gina. "You've got a lot of explaining to do, Gina. What were you thinking? Are you trying to get arrested?"

Mae had regained her composure and glared at Gina. "I gave you a chance, Gina. How could you—"

"I'm sorry, Mae. I wasn't thinking, I—"

"It was my fault, Mae. I—felt bad that she looked so uncomfortable, so I said we could go back to the house. I was gonna call you when we got in, but I forgot my key. Then we got distracted by the goats, and well—"

"It's—it's okay, Feather Anne," said Mae, pressing her fingertips to her forehead, her eyes closed.

The officer who'd gone outside to make the calls, poked his head back in the doorway. "Sarge? Can I talk to you outside a minute?"

Joel Asheby excused himself, leaving Mae, Gina, and Feather Anne alone.

Mae spoke first, her voice shaking with barely controlled anger and upset. "I thought she kidnapped you, Feather Anne. We had people searching, the police set up roadblocks, William—shit."

She jumped up in search of her phone. It rang just as she pulled it from her purse. "William! She's—they're—" Mae paused, listening to William on the other end, then exhaled and said, "oh, good. Yes, I'll see you when you get here. Thank you. Yes, I'm fine."

Mae disconnected and returned to the couches, lifting a strand of hair to her lips as she crossed the room, back to her sister and biological mother. Feather Anne sat cross-legged, brushing a strand of black hair across her lips like a paintbrush. Gina stood, hair to lips as well. The trio passed looks between them and their mirrored habit and they dropped their hands to their sides. Gina had yet to speak again since her attempted apology.

Mordantly, Mae said to Gina, "You're supposed to be the adult, Gina. Jesus."

"I—I know. I—listen, I know I've overstayed my welcome. So, I'll, uh, pack up my sh—stuff and get out of your hair," said Gina, her head bowed and hands twitching at her sides.

At first, Mae said nothing. She wanted her gone, her life back to the new normal they'd created. Gina upset the hard-won balance and structure she and William had fostered for Feather Anne. The woman was a jobless, barely functioning woman-child on her best days, and a lying, thieving addict at her worst. They didn't need her in their lives, damn it. But one look at Feather Anne's huge gray eyes— eyes that were nearly identical to both Mae's and Gina's—and she knew what she had to do.

"You don't have to leave, Gina. Not yet at least. You—"

"I'm afraid she does, Mae," said Joel from the doorway.

William had returned, looking both harried and relieved. He met Mae's eyes with a sad, apologetic head shake.

Mae stood and frowned at Joel and William. "What are you saying?"

Joel glanced at Feather Anne and winced. He gave Mae an apologetic head shake, just as William had done. Then he turned a hard stare to Gina.

"There's a warrant for your arrest. In New

Hampshire. A woman by the name of Suzanne Montgomery says you stole some belongings of hers."

Gina sputtered, "I didn't do no such thing. I don't even know a Suzanne Montgomery." She was genuinely puzzled.

Joel looked at his small, rectangular notepad and read, "Goes by Zuzu? Owns a hair salon in—"

"Shit," said Gina, all but admitting guilt.

Feather Anne scoffed and shook her head in disgust. "Mother of the Year yet again, huh, Gina?" and stormed off to her room.

"Feather Anne, wait. I—"

"Leave her be, Gina. Just..." Mae trailed off and waved her hand dismissively and looking away.

Joel glanced at his notes and said, "There's a proviso here. The woman is willing to drop the charges if you return the necklace you stole."

Gina's brow drew together, and her head pulled back. "Necklace? I don't remember any—wait."

Gina reached under the couch she'd slept on the night before and pulled out her bag. Mae rubbed her temples. Had it actually been less than twenty-four hours since Gina had shown up on their doorstep? It seemed like months.

"Just—" she fished around in the ratty brown leather bucket style purse, "hang—" she shoved her hand deeper, then gave up and dumped the contents onto the coffee table. Half a roll of Lifesavers, three packs of cigarettes, a hot pink bra, a dozen or so pennies, two nickels, four crumpled dollar bills, a tampon, gas station receipts, a book, a paperclip, a pair of sunglasses, and lastly...a gold necklace with a round, ornate pendant the size of a silver dollar.

She held up the necklace and shouted, "Ha, still got it!"

As she looked around the room at the somber faces staring back at her, Gina's triumphant smile faded, and she remembered her audience. These people were neither amused nor impressed. She saw herself through their eyes. Gina Byrd, trailer park trash. Addict. Loser. Dirty, scraggly, shit for a mother, waste of space. That had been her own mother's nickname for her growing up—waste of space. Her vision blurred, and she swallowed hard. Ain't no way she'd cry in front of them cops.

Defiantly, she said, "I didn't mean to take it. I was trying to get my due, what she owed me for workin'. The stupid thing," she shook the necklace in her hand, "must've been stuck to one of the wraps—you know, the kind they put around money—or, I don't know. I just know I didn't mean to take it. I can send it back to her. Tomorrow, first thing."

"That's the thing, Gina. Her condition runs out today. She wants it back by tonight, hand-delivered by you, with an apology. It's the only way she'll drop charges," said Joel.

Gina's heart sank. She had four dollars and a handful of change left. No car. She could hitchhike as she'd done getting back to Chance, but that took her three days. She would be going to jail.

"Well, then," said Mae standing, "I guess we'd better get moving, shouldn't we?"

She gazed at Gina with dark eyes, a myriad of emotions passing through them plainly. Anger. Pity.

Resentment. Hope. Yes, hope. Or something like it.

"We?" asked Gina.

At the same time, William stepped forward and said, "Mae, I don't think this is a good idea. The stress of—think of the—"

"I'll be fine, William. I promise."

Gina's head cocked, and she appraised Mae anew. *She's pregnant. Of course.* The near fainting, the roller coaster emotions, the new softness over her cheekbones. It was almost exactly how Gina had looked when she was pregnant with Mae. It had been different with Feather Anne—she'd been sick the whole time—but this was how she'd been as well. Ironically, she'd given her own mother a second chance at the time too. Rayna Byrd had failed Gina miserably, just as she always had. Well, Gina wasn't going to repeat history anymore, damn it.

From behind them, a small, fierce voice. "Then I'm going too," said Feather Anne.

Her hands were splayed on her narrow hips and her pointy jaw was thrust forward, daring anyone to try to stop her.

Mae looked at William imploringly. His head drooped, and he lifted his hand in surrender. "As if I could stop you two?"

Chapter 20

Love Me So

"Well, hello you."

"Hey, yourself," said Miles, a broad grin spreading across his face.

Rosabelle narrowed her eyes. "What's that smile for?"

"What, can't a man just be happy to be alone with his bride-to-be?"

"Miles, we talked about—"

"Ah, ah, ah," said Miles wagging his finger in front of her face. "None of that right now. Besides, I have every confidence that everything will work itself out."

Rosabelle groaned and threw her hands out. "But how, Miles? My parents leave in two days, and they are nowhere near ready to accept you."

"Ouch, um, harsh, Rosie. Come on, babe. Have a little faith in me—"

"Oh, God. Please don't start singing," moaned Rosabelle.

He sang anyway. Rosabelle covered her ears and laughed. Oh, if only her parents could see this side of him—the silly, sweet, genuinely charming Miles—instead of the Miles he was for everyone else. *That* side of Miles was a façade, and this side was his true self. One reserved for her alone. Not even his own family saw this version of him. She stopped laughing and dropped her hands in her lap and gave him a look of pure love.

"Come sit with me, Miles," she said.

He sensed the change in her demeanor and sat carefully beside her, mindful of the pain she still felt.

"What is it, Rosie? Are you hurting? Maybe we weaned you off the good stuff too soon. Should I call Dr.—"

"Miles, shh." She put a finger to his lips and giggled. "I'm fine. I just want to say something to you, that's all. I—I've changed my mind."

Miles looked as if he'd been struck. "You mean you don't want to marry me anymore?"

"Oh, Miles, of *course,* I do, silly. I mean I've changed my mind about my parents' approval. Forget them, and anyone else who doesn't approve."

She folded her arms over her chest for emphasis and scowled at the imaginary haters. Miles plunked his head on her shoulder and blew a gust of hot air down her shirt.

"Jesus, you gave me a heart attack, Rosie. Don't scare me like that again." He popped his head back

181

up and pressed his forehead to hers. "You mean it? You'd really marry me even if it means going against your parents, Rosie?"

She nodded, moving both their heads up and down. Then Rosabelle took his face in her hands and looked into his bright blue eyes and said, "Fuck 'em. Fuck 'em all. Someone's always going to think I'm too plain for you, or you're too much of a gigolo for me. But they don't *know* us. They only know what they think they see. I see *you*. You see *me*. That's all that matters. You and me, Miles."

"Us against the world, Rosie," agreed Miles. Then he gave her a rueful cockeyed look and asked, "Gigolo, huh? Ouch, Rosie."

She patted his cheek, then playfully shoved his mock-chagrined face away. "Yep. Now be a good gigolo and dance for me or do whatever you gigolos do to be charming. On second thought, can you just get me an ice cream?"

"Geez, Rosie. You'd pick ice cream over my killer dance moves? You sure you haven't been sneaking any of those leftover goofballs from the medicine cabinet?"

Rosabelle flung a throw pillow at his head and sent him off to the kitchen. When he was out of sight, her smile faded. Yes, she'd meant every word of what she'd said to Miles. But what Rosabelle had left out was her *other* motive. The one that gave her away as the pathetic and deceitful nerd she really was and always would be. She couldn't let that happen even if it meant disappointing her parents by marrying Miles. In time, they'd get over it. She hoped.

Chapter 21

Let's Be Jolly

Bruce eyed Elise as they turned down the duvet, trying to mute his surprise and failing. "So, just like that, huh?"

"Yeah, well, no," she said, throwing the decorative pillows onto the bench at the foot of the bed. "I mean, Brianna and I still have stuff to work out, of course. But I don't know, it felt good to have us all together again," said Elise with a shrug.

Two days ago, she'd sworn to Bruce that hell would have to freeze over before she let Brianna Baker back into her life. Two days. Yesterday, Katie had staged an ambush lunch—successfully—and today, they were going to yoga together, just like the old days before Brianna had tried to destroy both their reputations. He and Ricky had hardly hung out at all since the girls had their falling out, and every time they did, it had been strained.

183

Women, man.

"It's just, you know, all that shit she pulled last year. I lost a roofing job because of her. Remember? Father Jarvis? He made up some B.S. excuse, but I knew it was because he thought we were having an affair."

"Oh, now," said Elise, raising her eyebrow at him, "you only lost the job *temporarily*. As soon as Ethan and Jack came out, Father Jarvis asked you back. All's well that ends well, right?"

Elise tried to coax a conciliatory smile out of Bruce. He obliged, but it wasn't as genuine as she'd hoped. She had the feeling that if she didn't change the subject quickly, the conversation could turn into an argument. Not that a little spat worried her—she was the daughter of a lawyer, after all—but she wanted to have a talk with him regarding a much more important matter.

Ever since Katie's baby announcement, then Charlotte's news of their impending pregnancy, Elise had been struck by baby fever. Suddenly, everywhere she turned babies, babies, and more babies. Just as abruptly, Gianna had started to seem so big to her. It was psychological, of course, but still.

"Well, obviously it's your call, Elise," Bruce was saying as he folded his jeans over the chair in the corner, "but you'd better keep—"

"I want another baby," blurted Elise.

Bruce stopped mid-fold, puzzling out her words. "I'm sorry, what?"

Elise exhaled loudly and dropped on the bed. She quickly got under the covers and pulled them over her face. She repeated, muffled by the sheets and comforter, "I want us to have a baby."

Silence, then the creak of the bed as Bruce sat down. With a whoosh, he was under the sheets with her, his breath warm and minty on her cheek.

"Me too," he stage-whispered in her ear.

Elise yanked the covers away, leaving their hair staticky and wild. She laughed, covering her mouth. Bruce grinned back at her, nodding his head.

"You do? Really?"

Bruce playfully jumped on top of her, pinning her under his weight. "Of course, I do, dummy. How could you not know that?"

"I—I don't know. I mean, we've never actually talked about it. You and Gianna have such a sweet bond, and I guess I just thought maybe you felt like she was enough for you, or—"

Bruce rolled off her and slapped his hand over his eyes. "Ah, man. Now I feel stupid. I kinda thought *you* might not want any more kids."

He sprang up again, worry etched in his face. "Hey, listen. I love Gianna like she's my own. I know she's Ethan's and yours, but I'm happy to be her—I don't know—bonus dad. If you didn't want any more kids, I was ready to be okay with that too."

This time, Elise climbed on top of Bruce. "I couldn't possibly love you more than I do right now, Bruce Grady."

A devilish grin spread across Bruce's face, "Couldn't you, though?"

"Okay." Elise grinned back. "Maybe I could…"

After they'd made playful love, they curled

toward each other and laced their fingers together.

"Four weeks," said Elise.

Bruce said, "Till what?"

"Until your lease is up, and you move in for real," said Elise.

"Ah, that's right," said Bruce.

Elise let go of his hand and turned onto her back, pressing the sheets between them. They both stayed silent. There were two bones of contention in their relationship. Mae and moving into Elise's house. Bruce had won the first battle, Elise the second. However, both had been hard won wars of will and persuasion.

Where Elise struggled with accepting the friendship between ex-lovers, Bruce struggled with moving into another man's house. They'd volleyed points and counter-points, facts and feelings, until finally, surrender rather than compromise. Contingencies, by a matter of course, were declared.

Elise had to accept Mae and Bruce's continued friendship and working arrangement for as long as Mae was with William. She could not bear the thought of a single, available Mae Huxley, with her Disney princess eyes and silky fawn-colored hair, not to mention those damn long legs of hers.

In turn, Bruce planned on move into Elise's house—instead of buying a new house together—and do the renovations to make it more his own and no longer Ethan's old house. He had nothing against Ethan, and in fact, liked the guy well enough. It was simple, basic man code. A man can't just move into another man's house as if the previous man had never been there. He can't shave in the same sink, sleep in the same bed, or eat off the same dining table. It was weird.

"But you can sleep with the same woman," Elise had said wryly when he'd explained his point of view.

"Jesus, Elise," Bruce had replied, covering his ears and wincing.

That sparked a three-day fight, which was more of a mutual silent treatment. In the end, it came down to practicality and a touch of Bruce's unwillingness to put any money in Miles Hannaford's pockets by giving him another sale at his expense. It was petty, sure. Bruce didn't care though.

"You *said* you were fine with it," said Elise with a hint of a whine.

"I am," said Bruce, his tone resigned. He reached for her hand in the dark. "I *am*," he said again, this time reassuringly.

"Good," said Elise, turning back toward Bruce and hooking her foot over his ankle.

Bruce watched his fiancée—he still had to wrap his mind around the fact that he now had a fiancée—as her eyes fluttered closed and her breathing deepened and slowed. He marveled at how easily and quickly she fell asleep and had even teased her for it on occasion. She told him he was jealous of her 'mad sleep game' and he heartily agreed.

Bruce had been an insomniac ever since he was a kid. His folks often found him up on the couch playing video games or reading comic books under the covers with a flashlight at all hours of the night.

In high school, he'd taken to showing up at the football field to practice. He recited in his head, '*Elbow up, rotate, toe, target, release.*'

He'd once told Mae about his mantra and she'd laughed. "You said that *every* time?"

"Not out loud. Just in my head. Shut up, whatever," Bruce had replied, waving his hand dismissively. "You've got quirks too. Admit it."

They were in the café kitchen, putting away the last of the lunch time remnants.

"Okay, okay. Fine. I do have this one thing I do."

"Just one?" said Bruce, giving her the eye.

"Be quiet. You want to know it or not?"

Bruce had nodded and pretended to zip his lips closed.

"Every time I take the teapot from the stove, I sing, *I'm A Little Teapot* as I pour it."

Mae had winced in anticipation of ridicule, and Bruce was happy to oblige.

"Huxley, that is weird as shit. Sing it for me."

"No, I'm not pouring tea."

"Come on, sing it." He drew out the word 'it' and prodded her with a wooden spoon.

Bruce found himself grinning at the memory, then caught himself short. He shouldn't be lying beside his sleeping fiancée, thinking of another woman. Even if it was completely innocent and meant nothing.

Chapter 22

Take The Road Before Us

"Can someone put on the radio? It's too quiet in here," grouched Feather Anne from the backseat.

Gina and Mae exchanged a look, Mae nodded, and Gina pushed the on button. Frank Sinatra's voice spilled from the speakers and Feather Anne groaned.

"Oh, my *God*, Mae. We listen to that stuff all the time. Put on the *radio*. I want to hear normal music for once."

"You know, no one said you had to come, brat," said Mae in a sing-song voice tottering on sharpness.

Gina almost chimed in, then remembered her precarious place in this sudden dynamic. In a car of biologically related females, she was still the outsider. The Interloper. The Intruder. The—

"Outkast, perfect. Leave it there, please," shouted

Feather Anne.

She began boisterously singing along with the talk/sing lyrics. Mae cringed instinctively, but within a few seconds, her head began to bob along to the beat and her fingers drummed the steering wheel.

Gina knew the song, thanks to Feather Anne's obsession with it when it first came out a few years back. Despite her intended reserve, she couldn't help but belt out the chorus along with Feather Anne. Mae gave a theatric eyeroll and grimaced. More notably, she was laughing when she did so.

Once that song ended, Feather Anne spent the next fifteen minutes giving station changing orders to Gina.

"Change it. Change it. Change it. Leave it. No, never mind, change it," said Feather Anne in her bossy monotone.

Secretly, Gina was glad for the distraction. There'd been a nervous, weighted tension from the moment they'd buckled their seatbelts, as if they all knew this trip had the power to make or break the fragile, budding truce that had begun to poke through the dirt that was their relationships.

"Hey, that's a good one, no?"

Mae cut her eyes from the road to meet Feather Anne's through the rearview mirror. Feather Anne heaved a put-upon, world-weary sigh and dropped her head against the seat in defeat. Gina's finger hovered over the tune button, waiting for her cue to either change or turn up the volume.

"Fine," huffed Feather Anne.

She liked the song too, but no need to give over

that detail. Gina had played Fleetwood Mac to death when they were living in the trailer. This song, *Dreams*, was her favorite, and she'd crank the shitty old boombox as loud as it could go whenever it came on. Feather Anne had no choice but to know every word.

As for Mae, she too always loved that particular band, something she unwittingly shared with her biological mother, and *not* her father, who claimed Stevie Nicks' voice made him feel as though shards of glass were being stabbed in his ears. They'd had heated debates over the subject—Mae proclaiming Stevie as her own personal idol and absolute goddess, and Keith denouncing Mae as his daughter—and never did see eye to eye on that one. The most Keith allowed was an ardent admiration for Lindsey Buckingham, which he claimed had everything to do with his musicianship, and nothing to do with his strange, smoldering, sexy looks.

Together—but very separately—the three sang along with the song. Mae's eyes were trained on the road ahead. Gina's were fixed out her passenger window. Feather Anne, behind Mae, watched the trees and cars whiz by. As the song progressed, their voices rose in a stunningly perfect harmony.

No one dared speak when it ended, not at first. Then, shyly, Mae said, "I didn't know you sang," to Gina.

Gina shrugged, embarrassed. "It's been a long time, but yeah. I used to sing pretty well. Before the smoking and…well, before."

"I remember you singing when I was little," said Feather Anne from the backseat.

"Yeah? You remember that? I, uh, kinda figured you only remembered the bad stuff."

Gina bowed her head and fidgeted with the zipper on her coat. *Mae's* coat—loaned to her.

The rustle of Feather Anne's puffy coat indicated a shrug. "Yeah, I remember that too."

The next forty minutes went by in silence but for the radio. It was neither comfortable nor uncomfortable, the quiet. It just *was*. Mae tried to imagine it as just a mother and daughters road trip. Three gals hitting the road. Laughs, music, and memories in the making. That's what it would've been if they were a different family living a different life. Mae found that she couldn't force herself to pretend otherwise, at least not for more than a fleeting moment.

Their truth was not pretty, or typical. Their truth began with an unwanted pregnancy, an adoption, and a secret that everyone except Mae had been privy to until last year. Gina Byrd, in her selfish, spiteful mind, decided the day of Mae's father's funeral was a *great* time to bring this bit of unexpected trivia to her attention.

The recollection caused Mae's grip on the steering wheel to tighten and her chest and cheeks burned with welling anger. If Gina were to speak in that second, Mae knew she'd jerk the car over to the breakdown lane and throw her ass out. But Gina sat quietly, like a child who'd been scolded and knew they'd better just shut up, or else.

"I'm hungry," declared Feather Anne from the back.

The child's husky voice snapped Mae back to

focus, and she blinked rapidly, unfurling her death grip and shaking the cramp out of one hand at a time.

"There's a town up a couple miles. It'll have food and restrooms. Ten minutes," said Mae.

Twenty minutes later, the trio sat around a scarred plastic table across from a McDonald's counter. Mae had found to her relief that the adjacent restaurant served salads, wraps, and fruit and vegetable smoothies. Gina and Feather Anne dove voraciously into their burgers and fries while Mae spread her paper napkin over her lap and snapped back the lid of her salad box. She gave her mother and sister a bemused look.

"What?" they simultaneously asked.

Mae shook her head and laughed. "Nothing. I just—I mean, are you people *sure* I'm related to you?"

Feather Anne threw a French fry at her and Gina laughed good-naturedly. After a pause, Gina shot a cautious glance at Mae. Mae was looking at her salad, unaware. Before she could lose her courage, Gina said, "Your, uh, dad? He was always a healthy eater. Even back when we were kids."

Mae looked up sharply, her face unreadable. "Oh?"

"Yeah." Gina shrugged, embarrassed now for saying anything, but she started, and it was too late to pull it back. "I mean, we didn't know each other well. But I remember that about him. And that he was so nice to me. I mean, he was nice to everyone, of course. But I always remember how nice he was to *me*."

In a gentle tone, Mae said, "Most people…weren't nice to you?"

Gina laughed. It was a hard, bitter bark. "*Nice* to Gina Byrd? You know what they used to call me when I was a kid? Turd-Byrd. Creative, right?"

Mae winced.

"Ah, listen," Gina said dismissively, "that was then. Water under the bridge, right?"

"Gina, that must've been awful."

"Yeah, Gina. Kids suck," said Feather Anne matter-of-factly. She'd persevered through ridicule and humiliation and could empathize way more than Mae ever could.

"Yep, they do," agreed both Mae and Gina.

"Well, not *all* kids. My friend Brandon is different," said Feather Anne, jabbing her French fry into a blob of ketchup. She looked up to see her mother and sister staring at her with knowing smirks. "What? Oh, shut up."

Feather Anne jumped up, grabbed her crumpled napkin, and ran it to the garbage can behind them. Mae and Gina pretended not to notice the rosy blush that had crept up her neck, all the way to her scalp. Feather Anne pretended to be extremely interested in her straw.

Tentatively, Mae asked, "Brandon? As in Brandon Bourdreau?"

"Yeah, and I know, he's the ice queen's brother. But he's nothing like her."

Gina looked between her daughters…pausing mentally over the word daughters, and puzzled, "Did you say Bourdreau?" Then, almost immediately after asking, she smacked her forehead and said, "You're talking about Gordon and Martha Bourdreau's *kids*? Jesus, they had a second one?" She shuddered.

Mae would've called the shudder theatric, but for the furious set to her jaw and the glint in her eyes. They'd instantly turned from smoky gray to steel, just as hers and Feather Anne's did when they became angry or agitated.

"What's *that* for?" Mae was half curious and half defensive on behalf of Gordon and Martha, who despite having raised—as Feather Anne called Brianna, the Ice Queen—was decent as far as she could see. "The Bourdreaus are very nice people. Highly respected too," said Mae with a look of reproach.

Gina chortled unladylike and scoffed, "*Psh*— yeah, whatever you say."

"Oh, for God's sake. Gordon is a *deacon* at First Baptist. He's on the Board of *Education*. Martha leads a women's group to help *Haiti*. They're *good people*," said Mae, emphasizing her points to show she was appalled that she even had to spell out what good people the Bourdreaus were.

Gina stood up abruptly from her seat and gripped the edge of the table with both hands as if she might flip it. Her eyes blazed, and her voice shook. "Sure. People like Gordon," she spat his name out as if it tasted disgusting in her mouth, "and Martha Bourdreau are real salt of the earth folks." She mimicked Mae's intonations. "Pillars of the *community*. Always ready to help a neighbor in *need*. Fine, upstanding *citizens*."

Mae and Feather Anne stared, mouths agape.

Gina, suddenly aware of her surroundings, deflated and reached for her purse. Without looking at either of them, she said, "I'm not hungry anymore. I'll be outside havin' a smoke."

She began to walk toward the exit, then stopped and returned to the table. At first, Mae thought she returned to apologize for her outburst, but she was wrong.

"Last thing I'm gonna say on *that* topic—" She pointed a finger at Feather Anne. "*You*. I know I don't have the right to talk to you like a mother—either of you—but I'm telling you now. Stay away from the Bourdreaus. And *you*—" she pointed at Mae, "you keep her away if you want to do what's best."

After she'd gone, Mae turned to Feather Anne. "What do you make of *that*?"

Feather Anne threw her hands out and gave an exaggerated shrug. "Hell if I know."

"Language, Feath—"

"Wait, I *do* remember something. Gina had a boyfriend for a while—Hector—and they got into a big argument one night. Well, they got into fights almost every night, but this time Gina totally lost her shit—sorry, I know, language. Anyhow, I think it was about money. He suggested she go to the church and ask them for help like she'd done before I was born. Next thing I know, she's throwing stuff and screaming at him, 'you know I'd never go back there. I told you what happened to me. How dare you…' and blah, blah, blah."

"Wow, you had to hear all that, huh?" Mae felt sadness and guilt anew every time Feather Anne shared memories of her childhood.

Feather Anne gave one of her infamous 'whatever' shrugs and said, "Yeah, well, when all you got is a ratty curtain separating your bedroom from the rest of your trailer, privacy isn't really a thing."

Mae stood and gathered their trash, a thoughtful expression on her face. The next hour of their ride was spent in silence. Feather Anne had fallen asleep, her head bobbing and rolling and mouth open. Gina stared out her window, somber and stoic. As for Mae, she imagined various scenarios in which Gina Byrd could have had an interaction with Gordon Bourdreau that caused such a visceral reaction from her, even years later.

He'd been the deacon at First Baptist for as long as Mae could remember and had often stood in for Pastor John. Had Gina gone to the church for help and been treated poorly by Gordon? What else could have happened to make her so bitter? She glanced at Gina's profile. If Gina wasn't going to tell her then Mae had to find out another way.

Chapter 23

Good Will

"Rosabelle, Mrs. Waterman, so lovely to see you both," said William with genuine fondness.

"Hello, William. Nice to see you too." Rosabelle smiled warmly.

"Please," said her mother, smoothing her hair and smiling coquettishly, "call me Ruth. What brings you to the library today, William?"

Rosabelle looked up from her wheelchair at her mother's behavior. She'd never seen her act so—so flirtatiously? So puerile? Who *was* this woman, and what did she do with her real mother?

Ruth caught her daughter's incredulous stare and straightened. Not before casting a dirty look in her direction though.

William smiled graciously, waved the small stack of books in his hand, and said, "Returns and pickups. The girls are on a road trip, so Mae asked that I take care of these. Wouldn't want any of those overdue fines looming over our heads and putting us in hock."

He laughed to show he was joking. Rosabelle chuckled. Ruth? Ruth giggled like a schoolgirl. Now Rosabelle had seen it all. They made small talk with William for a few minutes longer, then parted ways. Once Ruth had rolled Rosabelle far enough away, she hissed out the side of her mouth, "Now, that's one hunk of a man."

"Moth*er*! What has gotten into you today?"

"I'm married, Rosabelle, not dead. Don't be so uptight. Besides, I'm merely acknowledging a fact. Miss Mae has landed herself quite a catch. Even if he is much too old for her. What is he? Fifty, fifty-two?"

Rosabelle squeezed her eyes shut for a second then said, "I don't know…fifty-six, I think. And please don't say that to Mae."

"Oh, come on, now. I would never. Anyhow, who am I to judge, right? Your father is older than me, and we worked out just fine."

"Mom, he's four years older. Can we just pick up my books and get back home? Miles is making dinner."

"It's *five* years, thank you very much. Oh, hey, we should check out that new little boutique that opened up on Main Street."

"Mom, I know you heard me. Miles is making dinner for us. He wanted to do something special before you guys left for South Carolina."

"Oh," said Ruth as she absently stroked Rosabelle's hair.

"Please stop doing that. You and Dad *are* coming for dinner, right?"

"Yes, yes. Of course. Wouldn't miss it for the *world*. Say, did William say Mae went on a girl's trip? What's that all about, you think?"

Rosabelle took a big breath and puffed her cheeks as she exhaled.

"Oh, honey, don't do that. Makes you look like a blowfish. What were we saying? Oh, you know what I've been meaning to ask you? That fella that hit you—what's his name, that Chris—has he even come to see you? What sort of man plows into a woman, nearly kills her, then doesn't come to see her? I have a mind to send your father over to pay him a visit, you know."

Mentally, Rosabelle counted the hours until her parents left. Thirty-six. A day and a half, then life could go back to normal. Or at least normal*ish*, considering she'd be starting physical therapy the day after they left. Thirty-six hours, and then she could breathe again without the constant strain of juggling Miles, her mother and father, her rehabilitation, and her secret shame.

"Don't send Daddy, please. He sent a card and flowers. He feels terrible enough as it is, so let him be. Bruce told Mae—who then told Miles—that Fat Chris was so distraught that he went to stay with his mother in Cromwell for a while. I feel so sorry for him."

"Aw, that's my sweet girl, always thinking of others, even when *you're* the one with the pain and suffering. But this is how you get taken advantage of, sweetheart. Don't you think that maybe Miles—

"

"Mom," said Rosabelle warningly.

"Okay, fine. Just trying to help, honey."

By the time they'd returned to Rosabelle's house, she was in need of a nap and ibuprofen, both to assuage her pounding headache. She calculated an hour and a half before Miles arrived with the groceries and her parents came knocking for dinner. Plenty of time.

Only, it wasn't to be. The moment her head hit the couch pillow, there was a knock at the door, then the unmistakable turn of the latch and her father's somewhat nasally call, "Hey-yo. Just your old Dad, buttercup. Your mom said you could use some company until what's his name shows up."

"You know his name, Daddy."

He batted a hand at her. "Yeah, yeah. Can I get you anything? Some tea? Maybe a magazine? You want your sketchbook?"

"Right now, I just need to close my eyes for a few minutes, but thanks, Dad."

"Your mother give you a headache? She has that effect sometimes, but don't tell her I said that, huh?"

"Daddy! That's not very nice," Rosabelle smiled slyly, "but, yes."

"I knew it."

Steven snapped his fingers together and shook his fist in victory. He shoved his hands in pockets and paced. Then he scratched his head.

"Daddy? Is there something you want to say, or…?"

"Hm? What? No, nope. Just uh, you know,

spending quality time with my girl."

Rosabelle cocked her head and waited. Steven sat beside her and made a few banal observations.

"Oh, you painted the walls since the last time we were here."

Rosabelle said, "Um, nope."

"No? I could've sworn they were blue before."

"No. They've always been mint."

"New lamp. That's definitely a new lamp."

Rosabelle shook her head, then groaned, "Spill it, Dad. What's on your mind?"

She was sure it had to do with Miles and the engagement, but she couldn't muster the energy it took to dodge and redirect. If he wanted to argue it out, so be it.

"All right. It's just—well," he took a gulp of air, turned to face her and said in a rush, "I'm so sick and tired of RVing and I don't know how to tell your mother. She loves it, the open road, the new places. But, Rosabelle, *I* do all the driving. If I have to listen to Carole King one more time, I swear to God, Rosabelle, I'll lose my mind."

He stood up and began pacing again, now gesturing wildly with his hands.

"Do you know how nerve-wracking it is to drive a recreational vehicle on the highways? And don't get me started on the city streets. I can't—"

"Whoa, hey, Dad," exclaimed Rosabelle. "Why don't you just tell her how you feel?"

"Oh, I know, sweet pea, I *know*. I should just tell her. But you know how your mother is. Has she said anything to you? Any indication she might be getting sick of it too?"

"Sorry, Dad. She hasn't said anything. I really think you should just talk to her. She'll understand. I even bet she'll be thrilled to settle down in the Carolinas."

Steven stopped pacing and blinked at his daughter. "Oh, honey bun, I don't want to live in the *Carolinas*. I want to come back *here*, to Chance. I mean, wouldn't that be great to have your folks back in town?"

A frozen smile adhered itself to Rosabelle's face, and her lips barely moved when she squeaked, "Here?"

"Surprise," said Steven, raising both hands and waggling his fingers, making Rosabelle think, 'Jazz hands, yeah!' She'd have giggled at the image, were it not for the sense of horror welling in her chest at the thought of Ruth and Steven Waterman living back in Chance.

Horror was too strong a word. Dismay. Apprehension. Yes, that summed it up nicely. She had to find a way to stop it from happening.

Her tone shrill, she said, "Daddy, you said you couldn't wait to get out of Connecticut, remember? You said the taxes were too high, the roads were atrocious. You—"

"I know, I know. All that's still true, by the way. But, with our little girl getting into that terrible accident and then getting engaged—" he twirled his hands in another dramatic gesture, this one indicating his sense of helplessness, "I just don't feel right about not being here for you."

Rosabelle bit back the admonishment for lumping her accident and engagement together as if

203

they were equally traumatic events and went for a mollifying tone instead.

"Dad, I am *fine*. I'm a grown woman, and I can handle whatever life throws at me. I'm not that same little girl, scared of her own shadow anymore. You must see that, don't you? And besides, you and Mom still have ten more states you wanted to see. You can't just quit now."

Steven's face softened. "Of course we do, sweetie. Your mom and I are so proud of you. It's just time, that's all." His face lit up with sudden inspiration. "I know, I announce it tonight, over dinner. She'll be on her best behavior with company."

"Oh, I—no, Dad. I don't think that's a good—"

"It's settled. Well, I'll let you get your rest. See you soon, pumpkin," and before she could say another word, Steven was out the door.

Rosabelle dropped her head in her hand. Ludo meowed. "Well, you're no help, are you?"

Ludo yawned and stretched, then hopped up onto Rosabelle's lap and curled up in a ball. She fell asleep petting his soft silky pate. In what felt like one second, Miles whistled and sang his way through the front door.

"Oops, sorry, Rosie. Thought you'd still be out with your mom. How'd *that* go?"

He set the two brown bags of groceries on the table and sat beside her. Rosabelle's face said, 'how do you think it went?'

He winced and said, "That bad, huh?"

"Let's see. I had to endure watching my mother flirt with William Grant. Then, she called me a blowfish and wanted to send Daddy to 'pay a visit' to poor Fat Chris. Oh, *then*, my father showed up and announced he was sick of traveling and wants to move back to Chance. I think that covers it." She looked up at the ceiling, tapped her chin, and then nodded briskly. "Yep, it does."

Miles squinched his eyes and said, "Well, at least they didn't try to talk you out of marrying me. That's encouraging, right?"

She dipped her head at him. "Seriously? That's what you got out of all that? My *parents* might move back. To *Chance*. I love them, Miles, I really do. But if they move back, I'll lose my mind."

"Aw, c'mon, babe. It wouldn't be that bad, would it? Once they get used to me, it'll all be great."

"My Miles, always looking on the bright side, aren't you?"

"Oh, shit, that reminds me." Miles smacked his forehead and grimaced. "The Brightsiders. I ran into them at the grocery store. Craziest thing. One minute we were talking—they asked after you, Rosie—and the next thing, Mrs. B. goes to reach for a jar of olives, and suddenly, she's weeble-wobbling. Like she'd just gotten off a roller coaster, or something. It was so weird because we were just standing still. Anyhow, I grab one arm, and Mr. B. grabbed the other to steady her. I said, 'You all right, Mrs. B.?' and you know what she said?"

Rosabelle shook her head and motioned him to get on with it. "She said—with the jar of olives in her hand—she said, 'My just got the lemons.' It was the weirdest thing."

"Oh, Miles, I think she may have been having a stroke. I hope Mr. Brightsider took her to the hospital. Call them right now. Hurry."

"It's okay, don't worry. Bruce Grady—of all people—was there too. He insisted on driving them himself. *Insisted*, as if he was the only one who'd think of it."

"*Miles*," said Rosabelle in a reproachful tone.

"Yeah, yeah. I'm the one who saved her from falling. She could've broken a hip or something, you know."

Rosabelle patted his cheek and stroked his ego with a few placating compliments on his heroism. When he left to start dinner, Rosabelle grabbed her phone and texted Mae. She hated to interrupt her trip with Gina and Feather Anne, but she knew that Mae would be devastated if anything happened to either of the Brightsiders.

After her text was sent, Rosabelle concentrated on mentally preparing herself for dinner.

Chapter 24

Relations

"I've been thinking," said Mae after a quick glance in the rearview to see if Feather Anne was still asleep. She was.

Gina tensed. Mae was going to tell her she couldn't be a part of her and her sister's lives anymore. She had that right, after all. There was nothing Gina could do about it, except hope that in time, she'd be able to prove to them that she'd changed for the better. For good.

"I think that you should move into the garage. And maybe start working at the café. Obviously, we'll convert the garage to an actual apartment. And I can only pay you minimum wage. Assuming you'd be interested in doing that, that is."

She was speaking in careful, choppy sentences, her hands tight on the steering wheel, her eyes locked on the road ahead.

Gina turned in her seat to study Mae's profile. "You—you'd do that? For *me*?"

"For Feather Anne," corrected Mae. Then, in a quieter voice, she added, "and for me."

"For…you? You mean, you want to get to know me?"

Mae nodded as if it were just dawning on her. "Yes. Yes, I think I would. I think I need to."

"I, uh, I'd like that. But Mae? I'm—it's not pretty, my story. I can't promise you're gonna like me very much by the end. Not that you do much now, of course."

She wasn't looking for pity, or for Mae to dispute her words. She merely stated the facts as they were. Mae had no reason to be fond of Gina Byrd. But at least maybe she could understand her. Gina could do at least that much for her.

Echoing her thoughts, Mae said, "I want to at least understand you. How you got to where—where you are now."

"Can I ask why? Is it because you're going to have a kid of your own?"

Mae shot a surprised look at Gina, then said, "In part. I see the way Feather Anne looks at you when she thinks no one's paying attention. I've heard her call you 'Mom' when she forgets herself and that tough kid act. I can do your job, Gina, but I can't take your role. She needs her mother in her life. Plain and simple."

"And you? What do you need from me, Mae?"

"I need you to not fuck it up, Gina. Okay?"

"I won't, Mae. I promise you. I won't."

Mae nodded once. Her white knuckles regained

their color and her posture relaxed. In the backseat, Feather Anne kept her eyes closed and her breathing steady, but she smiled.

They'd passed the Pellier town limits sign, with less than a mile to the hair salon. Gina requested that Mae and Feather Anne come in with her. She wanted them to see her humiliation, use the moment as part of her punishment. After Mae had exhausted a short list of misgivings on the idea, she finally agreed.

The threesome climbed out of Mae's Volvo, closing their doors quietly as if it were four in the morning and not the afternoon. Deep breaths were taken, damp hands wiped on jeans, then Gina led the way, with Feather Anne behind and Mae holding up the end.

A jangly bell rang above the door as they entered the brightly lit, compact salon. Immediately, their noses twitched with the perfumy aerosol haze of hairspray and chemical sharpness of dye and bleach. A plump, blonde, shellacked, helmet-haired woman swept tufts of dark brown hair into a pile with a leopard-print handled broom.

She looked over her shoulder at Gina and her daughters, and gave a small, self-satisfied grunt. "Kept me guessing all day. Made it with time to spare though."

The woman walked the broom to a dustpan against the far wall, pushing the pile of hair with her as she went. Gina, Mae, and Feather Anne remained in the doorway. An elderly woman sat under a dryer dome reading an old, curled *Cosmopolitan* magazine. She hadn't heard or seen them come in.

She had on bright pink pants and winter boots, which for some reason made Feather Anne want to laugh. Instead, she busied herself with counting the colorful bottles of nail polish on the lone nail technician table. It was wedged between a product tower and a fake palm plant, making Feather Anne think it'd been some time since anyone had come in to get a manicure.

After the woman had secured the broom in its slot and checked the status of her client's hair, she made her way to Gina, appraising her as she did.

"Mhm," she harrumphed at last. "Doin' all right for yourself, I see. You got the necklace with you, I assume?"

Her tone suggested that she assumed no such thing. It suggested the opposite, in fact.

"I've got it, Zuzu."

Gina reached inside her coat pocket and pulled out the ugly necklace. She held it out shoulder high and balled up in her fist, and when Zuzu put her hand out for it, Gina let it drop from her fingertips, dangling it just by the clasp so that the medallion reached the woman's palm first and the chain coiled languidly over it.

Zuzu pulled it greedily toward her chest as if Gina might try to steal it back again. She lifted it to her lips, then studied it for a moment.

With bright eyes, she explained. "It was my husband's. We went through AA together. Both of us got sober, twelve years. Cancer got him though. Beat the booze only to get the damn cancer," she said with bitter irony.

Zuzu continued, "He always had this with him.

After he passed"—she paused and collected herself—"I had the urge to start drinking. Real bad, you know? Anyhow, I found this in my nightstand. Somehow, he'd snuck it in there before he went into a hospice. Left me a note, said I was to keep this as a reminder. That he prayed all his will and strength into this medallion to help me stay strong. So, you see why I needed it back, don't you?"

"Zuzu, I'm so sorry. I—"

"I know you are. For the record? I wouldn't have pressed charges on you. Not once I calmed down. I know you wouldn't have taken this cheap trinket on purpose. And the money?" She waved a hand dismissively. "I owed you your pay, anyhow."

"We both know I took more than what I was worth. But I'm going to pay you back. Every cent."

"Well, look at you onto step number nine. That mean you got over your hump?" She nudged Gina conspiratorially.

Gina laughed and bowed her head. "Yes, ma'am, I think I have. These are—this is Mae and Feather Anne," she added, blushing.

Mae stepped forward and shook Zuzu's hand. "We're her daughters."

Chapter 25

Through The Woods

"Babe, what *is* all this stuff? What are you doing," asked Ricky from Brianna's newly converted office space, formerly the gift wrapping and craft room. Not that she'd ever gotten around to crafting.

The room had, at various times, served other whims. It had once been—respectively—her reading room, her meditation room, and her music room. Ultimately, it was the room that had become home to the detritus of Brianna's passing follies.

Now, however, it was to be the hub of Bourdreau-Baker Events. Or Events by B. Baker. Or—well, she had time to decide on a name. Her priority was setting up her office. A row of blue plastic storage bins stood against the wall like obedient soldiers awaiting their orders, and Brianna marched up and down the row dropping this paper here and that object there. Then she'd grab the next pile and begin the process again.

"What does it *look* like I'm doing? Isn't it *obvious*?"

Ricky looked around the small, cramped room, then at the determined, maniacal zeal in which she deposited her belongings—they were all hers—into the boxes. It could only mean one thing. His wife had found a new hobby. He briskly rubbed his stubbled jaw and cheeks.

"Babe? You, uh, want any help?"

Sharply, she said, "No, Ricky. I do *not* want help, thank you. And I don't appreciate your tone."

"No tone, babe. Just wondering what you're doin'. That's all," said Ricky tiredly.

"If you must know, I'm starting a new business. This will be my office. Obviously, everything here has to go first. Oh, and I ordered a new printer. And a desk. It'll be here this afternoon. And Skinny Chris is coming by to give me an estimate for painting."

Ricky wasn't sure where to begin, and he was too tired to get into it with her. Especially when she got all manic. He'd made the mistake once of saying, "How does someone who's obsessed with order and cleanliness have a pig pen room," and she'd lost her mind. Two hours he spent—a bathroom door between them—begging her to just come out, he was sorry, he didn't mean *she* was a pig pen, and he'd said the wrong thing.

They'd had more than a few similar episodes, each starting with Ricky saying the wrong thing and ending with him apologizing for hours after. It wasn't like she got crazy over any old thing. Only two very specific things. One, her need for personal cleanliness and order around her. Two, religion. It was an off-limits subject, period. Ricky, knowing her better than anyone—better than she knew herself, even—understood well the 'why' of her behaviors.

He even understood the junk room. It was the one, small exception she made. An allowance of sorts. She could go in that room and be messy, then she could walk out, close and lock the door, and resume her tidy life. At least that's the conclusion he came to. Either way, it didn't bother him any. This 'new business' notion. *That* bothered him. Not because he didn't want her working. Hell, he'd asked her a million times to come do the books at the shop. He was even willing to get one of those office trailers for her, so she wouldn't have to go inside the building. She wasn't interested.

What the hell kind of business did she want to start now? More importantly, how much was it going to cost him? Maybe if he just gave it a few days, she'd get over it like she did with the other stuff. Suddenly, he felt like a jerk. He was supposed to be supportive, not cynical. Ricky had a brainstorm. When Brianna left for Cassidy's playdate tomorrow, he'd clear out the rest of the room for her, set up her new desk, and hang the pictures she'd meant to put up in there.

***

"Ricky," hollered Brianna from the kitchen

doorway. "Ricky? We're back. I've got groceries, come help."

She set Cassidy in her highchair with a handful of Cheerios and her sippy cup. She listened for the sound of Ricky's boots plunking down the stairs, but there was silence.

"Daddy thinks he can get away with not helping carry in the groceries, doesn't he?"

Cassidy giggled and crammed several pieces of cereal into her mouth.

"You hang tight, Miss Monkey face. I'm going to find your Daddy and put him to work."

Brianna left the kitchen and went down the hall. She'd expected to go upstairs and find Ricky sneaking in a nap, but then her eye caught the open office—*office-to-be*—door. She always kept that door closed. She strode over, frowning. The sight of Ricky standing so unexpectedly in the room gave her a start.

"Jesus, Ricky. You scared the crap out of me. Why didn't you answer me when I called you? Ricky? What's wrong?"

She looked at the long, rectangular office envelope in his hands. An icy hand of fear gripped Brianna. *Why* had she kept that damning thing? Ricky's face bore an expression she'd never seen on him. It was indescribably horrible. Pain, physical pain pinched his features, and his skin looked ashen. But worst of all, his eyes. They looked right through Brianna as if he'd never seen her before. Like she didn't exist.

Even as she asked a second time, "Ricky what's wrong?" she knew.

215

His voice was flat. "I, uh, wanted to surprise you. Clean the room out. Set up your office. Your desk. I started to—anyhow," his Adam's apple bobbed visibly. He looked at the seemingly innocuous envelope. "Why did you get a paternity test done, Brianna? I don't—I don't understand why you would need to do that."

Brianna's knees went weak, and she gripped the door frame. "Ricky, I—"

Ricky barely controlled the tremor in his voice as he forced each word from his lips. "Why would you need to get a test to see if she was mine, Bri?"

Brianna's chin quivered violently, and she shook her head. "Let me explain. We—"

"Stop. Just, stop."

Brianna made a move to go to him, but he recoiled and side-stepped her, his hands up defensively. She couldn't bear the look—the *absence* of a look—in his eyes.

"Ricky, please. It was just—we were having problems, and I—"

His eyes snapped into focus, onto her face. "*We* were having problems? No, *you* were having problems. *You* were the one *struggling*. I was the one—I have always been the one waiting patiently for you to just—" He threw his hands up in frustration, then raked his fingers through his hair. In a voice scraped raw, he said, "I would've done anything in the world for you, Bri."

If he had raged, and yelled, and thrown things, if he'd punched the wall or demanded the guy's name—if he'd done any one of those things, Brianna might've thought, 'Okay, it's okay. We'll get through this,' but this Ricky was foreign, unrecognizable to her. This version of her high school sweetheart and husband—a man who'd literally lifted her from mud—looked at her as if they were strangers.

"Ricky, please. Just tell me what I can do. I'll do any—" Her voice broke as she reached for him again.

"No. Just—no."

He brushed past her and she spun around— maybe to follow, or to beg him to forgive her, she didn't know. She was wild with sheer panic—but before she could speak, he paused, giving her only his profile.

"I'll be at my parents'. Don't call unless it's about Cassidy. Don't come to the house. Just stay the fuck away from me, Brianna. If you want to do something for me, then just stay the fuck away."

A moment later the front door slammed, jolting Brianna like a slap to the face. She sat back hard against the desk and buried her face in her hands and wept violently. Down the hall, in the kitchen, Cassidy called, "Mom-my. Mom-meeee. Mom-meeee. More o-o's, Mom-mmy," her tone becoming more demanding.

Brianna dried her tears and sniffed. She had to pull it together. She could fix this. She *had* to. Yes, she'd fix all of this. It became a mantra in her head as she marched back to the kitchen, the words in time with the click of her heels.

I will. Fix this. I will. Fix this. I will. Fix this.

Even as she smiled brightly at Cassidy and refilled her tray with 'more o-o's,' it repeated. As she picked up the sippy cup that had either fallen or been thrown in toddler fury, it played on in her brain. While she brought in the groceries and put them away, made her perfunctory call to her mother, and confirmed her dentist appointment for Thursday—it carried on. She had to fix this. But how?

Chapter 26

What Is Right

"Rosabelle, hey it's Mae—sorry, of course you know who's calling. Caller ID. Ugh, now I'm leaving a stupid voicemail. Anyhow, I got your text about Georgie, thank you. We're on our way back home. I'll call Charles now and see what I can find out."

Mae ended the call and bit her nail. Tentatively, Gina put a hand on her arm. "I'm sorry, Mae. If you didn't have to come out here for me, you could already be at the hospital."

Mae smiled weakly. "I chose to do this, so don't blame yourself. My dad always said, 'You can't plan around possibilities, probabilities, or inevitabilities. You just have to *live* your life.'"

"What the hell does that mean?" asked Feather Anne.

"It means you can't worry too much on the

things that are out of your control. It does you no good," said Mae.

Feather Anne looked skyward, thrusting her chin sideways. After a second's thought, she shrugged and said, "Yeah, that makes sense. Can we get going now? I want to see Mr. and Mrs. B. Do you think they're home now? Hey, we should stop and get them maple syrup. Wait, is it New Hampshire or Vermont you get it from? Oh, you know what? Mrs. B. likes maple candy too. Let's get that too."

Mae let Gina handle the barrage of questions and comments hurled by the suddenly chipper Feather Anne. The poor kid had been more anxious about the trip than she'd let on, and now that everything had been resolved without her mother ending up in jail, her tension dissolved in a flood of pent-up chatter.

When they'd gotten back to the car, Mae had picked up her phone to call William, and that's when she saw Rosabelle's text. They agreed to head straight back to Chance even though Mae had downplayed the possible seriousness of Georgie Brightsider's condition.

Eventually, Feather Anne exhausted herself and pulled her headphones on to listen to music. Mae used the opportunity to tell Gina her concerns.

"It sounds as if she may have had a stroke. I don't want to say anything more to Feather Anne until I know more. If it's bad, I have to forewarn her."

"She's always been close with them," said Gina, nodding.

"You knew that?"

"Yeah." Gina chuckled. "Old Georgie B. wasn't fond of me, but she was very fond of propriety. She sent me a letter every time Feather Anne paid them a visit. You know she was my fourth-grade teacher?"

"What?" exclaimed Mae. "No, I never knew that. She never mentioned it."

"Eh, she had so many students over the years. Doubt she remembers every single one. She gave me a book once, my favorite story. First gift I ever got."

Mae smiled, suspecting the answer to her question, but asked it anyway. "What was the book, Gina?"

"*The Secret Garden*. I still have it." She patted her purse and smiled fondly.

"She's a cheeky one, that Georgie. She gave me the very same book." Then in a quieter voice, she added, "It's my favorite too."

"You think that was intentional? Like she was— I don't know—connecting us in her own way?"

"It explains her inscription on the inside cover. I'll show it to you when we get back home."

Chapter 27

From Now On

It started out well enough. Miles had prepared a surprisingly good stroganoff. So good, that even Ruth complimented him—it was in a back-handed way, but still a compliment—and Steven had a second plate. Neither Ruth nor Steven had uttered a single disparaging or snide remark in Miles's direction. Miles only spoke of safe topics—the weather, the stroganoff—and avoided all mention of politics, the economy, and global warming. Rosabelle was beginning to relax. And that was her mistake.

She was the one to slip, Rosabelle. Such an innocuous slip, it was, but it was just enough to start an avalanche. The second the words left her mouth, she knew it.

"Miles just took a new listing. You remember Brian Donovan, right? He's moving to Florida."

"Oh?" Steven perked up comically.

"Ugh, I bet that place needs a ton of work," said Ruth dismissively. "Steven, pass the salad, please. *Steven.*"

Steven's eyes were squinted and gazing off into the distance, his jaw at a jaunty angle, and his fingers tapped rapidly on the table. Rosabelle could practically see the proverbial lightbulb flash on over his head.

His voice unnaturally high and forcefully nonchalant, he asked, "How much is he asking?" as he passed the salad bowl to Ruth.

Ruth scoffed, "Don't be nosy, Steven. What do we care what Brian Donovan gets for his house?"

Rosabelle tried to signal Miles, but he was oblivious.

"Well, Ruth's right, it needs a little TLC. If he sells it as is, we won't get more than two-twenty-nine for it. We'll start higher, of course, but—"

Steven leaned forward. "Is it on the market yet?"

Now Ruth narrowed her eyes. "Steven? What's this about?"

Before Rosabelle could stop him, her father blurted, "We need to move back home, Ruth. Rosabelle needs us."

Miles, both flabbergasted and insulted, said, "All due respect, sir, but Rosie has me now, so—"

As dismissively as he would a pesky fly, Steven said, "Oh, you've broken her heart once, who's to say you won't do it again?" then he returned his attention to Ruth. "Ruthie, sweetheart, come on. Be reasonable. We've done the traveling, we've seen the things. Don't you miss home?"

As Rosabelle's parents argued, she watched Miles. His bafflement shown in his drawn brow and upturned hands. He turned those hands and that expression on Rosabelle, who could only stare mutely back at him.

"Rosie, what—" A look of boiled over frustration came over him and he turned his question to the Watermans. "I'm sorry, but for once and for all, can you people tell me what you think I've done to your daughter in the past?"

The Watermans paused their dispute to turn a jointly contemptuous scowl at Miles. Ruth spat, "Oh, don't act like you don't know what you did, Mr. Secret Loverboy."

"What are—"

"Yeah, nice try, Romeo," added Steven, clearly relieved to have Ruth's anger pointed away from him, even if for a moment or two. "You think we don't know about you dating our daughter back in high school? How you made her keep it a secret because you couldn't have all your cool friends know?"

Ruth tapped into the imaginary ring. "And let's not forget how you dumped her just before we were supposed to have you over for dinner. Rosabelle cried for weeks over you. We couldn't even say your name, she was so upset." Then, suddenly remembering her argument with her husband, pointed at him and said, "Don't you try to deflect here, Steven Jacob Waterman. We're not done with this conversation."

Rosabelle, her cheeks aflame with hot mortification, watched it all, helpless. She could hardly bear to look Miles in the eye for fear of the hurt and disgust she'd surely see there, but she forced herself to meet his gaze. He looked neither angry nor contemptuous, but puzzled, sad, and then—dare she believe it—understanding.

Miles stood and addressed them. "Mr. and Mrs. Waterman, I owe you both—and Rosie—a sincere apology. My behavior and actions back then were wholly inexcusable and unacceptable. I was an immature, egotistical jerk. You have every right and reason to despise me, however, I humbly ask your forgiveness and I can assure you, on my life, that I will never again do anything to hurt your daughter. With that said, I must forewarn you—with all due respect—that I am going to marry your daughter…with or without your approval."

Steven blinked up at him. Ruth's mouth was agape. It was Steven who recovered first. He stood and extended his hand to Miles and said, "Well, son. Much appreciated. That's all we needed to hear, you know. A little remorse goes a long way, doesn't it?"

The men shook hands as the women looked on in disbelief. Rosabelle, stunned by his admission to a disservice he'd never been guilty of, mouthed the word 'why' to him as Steven spoke quietly to his wife.

Miles leaned in and whispered in her ear, "Because I love you."

Later that night, after dessert and several rounds of Rummikub, Miles and Rosabelle snugged on the couch.

"Miles, I'm so embarrassed. I don't know why I

made up such—" she shook her head and started over, "that's not true, I do know why I made up such a ridiculous story."

"Rosie, you don't have to explain anything. We were kids, we all made up shit to our parents."

"Yes, but *I* didn't. Not normally, I mean. I was their good, boring, extremely average in every way, daughter. I saw the way they watched the football games—we saw you guys play every week, you know. Home and away games—and it wasn't just the football players, it was the cheerleaders too. Brianna, Elise, Brittany…all of them. My mother made comments."

Rosabelle affected her mother's nasally tone, "Look at how gorgeous Brianna Bourdreau's hair looks." Or, "Oh, that Brittany has such perfect skin."

She shifted to look up at him. "She pointed you out once too. She said, 'My, that Hannaford boy is handsome.' My father had said, 'Yep, the kinda boy every father dreams of having.' They probably don't even remember saying it. But I do. I guess that's what started it all. I started writing this whole fantasy life in my journal, and then one day, my mother found it, and—"

"And the rest is history. It's sweet what they said about me, though. Even if they did end up hating me." He laughed.

"Well, they hated an imaginary version of you," corrected Rosabelle.

"Eh, well, unfortunately, they weren't far off the mark. I was a real jerk, Rosie. That's no secret. When they said all that stuff tonight—I don't know—it was like really hearing for the first time the damage I might have done to other girls. I had a moment where I put myself in your dad's shoes—any father's shoes, actually—and I just thought," he cast her a sheepish glance, "I wouldn't let a guy like me near my daughter."

"Oh, Miles," said Rosabelle, full of affection.

"Rosie, you've changed the way I see myself, or more so the way I *want* to see myself. I want to be who you think I am."

"But you *are*, Miles. You've always been this guy, deep down." She poked his chest, over his heart. "This has always been as huge as it is right now."

"No, I—"

Rosabelle held up a finger, shushing him. "Sophomore year. Danny Feltzer. I was at my locker, minding my own business and Danny thought it would be fun to flip my books out of my hands. Total juvenile crap. When I bent over to pick them up, he grabbed my ass."

"Oh, shit, I remember that," said Miles, the recollection dawning.

"Yeah, and do you remember what you did?"

Miles looked proud as he smiled. "I kicked his ass."

"Yes. You did. He got in a punch too, tough guy. You had a bloody lip, I remember. Mr. Vianno pulled you down to the principal's office, but you stopped in front of me and said, 'You okay, kid?' Rosabelle shook her head in wonderment. "You'd just gotten into a fight, had a bloody lip, and would've gotten suspended, but you were asking me if I was okay. That's when I knew, Miles. That's when I saw *you*."

Miles gently pinched her chin between his fingers. "I didn't get suspended because a particular girl went to the principal and told him what happened. I'd have gotten kicked off the team if you hadn't done that, Rosie."

"Hmm, then I guess we're even, huh?"

Miles nodded and drew her in for a kiss. "Now can we start planning our wedding, please?"

It was Rosabelle's turn to nod. "Summer."

"Next week?"

"Miles. Spring?"

"Two weeks?"

"Valentine's Day?"

"Too cliché. Three weeks?"

Rosabelle studied him to see if he was serious. He was. "Get your calendar out."

Twenty minutes later the date was set, and a very giddy Rosabelle and a barely contained Miles called their parents with the news.

Chapter 28

Take Each Moment

"Sweetheart, you must be exhausted." William greeted Mae at the front door, concern darkening his warm molasses-colored eyes even more.

"A little," agreed Mae, walking gratefully into his arms. "Have you heard any more news on Georgie?"

William shook his head and glanced over Mae's shoulder at Feather Anne and Gina trudging up the driveway with their overnight bags.

"You girls should've just stayed in New Hampshire, then come back in the morning," admonished William.

"I couldn't, William. Not with Georgie in the hospital. If she—well, I couldn't bear to think of Charles all alone."

Mae's voice shook, and her eyes brimmed with tears at the image of Charles bent over Georgie's

229

bedside.

"Say no more, my love. There's still an hour or so for visiting. I'll drive you, yes?"

"Me too," chimed Feather Anne.

"Sorry, sunshine, no one under twelve. Perhaps we'll be able to sneak you in tomorrow, yes?"

"That's not fair." Feather Anne stomped her foot.

"Hey," said Gina cautiously, "if it's all right with Mae and William, maybe you and I can make dinner for when they get back. What do you say?"

Feather Anne pouted a moment longer, then unclenched her fists, slumped her shoulders, and gave a perfect, pre-teen utterance of, "Fine," before stalking into the kitchen.

"Thanks, Gina. Feather Anne knows where everything is. Call if you need anything."

Gina beamed, and the change to her face, normally drawn and world-weary, was extraordinary. It was the first time Mae could see the Gina she could've been—and could become— with different circumstances. Had no one ever shown her the simplest kindness?

It caused Mae's misgivings to lessen. The decision to ask her to move into the garage—once converted—had been discussed in length the night before. William, as always, was willing to defer to her regarding her family. In his calm, pragmatic way, William laid out the pros—building healthy relationships between mother and daughters, helping a fellow human in need, and keeping an eye on her—as well as the cons. The biggest con being that Gina might very well be *conning* them.

Gina's shift from hard, cynical, untrusting, and

untrustworthy derelict to reticent yet hopeful, apologetic, and remorseful mother figure was jarring. Mae found it a challenge to reconcile the two very different people that Gina presented herself as. So, what had changed, and why?

William, ever intuitive, said quietly, "We trust until we're given a reason not to, yes?"

Mae breathed out and rested her head against his chest. "Yes."

The second they pulled up to the hospital, the familiar wave of sadness swept over Mae. From beside her, William said, "In a matter of months, we will be here for the second happiest day of our lives."

A slow smile stretched across Mae's face. She hadn't thought of that. Instinctively, she rested her hand over her stomach, which was of course, still flat. It made the baby seem more an idea, and not yet a reality. But it *was* a reality. There was a teeny-tiny person growing inside her. She, William, Feather Anne, Katrina, and now—if everything went well—Gina, were going to have this new human to love and cherish. Surreal was the only word she could come up with. Then a new worry struck her, and as irrational as it may have been, the second it hit her, she couldn't shake it.

"William? What if this is like that saying—or maybe it's a wives' tale, or something—you know, about someone dying just before a new life comes into the world? What if—what if this means Georgie is going to die?"

William began to chuckle and say, "Oh, come now, you don't seriously believe in—" and stopped frozen at her very serious expression. Clearly, she very much believed. "Oh, my sweet. Here's what I believe. Do with it as you must. I believe we come into the world, live our life, and when we die, it's because it is our time."

Mae frowned. "I know, I suppose. And I *know* everyone must die sometime. I'm just not ready for it. I'm not sure I know how to *be* ready for it."

"None of us are, my dear. Come. Let's go see the Brightsiders."

Chapter 29

Do You Know What I Know

Craig Henry Davidson smoothed back what was left of his hair and looked up Old Main Street, then down it. He pressed the lock symbol on his car key, buttoned up the top button of his navy peacoat, and jogged briskly across the street to the promising warmth of the café called Mae's. He'd seen the pictures online, read the bio, and noted the hours of business. He'd timed his arrival with the end of the breakfast rush.

The door opened with a dainty jingle of bells and Craig stepped aside to let a fivesome of attractive young women out. They were deep in a tense, hushed conversation and paused only to murmur a quick 'thank you' and 'excuse us.' Craig gave them a tight, polite smile. He too, felt a particular sense of tension on that January morning. Craig Henry Davidson was going to meet his birth mother for the

233

first time.

Craig followed the sign's request to 'seat yourself,' and chose a table near the back corner. A gentlemanly looking man sat in the corner—at the table he *would've* chosen, had it been available—and raised his coffee cup in salute before returning his attention to his open laptop. Craig raised his hand halfway in return then sat facing the entrance. Immediately, he stood again to remove his jacket and hang it over the chair next to him. A few seconds after *that*, he slid the coat off the chair and draped it over his own. As he stood for the third time, a waitress approached.

"Hello, welcome to Mae's. Can I pour you some coffee to start?"

"Oh, hello. Yes, please. Decaf, I think. No—yes, decaf. Oh, and there'll be one more joining me. Maybe I should wait until she arrives before I get coffee?"

The waitress, an especially attractive woman with unusual eyes—they were true gray—cocked her head, then smiled encouragingly. Craig berated himself mentally for his obvious nervousness. He was a schoolteacher, not a schoolboy, for heaven's sake. He took a calming breath and smoothed back his hair.

"Coffee would be very nice, thank you."

This time his voice was steady and assertive, just as his Tony Robbins CD told him to be. He'd spent forty-five minutes of the hour and a half drive listening to the motivational speaker. The other forty-five were spent listening to his wife, Marianne, on the Bluetooth. She had *trepidations* about his pending meeting. She had *concerns*.

Marianne was a woman of many trepidations and concerns, most of which revolved around Craig now that the boys were grown and out of the house. Nate, the youngest at twenty-two, hinted at moving back in, but he was probably hoping for a loan to hold him over. Dylan, the middle boy, was spending his twenty-fourth year abroad, backpacking with his girlfriend, Lotus. Craig had a hard time believing her name was really Lotus. Marianne was having a hard time believing her breasts were real. Craig made the wise choice to have no opinion on that matter. As for their oldest, twenty-six-year-old Thomas, he was busy getting his bachelor's and student teaching. Chip off the old block.

They were good boys, all three. Nate got into a spot of trouble here and there, but nothing out of the ordinary. Even when they were little, they were an easy lot. Craig would've kept trying for a girl, but after Nate, Marianne had woman troubles that ended with a hysterectomy. So, that was that. He'd had his heart set on a big brood, being both an adopted and an only child, but he'd never intentionally say anything to make Marianne feel bad.

"Here's your coffee and I'll leave you with a couple menus. Specials are on the board. Is your…breakfast date running late, or—"

"Oh, it's not a date. It's, well—I'm meeting my biological mother today. I guess I'm a bit nervous." Craig laughed.

It was a self-deprecating, apologetic laugh. Tony Robbins would not be impressed.

"I see," said the woman. "I'm sure it will go wonderfully."

Craig looked up with a hopeful grin and said, "Fingers crossed," and crossed his fingers.

Twenty minutes later, the waitress tentatively returned, apologetically, biting her bottom lip. "Maybe she's just caught in traffic? Or got lost?"

Craig tried to make his face look smooth and untroubled, but he could feel the pinched, tight skin around his eyes. "I'm sure that's all it is. Maybe I could just get a blueberry scone for now? While I wait."

"Of course," breathed the woman.

He wondered briefly if she were single. Thomas would be instantly smitten by the leggy, long-haired woman. Right after he had that thought, he saw the ring on her finger. She strolled over to the man at the corner table and Craig watched through the wall mirror as she leaned down to kiss him on the lips.

So, that's the husband. He'd never have guessed the older man—Craig guessed him to be about his own age—and the stunning young woman were together. But who was he to judge?

As the waitress walked away, she called over her shoulder to her husband, "Oh, and I updated the Facebook page with the latest news. Everyone's been asking, so it made sense."

"Good thinking, love," said the dapper husband.

Of course, he'd have just the hint of an English accent. Craig had always wished he had an English accent. Instead, he taught English class to six-graders. With nothing better to do, he decided to be nosy and see what the café update was all about.

He'd 'liked' the page and didn't have to scroll far to see the post in question.

UPDATE: Since so many have been asking, we wanted to give you an update on Georgie Brightsider. She is at Hartford Hospital. The doctor's determined she had a mild stroke. She is still being observed and will remain in ICU until the doctors feel she is stable enough to be moved. They send their love and thanks to all who've called and come to visit.

Craig's heart sank. All these years. Why now? Not that he'd wished her ill on another time, of course. He wasn't the kind of man who wished ill on *anyone*. Hastily, he stood and fished his wallet from his coat breast pocket and set a twenty-dollar bill on the table, beside his half-full coffee cup. The waitress arrived with the scone and a confused expression as he swung his coat over his shoulders.

"Is something—" asked the waitress.

He noticed her nametag and said, "Oh, you're Mae. Of *course*, you are, I—what am I doing? I have to go." He shook his head at his own distractibility. "My—my mother's in the hospital."

"Oh," said Mae, putting a hand to her chest, "I'm so sorry. Please, no charge. Put your money away. Wait one sec."

She rushed behind the counter, tore off a piece of foil from the large roll under the counter, and wrapped the scone. Before Craig had even made to the door, she was back and handing him the neatly wrapped package.

"On the house. I hope your mom is okay," said Mae earnestly.

"Why, thank you. Very kind. And I hope so too."

Craig was across the street and climbing into his car before Mae could respond. William came up behind her and watched the tense man drive off.

"What was that all about?" asked William.

"Huh," huffed Mae. "He was going to meet his mother for the first time. Here."

"Really? That explains the fidgeting. Did you notice?" William chuckled, but not unkindly.

"Impossible not to," said Mae. "Didn't he look so familiar? Something around the eyes." She puzzled over it a moment, then was distracted by the phone.

As Craig drove along the street, he pressed the Bluetooth button and enunciated as clearly as he could, "Navigate to Hartford Hospital." It took three attempts before his system recognized the command, adding to his agitation.

His phone rang, startling him. "Hello, Marianne."

"Craig? Why are you answering? Aren't you at breakfast with—aren't you at breakfast?"

"If you thought I was at breakfast, then why did you call?"

"Well, I intended to leave you a nice message. You know, words of encouragement and whatnot."

Craig dutifully said, "That was very thoughtful of you."

"Yes, well, now it's ruined because you answered the phone. You know, I read an article last week that said couples in their golden years need to—" she adopted an authoritative tone, "make more of a conscious effort to connect and empathize with one another." In her normal voice, she said, "And that's what I was trying to do. But now it feels weird, Craig."

"It's the thought that counts, dear. Are we really in our golden years? I don't think we're old enough to be there yet. Maybe our silver years? I—"

"*Craig*," wheedled Marianne. "Why are you answering your phone? Did you go to the café? Ooh, did you see the author? Oh, Craig, you didn't stand her up, did you?"

"No, of course not, Marianne. I was there. She didn't show up—"

"That terrible woman," exclaimed Marianne, full of indignation and hurt on her husband's behalf. "You should—"

"It's all right, Marianne. Turns out she's in the hospital. A stroke, for God's sake. It might be—I'm afraid I'm going to be too late. What if she's lost her memory, or can't speak? What if—"

"Now, now," Marianne's tone took on the calm, rational tone mothers used with their children. "Let's not get ahead of ourselves."

"It *was* a mild stroke," he conceded.

"There, you see. And, Craig, remember, the husband doesn't know. That was what her email said. You're likely to see him at the hospital, so be mindful. He's elderly, so, you can't go giving him a heart attack. Although, I suppose the hospital is the best place to be if—"

"Marianne, how did you know I was heading to the hospital?"

"Oh, *please*. We've been married thirty years. I know what you're thinking most of the time before you even think it."

They both laughed. They chatted—mostly about the boys—the rest of the car ride. Marianne had a way of settling his nerves. He liked to think he did the same for her when the roles were reversed, but he wasn't sure.

"We're perfectly suited for each other, aren't we, Craig? After all these years, we're still peas and carrots," said Marianne warmly.

"Yes, I believe we are," said Craig as he parked in the hospital garage. "I'm here now."

"All right then. Go see your mother. Call when you can, dear. I love you."

"Love you too. Marianne?"

"Yes?"

"Thank you."

"Go on, now. Stop stalling." Marianne chuckled.

At information, he received a visitor's badge. When the elevator door slid open, he peeked out, looked both ways as if crossing the street, then stepped out. At the nurses' station, he confirmed the room number and direction. Sweat ran from his armpit down his side. He'd stopped in the gift shop and bought a bouquet of tea roses.

Craig knew from Facebook that she loved tea roses. In his mind, he saw the photo of her flower garden, a wide brimmed hat on her head and a pair of pruning shears in her hand. She was bent, looking at the delicate swirl of pale yellow rose between her finger and thumb, giving only her profile. She was smiling the type of smile one gives

240

a small child. Two small dogs with long, silky hair sat panting happily in the foreground. Craig loved his flower garden and his yellow tea roses as well.

Just outside the door, Craig halted. Light spilled from the room, but no voices drifted out into the hall. Around him, the business of caring for the infirm carried on, oblivious of the monumental, life-changing event that was about to occur. Craig allowed for the possibility that the moment could be anticlimactic. He was a grown man, after all. Fairytales and fantasies were for children. Not adult males with families of their own and responsibilities.

He didn't *need* this woman in his life, he'd had a perfectly fine life before and still now. There was no 'hole' or 'void' that had to be filled. That was untrue. He knew this even as he told the lie to himself. Edward and Viv Davidson had done a solid job raising their adopted son, Craig. They were a middle-class, suburban, blue collar, picket fence family of three. He had tennis lessons and piano lessons. Birthday parties and yearly vacations in Maine. They bought him a car when he was sixteen—which he drove responsibly and carefully—and paid his college tuition. It was a good, solid, comfortable life.

When Craig was five, Viv and Edward sat him on the couch with a huge bowl of ice cream. A card envelope sat beside the bowl on the coffee table. It was blue. They exchanged nervous glances. Viv haltingly explained how they picked him out over lots of other little babies because he was extra special, and he had another mommy who loved him enough to give him to people who could take care of him. Craig spooned mounds of vanilla fudge ice cream into his chocolate ringed mouth, his eyes traveling back and forth between his father and his mother. Only—his five-year-old mind thought—they're *not* my mommy and daddy. He had two *other* people in the world that were his.

At the end of the talk—given almost entirely by Viv—she pushed the blue envelope toward young Craig.

"That's from your—your biological mother," said Viv. She said 'biological' slowly, breaking down the syllables.

Craig stared at the envelope. Their neighbor, Mrs. Miller, had given him a card for his birthday last month with a dollar in it. He got to spend it on candy in the grocery store. Maybe *this* card would have a dollar too. He opened it, anticipating the crisp dollar bill slipping into his small hand. Instead, a picture fell out.

It had landed face down in his lap, the words—he'd had his mother-who-wasn't-his-mother read it to him after—in cursive, 'Georgie, nineteen-sixty-two' written on it. He flipped it to the front side. The picture showed a woman leaning her elbow on a piano, her chin on her palm. She pouted, but there was the hint of a smile teasing her mouth, so Craig knew that the woman wasn't *really* grouchy to have her photograph taken, she was just *pretending* to be grouchy. Craig did that sometimes too.

His eyes traveled to hers. They were fixed directly at the camera, so it appeared as if she was staring right at Craig. Their eyes were the exact same color. He looked up at Viv and Edward, at their almost matching brown eyes, then back at the photograph. Next, he looked at the woman's—*Georgie's*—hair. It was dark brown, like his, and she had a cowlick in front just like he did. His mom—Viv—always tried to comb it over, but it never stayed put.

After he'd studied the picture for a minute, he said, "Am I going to meet her?"

Viv and Edward exchanged pained expressions. "Maybe someday, sport," said his father, "but not until you're much older. That okay?"

Little Craig shrugged. He had more questions, but Viv looked ready to cry, and Edward's face had gone a funny color, so he just said, "Okay. Can I keep the picture?"

"Sure, honey, sure," said Viv too loudly. "She wrote on the card too. Would you like Mommy to read it to you?"

"No thanks," said Craig. He scooped up the card, slipped the photo back inside, and ran it to his bedroom. Later, he slid it out from under his pillow and studied it better.

Craig startled out of his reverie at the sound of a man's voice saying, "Can I help you?"

Craig blinked up at the tall elderly man. He reminded Craig of the famous actor, Clint Eastwood, but his eyes weren't steely and hard glinted. This man had kind, denim-blue eyes. The lines around them guaranteed that those eyes had crinkled in many years of laughter. However, they held none of that humor now.

"Oh, I—" stammered Craig.

Something in the man's expression changed. A clearing of sorts, a recognition. He straightened, put his hands in his pockets, and appraised Craig with keen interest. Then he nodded as if confirming something in his own mind.

"You're Georgie's son, aren't you?"

Chapter 30

Friends You Know

"Bruce, it's awful. I've never seen Brianna this way. It seems—"

"Lissie, what do you expect me to do? He doesn't want to talk to her. The best thing she can do is give him space."

Elise plunked down on the floor beside Gianna and handed her a block, smiling distractedly at her. Another idea occurred, and she sprang up again.

"I know. What if you and I—"

"Elise," said Bruce warningly, "don't get involved. See, I knew this would happen. She's going to drag you into her shitstorm—one that she created, by the way—and somehow, I'm going to get dragged in too."

"Oh, come on. They're our friends, Bruce. We can't just not try to help them."

"Lis, this isn't kid stuff anymore. It's not like the

245

time what's-his-face hit on Bri after the football game, and Ricky kicked his ass. This is way bigger. She cheated on him and thought their kid might belong to another dude. And Miles Hannaford, of all people?"

Elise grimaced and shuddered. She left out the fact that she'd known this information for a long time. It could only cause a fight, and one fighting couple was enough.

"Well," said Elise stubbornly, "if you and Ricky are such good friends, then I'd think you'd at least want to try to help him."

Bruce cut her an exasperated glance and said, "Hand me the Phillips."

She handed him the flathead. "Don't give me that look, Moosie. You—"

"The other Phillips, please," interrupted Bruce. "You are going to know the difference between these by the time I'm done with this."

"Hmph," replied Elise, sticking her tongue out at him.

She knew the difference. In fact, she could've put up the shelves for the playroom on her own, but he didn't need to know that. She changed tacks.

"Hey, did you forget to tell Mae you weren't coming in to help her today?"

"Hmm," he mumbled around a screw in his mouth.

"Eww, don't put that in your mouth, it's filthy. I said, did you forget to tell Mae—"

Bruce opened his mouth and let the screw drop into his hand with a sardonic look. "There, happy? I guess I did forget. I'll text her later." Bruce shrugged nonchalantly.

It was the nonchalance that caught her attention. "Are you two fighting?"

"Who?" asked Bruce, tightening the screw with a quick zip of his power tool.

"You and Mae," said Elise deliberately. He was being obtuse, and she knew it.

"Oh, no. Why?"

"Because you're acting weird."

"What are you talking about? I'm not 'acting' like anything. Calm down."

If there was one thing she hated, it was being told to 'calm down,' especially when she *was* calm.

"Do not tell me to 'calm down.' I am calm. I'm just asking you a simple question, which you are avoiding answering."

"Oh, you sound calm. Listen to yourself," said Bruce.

"Okay, you know what? I'm not fighting with you over this. Gianna and I are going to visit my mother."

She scooped up Gianna and stomped out, leaving him staring after her in disbelief.

"Crazy woman," he muttered to himself once he was sure she was out of earshot.

Truthfully? She was right. He was acting weird. And he didn't 'forget' to call Mae. He'd opted not to call. Bruce woke up that morning, looked at the alarm clock, and decided not to go to the café. He decided not to tell Mae. Part of him wanted to see how long it took before she called or texted him. Part of him—well, that was the thing. He didn't know what the other part of him was thinking.

Elise had been sound asleep beside him, snoring softly. Through the baby monitor, he heard the cheery babble of Gianna in her crib. She was ready for a toddler bed, but Elise resisted the transition. In a few minutes, the happy babble would become an insistent call for, 'Momma, get me.' Bruce sat up, careful not to disturb Elise. He'd get Gianna, make her breakfast, and do some long overdue projects around the house before he had to check on Brian and the guys at the Villeneuve house. They had three unseasonably warm days to get the job done, so they'd better be moving quickly.

"Hey there, munchkin. Can Moosie make you your breakfast today?"

"Moosie," agreed Gianna, stretching out her plump arms and opening and closing her little fists rapidly.

"Atta girl. We'll let momma sleep. You want panny-cakes?"

"Momma, seep. Panny-cakes."

Bruce carried Gianna down the stairs and Gianna patted his cheeks and giggled every time he squeezed his eyes shut in mock pain. Probably not supposed to encourage little kids to think it's funny to hit someone, but she was so stinkin' cute, this kid.

He got Gianna in her highchair, found Elise's apron, and began making 'panny-cakes' for the three of them. Gianna started to get bored, so he began singing one of those goofy songs from the CD they were always playing in the car.

"Well, isn't this a sight?" Elise laughed from the kitchen doorway, her eyes still sleepy.

"Ah, shit, babe. I wanted to let you sleep in."

"Language. And I heard you through the monitor. But hey, by all means, carry on with the show. We're loving it, right, Gigi?"

Gianna clapped and said, "More sing, Moosie," drawing out the 'o's in Moosie.

It had been such a fun morning, and now, just hours later, they were fighting again. Over nothing. Bruce set the new shelf on top of the brackets. And started the next one.

Chapter 31

Near And Dear

"Here? At the Café?" Mae stared at Rosabelle in surprise, then hugged her. "Of course, you can have the wedding here. I'd be honored.

Rosabelle waved a hand to encompass the café. "Well, it *is* where it began, and all thanks to you."

She glowed with happiness. Best of all, she was walking and standing. It was for short periods of time and not without discomfort, but it was a start.

"Are you sure we'll have enough room? You *know* Miles's parents will want to invite half the country."

"Oh, don't I know it. We've made a compromise with them. Well, *I've* made a compromise—"

"Ooh, you're brave. Standing up to the Hannafords?" Mae made the face of someone stepping into a haunted house.

"Yep. Poor Miles, he was so nervous. And I'd

250

already dealt with my parents, so I was on a roll, I guess."

She shrugged. It was both dismissive—as if it was no big thing to go head to head with Jeannie Hannaford—and proud, that shrug. Rosabelle Waterman had come a very, very long way from the timid, shy girl she used to be, there was no doubt of that.

"Anyhow," said Rosabelle, "I told Jeannie she could host the engagement party if she wanted. Gave her full rein too. 'Invite whoever you want,' I said. That seemed to make her happy enough."

"But what about your parents?" asked Mae.

"Well, they'd never admit it, but I believe they were relieved the Hannafords took on the engagement party. Looks like they'll be stretching their finances in the coming months," said Rosabelle, resigned.

"Oh? How come?"

"Well, Steven has convinced Ruth to move back to Chance, effective immediately." Rosabelle gave Mae a plastic, ultra-cheery smile, then slumped theatrically.

"You're kidding? In the motor home? I don't understand."

"Not exactly. My darling husband-to-be is brokering the sale of Brian Donovan's house. The closing will be sometime next month. So, yay. Right?"

"Aw, it'll be fine. You'll see. Hey, speaking of Brian Donovan, that reminds me—have you heard or seen from Fat Chris since the accident? Bruce said that Brian and Skinny Chris have been working extra because Fat Chris still hasn't come back from his mother's house. I hope he's all right."

"No, nothing since the accident. You think I should reach out to him? Let him know everything is fine? I mean, honestly, I don't blame him. It was an *accident*. The road was icy and, well, it happened."

"I'm sure he'd appreciate that. Bruce said he was a mess after."

With that settled, the pair moved on to excitedly planning the March wedding details. The ceremony could be held on the patio, reception inside. Mae would, by a matter of course, cater the event.

"Do you think Charles Brightsider might be willing to play the wedding march?"

"I'm sure he'd be thrilled. I'm going to see them later, so I can ask."

"How *is* Georgie? I think Miles was more disturbed than he'll admit. He keeps reading me things from the internet like 'surprising warning signs' of a stroke, and 'things you should do immediately after someone suffers a stroke.' I swear Miles thinks *he's* going to have a stroke now that he's seen someone having one. God, I hope I'm not marrying a hypochondriac."

To herself, Mae thought, '*No, just a narcissist*,' but what she said was, "Oh, I'm sure you'll nip that right in the bud. And Georgie is stable right now. They want to keep her in the hospital for observation and testing though. There's a blood clot they're watching. I guess they're hoping the medication will help."

"He commissioned a painting from me just

before my accident. It's from a photograph of them when they first met. I started working on it last night."

"How sweet," said Mae.

"Isn't it? He wants to surprise her for their fiftieth wedding anniversary in May. I hope—"

"Me too," said Mae, not wanting to hear the words she knew Rosabelle intended to say.

Rosabelle put her hand over Mae's. "You're very fond of them, I know."

"They've been honorary grandparents to me. Even more so to Feather Anne. Did you know she's been visiting them since she was six years old? *Six*. I still can't wrap my brain around how Gina could be so negligent."

"Speaking of..." Rosabelle trailed off expectantly.

Mae lifted her shoulders and dropped them. "All right so far. It's an adjustment. My instinct says I'm doing the right thing, but I can't help having my reservations. Thank God for William. He's been a saint with all the madness."

"I think we may need to get the Queen of England to bestow him his knighthood. Do you think she can make it on short notice?"

The twosome laughed. They spent the next hour catching up on the latest news and goings on as well as Mae's burgeoning morning sickness symptoms and Feather Anne's obsession with the gestation cycle. All the while, Mae's thoughts hovered on the Brightsiders. At Charles's request, she'd downplayed the seriousness of Georgie's condition.

253

Chapter 32

Those Who Know

"How long have you known?"

"I think," said Charles, running a mildly arthritic finger around the rim of his coffee cup, "it was the from the moment I saw your face on the internet. The, uh, face book." He said it as two words. "Subconsciously, that is. Consciously, I remember thinking, my, he has such a familiar face, that young man on my wife's list of friends."

"Young." Craig chuckled, smoothing his thinning hair. "Been a long time since anyone has called me young, Mr.—"

"I think you can call me Charles, don't you?"

Craig nodded, then tried it out. "Charles. You know, we almost named my youngest Charles. That would've been a funny coincidence, wouldn't it?"

"Indeed," agreed Charles.

Hesitantly, Craig asked, "You—you didn't know

about me, did you?"

Charles face contorted in a brief flash of anger, then settled into sadness. Craig assumed he was angry at Craig's very existence, so he was surprised at his reply.

"All those *years*. My Georgie thought she had to carry that—that shame on her own. How it must have hurt her." He glanced up, apologetically at Craig. "The shame of giving up a child. Not the shame of having you. Also, I suppose, at the time that was part of it. Back in our day, good girls didn't—well, they—"

Craig let the poor man off the hook. "I understand, Charles. Really, I do. Georgie—it feels so strange saying her name out loud—she left a card and a picture with the foster home, to be given to the adoptive parents. She explained everything. Her regret, her hopes for the best life possible, her heartbreak."

Charles' eyes welled, and Craig looked away. He didn't have tears for this story. It never felt real to him. More a fairytale or someone else's story. Not plain old Craig Henry Davidson, schoolteacher, husband, and father of three. He'd read Georgie's words numerous times over the years. Studied her picture. He'd even made up fantasies of meeting her. But it never seriously occurred to him to seek her out. She gave him up. She didn't—or felt she couldn't, to be fair—keep him. He was Edward and Viv's, not Georgie Perri's kid.

It had been Marianne's idea, ultimately. She'd been the one to read William Grant's book, and to research the real-life people it was based on.

"Craig, honey," she had said from her side of the kitchen table, "did you know the elderly couple in 'A Summer in Small Town' is based on a couple named Charles and Georgie Brightsider?"

Craig, opposite her, had answered, "No, Marianne, I did not. I haven't read the book, remember?"

Marianne waved him away impatiently. "That's why I'm telling you, dear. Did you hear what I said? *Georgie* Brightsider."

"Mhmm, that's true, dear. It *isn't* a common name."

Craig feigned a mere casual interest in what Marianne was suggesting. Marianne knew better.

"I have a *feeling*, Craig. You know I'm almost always right when I get one of my intuitions."

"That's true, dear, you often are." Craig tried to go back to grading papers. Then, "I'm sure if there's anyone who could find out, it would be you."

It was his way of asking her to check, and Marianne, knowing her husband as she did, took the statement as permission. She'd opened her laptop and began typing rapidly. Twenty-five years as a stenographer gave her very fast hands.

Craig continued his pretense of disinterest and tried to read Kristy White's heinously written composition titled *Why American Literature is Important to Me*. It had been a punishment assignment for the class, a consequence for poor behavior in class the day before. He couldn't seem to get past, 'American literature is important to me because...' as he waited for what Marianne found.

"Ha, I found her," exclaimed Marianne triumphantly. "Easy-peasy. She's on Facebook. How about that?" Before Craig could answer, she said, "There, all set."

"What do you mean, 'There, all set?'" asked Craig, alarmed.

"I sent her a friend request. Well, you did. I'm on your account."

"Oh, Marianne, I wish you hadn't."

"*Pshht*, stop. This could be a good thing for you, Craig. You wouldn't have hung on to that photograph and that card if it didn't mean something to you."

Craig ignored her statement, and with a hint of petulance said, "How do you even know it's the right Georgie?"

Marianne turned the laptop to face Craig. A photo of an elderly woman stared back at him from the center of the screen. Platinum-white hair cut in a neat bob framed a well-lined, sun-weathered face. Her cheekbones were high and pink-tinged. Her lips, set in a polite smile, bore a hint of pale pink lipstick. She was a lovely, grandmotherly looking woman who probably gave the grandchildren cookies, but made them use their manners and sit up straight. Most striking, though, were her sharp, clear, denim blue eyes gazing steadily into the camera lens. They matched Craig's eyes exactly.

He could see the hint of the young woman she once was in those eyes. The defiance, the feistiness. Craig stood abruptly and went to the bedroom. From his bookshelf, between Faulkner and Hemingway, he pulled the card and slipped the old photograph out.

A silent Marianne watched as he held the picture up beside the computer screen, his eyes volleying between the two. There was no mistaking. It was the same woman.

Marianne had stood and was now behind him, one hand light on his shoulder. She said, "And she was a schoolteacher. English, same as you. No children, Craig. She only had you."

Craig had done nothing with the information, not at first. A day later, he saw that Georgie Brightsider had accepted his friend request. Two weeks after that, he received a message from her. After several exchanges, they decided to meet in person.

"So, you see, Mr.—Charles, I mean, I guess a part of me did always want to meet her, even if it was just once. But if I'm to be finally honest, I was afraid she wouldn't want to see *me*. When I got her last message, asking if I'd be willing to have coffee, something—I don't know, something in me just…" Craig was at a loss for words.

Charles helped him. "Opened. Something in you opened, and you decided to let Georgie in. That's very kind of you. I almost messaged you myself. I had this niggling feeling that I *knew* you, somehow. Your face had looked so familiar. And then, well, I guess I'm like your wife in that regard. Something in me just knew. Or suspected, at least. When I saw you in the hall, I was positive."

"Well, you're very gracious, sir. I'm not sure how I'd react if my wife—"

"Fifty years, son. Georgie is my world, and I'm hers. To be angry at her for something that happened before me, well, that'd be plain stupid. And cruel. I'm only sorry she thought she had to hide this. You."

"Is she—is she well enough to see me, you think?"

Charles smiled. "I think you're just the medicine she needs right now. Come on, I'll bring you in and then give you two time alone together."

Chapter 33

In The Frosty Air

Brianna grabbed the handles of the large picnic basket in the backseat, balancing Cassidy on her hip as she did. Elise had offered to babysit but having Cassidy with her was the only way Ricky would let her stick around.

"Okay, baby girl, you ready to visit Daddy at work?"

"Da-ddy, work," agreed Cassidy cheerily.

"That's right, we're going to see Daddy at work. We're bringing him lunch. How does Mommy look?"

Usually, when Brianna asked Cassidy this question, she would yell, 'Pri-ty. Momma yook pri-ty,' and clap. Today Cassidy appraised her curiously, patted her cheek and elected not to answer the question.

"Thanks a lot, kid," huffed Brianna, hooking the

basket in the crook of her free arm.

Both Cassidy and the basket were heavy, and the auto body lot was pot-holed and uneven, with patches of slushy, dirty snow in many spots. It was a surprising relief not to be wearing heels for once.

When Brianna awoke that morning after a mostly sleepless night, she'd decided—with a manic zeal—that she and Cassidy would surprise Ricky at work. Elise called it an ambush, which she chose to ignore. She hurriedly showered, thrown her hair in a short, sprouty-looking ponytail, and prepared a king's feast. She was well aware of Mrs. Teccio's disapproving bafflement as she tended to Cassidy.

"Missy Brianna, you no wear a dress today," asked Mrs. Teccio in a way that sounded less a question and more an admonishment.

"No, but thank you, Mrs. Teccio. These jeans are fine."

"But this," she fanned her plump hand at Brianna's face and sweatshirt—technically Ricky's sweatshirt—and clucked her tongue several times, "this a no *good*, Missy. You put on a the makeup, yes? Fix a the hair. Look a *nice* for you husband, no?"

"Please, just get Cassidy ready for me, Mrs. Teccio?"

Brianna couldn't tell her nanny that her husband despised her, and she was desperate and that no amount of makeup or pretty clothes would change anything. She was in full panic mode and virtually pathological in her need to save her marriage. Her only hope now was that persistence would wear him down, eventually.

Brianna stepped carefully through the muck, glancing nervously around in mixed hope and fear of seeing Ricky. It had been nearly a week, and he still refused to see her, sending his sister and mother to pick up and drop off Cassidy. They were polite but aloof with her. She'd avoided meeting their eyes as shame and mortification consumed her, recalling her past humiliations and feelings of self-loathing and disgust.

"Bri? What are you doing here?"

She looked up sharply at the sound of Ricky's voice and lost her balance. He hurried to her and took Cassidy from her arm, glancing around warily, as if all eyes were on them. Conceivably they were, she realized. Had he told them about her...transgression? How she thought—wrongly—that Cassidy was another man's child? Her face flushed a violent shade of red, then drained as quickly. She felt a wave of nausea.

Ricky grabbed her arm at the elbow and led her toward the new section of the building. He didn't exactly pull her, nor was he especially gentle. Still, he hadn't let her fall, so that was something.

"I—sorry. I just thought I'd bring you lunch. And, well, Cassidy's been asking for you, so—"

"Don't use her to guilt me, Brianna. I thought I told you to stay away."

She pretended not to hear him. "Hey, the addition looks great. Is that your office over there?"

She pointed to a large, square, windowed section at the far-left corner of the spacious room. It abutted the auto body shop and had two doors, one to the shop, and another to the showroom. For maybe the first time, Brianna realized just how good Ricky was at what he did. The addition was his idea and design, and the initiative his too. His father had been instrumental in moving the process along, but ultimately, it had been solely Ricky's hard work.

He avoided eye contact and shifted Cassidy to his other hip, so he could point. "Yeah. Over there I'm having a coffee and snack station put in. Right there is gonna be a playroom for when people want to look at cars and need the kids to be distracted. Plus, it'll be perfect for when Cassidy is here. I'm putting in a playscape out back in the spring too."

Brianna's eyes stung. "You're a great Daddy, Ricky. Cassidy's a lucky little girl."

It was the wrong thing to say, a reminder that Cassidy had almost *not* been his little girl, and Ricky's face closed off again.

"Yeah, well…listen, I got a lot of shi—stuff to do. Thanks for the food." He kissed Cassidy, nuzzled her cheek and said, "All right, sunshine girl. You go with Mommy. Daddy's got to work, work, work."

He handed her over without looking at Brianna, but mid-pass, Cassidy decided to cling to both of them, drawing the threesome close.

"Mommy, Daddy, Cass-dee hug," said Cassidy, squeezing their necks.

It was a ritual, the Mommy, Daddy, Cass-dee hug, and it was always followed by, 'Mommy kiss Cas-dee, Daddy kiss Cass-dee. Daddy kiss Mommy, yayyyy.'

They followed their toddler's commands, but when it came time for Daddy to kiss Mommy,

Ricky's face turned to stone. Cassidy insisted, her little voice raised determinedly.

"Daddy kiss Mommy, *now*."

Cassidy pushed their faces together with surprisingly strong tiny hands. Ricky kept his eyes trained over Brianna's shoulder and his lips grazed the corner of her mouth. She reached up to touch his cheek, but he'd already pulled back, abruptly pushing Cassidy into her arms and turning away.

She started to call out, "Don't forget your—" but the shop door had closed with a metallic clank before she could say, "lunch."

The basket remained on the floor of the newly tiled showroom, lonely and dejected. Brianna knew she was projecting her feelings on the inanimate object, that it was just a basket of food on a floor. But the sight of it made her eyes and nose sting with the threat of tears.

Chapter 34

Under The Weather

"Your first ultrasound, how exciting," squealed Aunt Katrina through the phone.

"I know, I know. I'm so nervous. What if—"

"No. Nope, stop that. Everything will be perfectly fine. Oh, God, you're not one of those neurotic pregnant women, are you? I will take back that pregnancy book if you plan on behaving like a crazy lady. How many times have you called the doctor's office?"

Mae pouted, then giggled. "Three times. Okay, four. It said not to pick up cat litter. I got nervous."

"Mae, honey? You don't *have* a cat."

"I know that. But we have chickens, and goats, and I thought maybe if cat litter is dangerous, then maybe—"

"Let me guess. It's fine?"

"Yes."

265

Aunt and niece bantered and teased for several more minutes until William finally leaned into the kitchen, tapped his watch and motioned for her to wrap it up.

"Okay, gotta go. The boss-man has started the meter. Call you after the appointment."

As they said their goodbyes, the café phone rang. Mae motioned for William to answer.

"Okay, Gina. You shouldn't get more than a couple post-breakfast stragglers while we're gone. Bruce may or may not show up as usual. Claudia and Paulina will be here within the hour, and I'll be back in plenty of time."

William hung up the phone, his face set in a frown. "Little bit of a glitch in the plan. That was the school nurse. Feather Anne has a fever and needs to be picked up."

"Damn it, I *thought* she seemed off this morning," said Mae. She hesitated, then said, "Okay, then. You'll have to go pick her up, and I'll just go to the appointment."

Gina wanted badly to offer to help, but her license was still suspended, and the best she could do was watch the café while they were gone and then take care of Feather Anne when they brought her home. She told them, "I'm sorry I can't be more helpful to you."

"It is what it is," said Mae distractedly.

She was sorely disappointed, but making Gina feel badly wouldn't help anything. William, equally frustrated and disappointed—but equally practical—nodded his head in agreement.

"Are you sure you want to go alone? Maybe we

can reschedule the appointment?"

"Dr. Srinivasan is going away for two weeks as of tomorrow. I don't want to wait any longer, I'm going crazy with impatience."

"Of course. I understand. All right, I'll go straight to the school, get Feather Anne home, then meet you there."

"Perfect. See you soon."

William left out the front, and Mae out the back. Gina looked around, cursing her uselessness and trying to think of something to do that Mae might appreciate.

Out back, Mae turned the key in the ignition of her trusty old Volvo. Nothing happened. She tried again. Nothing. Her frustration boiled over and she slammed her hand against the steering wheel.

"Damn it. Now, what am I going to do?"

Just then, Bruce's truck pulled into the lot. He frowned at Mae. He hopped out and came around to her car as she was climbing out, swearing in a most un-Mae-like manner.

"Hey, aren't you supposed to be going to your doctor's thing?"

"My ultrasound, and yes." Her tone was curt.

"What's wrong?"

"My stupid car won't start, and William had to pick up Feather Anne at school, and Gina is useless because her license is suspended. Oh, and I—"

"Hop in the truck, Mae."

"No, Elise will get mad."

"Stop, it'll be fine."

Mae sniffed. "You don't mind taking me?"

"Get in the truck, Mae. Come on, move it."

Mae did as he said, smiling weakly. Her emotions were all over the place these days. One minute she was angry, the next weepy. She knew it was to be expected, but boy, was it exhausting.

"So, how've you been? Haven't seen you in ages," said Mae archly.

Bruce gave her a look. "You mad at me?"

"No." Mae shrugged, turning her head away.

"Yeah, you are. Sorry, kid. It's been hectic."

They both knew that was only partially true. The other truth was that something had shifted in their friendship, creating a chasm, and that thing was simply *life*. They both had others to fill their time and their needs. Others who loved them and depended on them. Others who tolerated the bond Bruce and Mae shared *because* of the love they felt for them. The pull was inevitable.

"It's okay. I get it." And she did. It didn't mean she had to like it though.

"All right, we're here." Bruce turned off the ignition and looked at her expectantly. "Aren't you going to—hey, what's wrong?"

Mae had begun to cry. "I have no idea. I have no idea why I'm crying." She covered her face. "I'm nervous, I guess. I'm scared that something is wrong. You hear that all the time. What if there's no heartbeat, or the baby is—"

"Whoa, whoa. Hey. Come here, knucklehead." Bruce pulled her into an awkward hug over the center console. It jabbed him hard in his side, but he didn't mind. "What do you say I go in with you? Just, you know, until William gets here. Okay?"

Mae, her head still in her hands and her forehead

against the cold coat button of his coat, nodded and mumbled, "Yes, please."

"All right, then. Wipe your face and let's do this."

Across the street, coming out of a Dunkin Donuts was Brittany Sheffield. "Hang on, I'll have to call you back."

She disconnected the call and hit her phone's camera icon and took several pictures. She made sure to get the signage above Bruce and Mae's head too.

"Women's Health Network, hmm? I'm sure Elise will appreciate *this*," said Brittany to herself. She drank her too hot coffee, burning her tongue.

***

"Thanks for coming so quickly, Mr. Grant. Her fever is one-hundred and two point three and I suspect she has strep. You'll need to get her to the doctor's office before they close. And remember, she can't come back to school until twenty-four hours after her fever has gone," said the school nurse firmly.

"Yes, of course, thank you," said William. "Hey, sport. How you feeling?"

"Like a poop emoji," said Feather Anne weakly.

"Well, I don't know what that is, but I assume that's not a good thing. Let's get you home."

"You mean the doctor's office, Mr. Grant. Strep is no joke."

"Ah, yes. Right."

William had a suggestion of where she could

take her tone but thought better of it. He fished his phone from his pocket instead and dialed Mae's number. It went straight to voicemail.

"I suppose you don't know where your doctor's office is, do you?"

Nurse Know It All gave him a censorious glare, to which he wanted to say, 'My wife handles these things,' which would have made him look chauvinistic, so he ignored her.

Feather Anne said, "Dr. Fleishman, on Main Street."

"Right, yes. Let's go see Dr. Fleishman, then."

It appeared he would not be making it to the ultrasound after all. William dialed Mae's number again, this time leaving her a message, then drove Feather Anne to the doctor resignedly.

Chapter 35

Loved Ones Are Near

"Georgie, sweetheart? I've brought someone in to see you," said Charles tenderly.

"Oh, Charles. My hair isn't—"

"Your hair is perfect. Now listen to me. Everything is fine. Wonderful in fact." Charles motioned for Craig to come forward. "I've had a lovely chat with this delightful young man and I suspect we're about to be fast friends."

"Hello, Georgie. It's very nice to meet you. It—it's me, Craig. Your son."

Georgie raised a trembling hand to her mouth and tears began to spill from the corners of her eyes. She looked from Craig to Charles. Fear mixed with relief, joy with pain. It was written plainly on her face.

Charles took her free hand and reassured, "It's all right, my darling. It's all right. I'm just so sorry you carried such a secret alone, my dear."

"Oh, Charles," said Georgie, overcome. Her eyes drifted to Craig, who stood shyly at the end of the hospital bed. "You're even more handsome in person."

Craig ducked his head and ran his hand over his hair. He was smiling though. "Why, thank you. I'm a little nervous, I must admit."

"Me too." Georgie smiled. "Come, sit beside me, if you would."

Craig obliged, pulling a chair close to the bed and sitting at the edge of it.

Charles patted Craig's shoulder and gave him an encouraging nod. To Georgie, he said, "I'm going to let you two get acquainted. I'll just run home and check on Rufus and Mabel, should you need me."

He kissed his wife's cheek and winked at Craig, then left them alone. In the lobby, he ran into Miles Hannaford, who acted excessively pleased to see him.

"Mr. B. How *are* you? How is Mrs. B.? I haven't been able to stop thinking about you both. After the thing at the store—you know, Mrs. B.'s stroke—"

"Yes, son, I knew what you meant. That's very nice of you to come by, but Georgie has a visitor right now."

"Oh," said Miles. "Bummer. Well, is there anything I can do for you? Anything you need?"

"All set for now, thanks. Unless…" Charles appraised Miles, "how are you with dogs, Miles?"

"Dogs? I love dogs. Um, why?"

Charles took out his house keys and gave instructions to the very eager to please Miles, secretly marveling at the changes in him. Had to be the Waterman girl, no other explanation for it.

"You think you can do that?"

"Yes, sir. No problem. Glad to help. To be honest, it was Rosabelle's idea for me to come see Mrs. B. You know, see that she's all right. I guess I've been driving her nuts."

"Well, seeing someone have a medical emergency can be upsetting. Totally understandable," said Charles sympathetically.

Charles's phone buzzed in his pocket and he lifted his finger to Miles. "One moment, son. I'll just see who this is." He recognized the hospital extension at once. His first and only thought was of Georgie. He shouldn't have left her side.

"Mr. B.? You okay? You look—shit. Hey! Hey, someone help," shouted Miles as Charles Brightsider crumpled to the floor.

Chapter 36

Tidings We Bring

Bruce pulled into the café lot beside Mae's car and turned off the ignition.

"You okay?"

"No. Yes. I don't know," said Mae, her eyes saucer wide.

"Everything will be okay, Mae. *You're* going to be okay. You got William and Feather Anne. Shit, you got me and everyone else."

"I know. Hey, I can't thank you enough for staying with me and coming in for the ultrasound. I couldn't have handled the news on my own."

"You're one of the strongest women I know, Mae. You could've handled it, but I'm glad you didn't have to. Now, let's close up shop and get you home."

***

"All right, my dear. Antibiotics taken, ibuprofen administered, DVD in, blanket on. How'd I do?"

"Perfect, William. When's Mae getting back?"

William tried to not be offended by Feather Anne's vaguely patronizing tone and the request for her sister. "Any moment now. Although she can't come near you, so you're stuck with me, I'm afraid."

"That's fine. I just want to see the ultrasound picture. Aren't you excited?"

"Indeed, I am," said William.

There was an ominous tone to Mae's text that raised an alarm in William. However, he would not concern the child with it until he knew. If Mae had been delivered unhappy news without him by her side, he'd never forgive himself.

When the front door opened and closed, he nearly tripped over his own feet in his rush to greet her. Gina came in with Mae and excused herself to her room, shooting William an 'I don't know anything,' shrug.

"Mae, sweetheart, I'm so sorry I couldn't get there. Feather Anne has strep, so she's in quarantine. Come, sit. You look white as a ghost."

William steeled himself for bad news, and he had to be strong for her. For both of them.

"You sit too, William. You're going to need to as much as I do."

From her purse, she pulled a rectangular paper the size of a photograph and handed it to him. It was, quite obviously, a sonogram. William felt a small surge of relief, there *was* a baby, this much he understood. He stared at the image, not comprehending.

"What are the two plus symbols? A and B? What is that?"

"It's not a that, William. It's a *they*."

"They? You mean—it's a—we're having…"

"Twins, William. Heaven help us, we're having twins," said Mae, shell-shocked, but beginning to grin.

A tremulous smile spread across William's face, crinkling his eyes. "Two for the price of one, huh," he said wonderingly.

"Oh, it'll be two for the price of two, you can bet on that," corrected Mae.

"This is—" William's voice broke, and he gave a small, shaky laugh. "What wonderful news, my love. We are so very blessed, aren't we?"

Mae hadn't realized how tense she'd been until those words. *Blessed, indeed.* Terrified, overwhelmed, but yes—blessed.

The house phone rang and William—after kissing his wife—went to answer.

"I see," said William after a pause. "Yes, of course. I will do just that. Thank you for letting us know, Rosabelle."

Mae stood and turned to William, her heart sinking at his somber expression.

"Sweetheart, Charles collapsed in the hospital lobby. Miles was there with him and called Rosabelle. It doesn't look good, I'm afraid."

Chapter 37

A Season To Remember
Three Months Later

The first day of spring came and went without much ado. The sun made fleeting appearances through the thin, bruised-looking clouds and daffodils stayed tightly shut and shuddering in the breeze. The ground still bore the remnants and reminders of a harsh, long winter in patches and stubborn mounds of ashen, dirty snow.

By the second week of spring, Mother Nature decided to give in and reward Chance with a true, postcard-worthy spring day. By mid-morning, the sun shone brightly from a clear blue sky, the gritty snow piles became sparkling puddles, and the bright yellow buds ruptured the thin papery casings.

"A new beginning," said Rosabelle, breathing in the fresh air. "I love spring, don't you?"

Miles grumbled. "Eh, not so much. Late spring,

sure. But right now, it sucks showing houses. Everything is muddy and blah. Everyone's grass looks like crap."

"Wow, thanks, Debbie Downer," said Rosabelle, rolling her eyes.

"Sorry, babe. Hey, how's the painting coming along?"

Miles left his laptop and listings to stand over Rosie's shoulder. She set her brush on the palette and leaned back against him.

"Final touch is done. What do you think?"

"You've outdone yourself, Rosie. I mean it. You captured Mr. and Mrs. B. perfectly. It'll look amazing at the ceremony."

***

"Mae, can you waddle over here and help me with my bow?"

"I do not waddle, thank you very much," said Mae indignantly.

"Feather Anne, be nice to your sister," ordered Gina from the kitchen.

From down the hall, William called, "Darling, could you waddle here next and help me with my tie?"

Mae scowled, told them both what they could do with their bow and tie, respectively, then went to help Gina in the kitchen. As it turned out, they worked well together.

***

"How long does it take—"

"Uh oh, stop there, my friend. I may not be able to give much advice here, but one thing I can say for sure is, never rush Elise when she's doing her hair," said Ethan sagely.

Bruce flopped back onto the couch and loosened his tie. Jack sprang up and said, "Shall I?"

Together, Bruce and Ethan said, "Be my guest."

Ethan sat across from Bruce and said fondly, "He's really found his calling. Who knew a travel agent could make such a damn good hairdresser?"

"Well, aren't all you gay guys good at that stuff," asked Bruce with a smirk.

"We're good at everything, honey. Except for being straight," deadpanned Ethan.

The men clinked beer bottles together and Bruce turned on the football game, resigned to the fact that they'd be late in getting to the ceremony.

***

Brianna waited in the car, fussing with the seam on her black pants. Cassidy had fallen asleep in her car seat and the quiet was deafening.

At last, the driver's side door opened, and Ricky sat behind the wheel. He didn't look at her, he didn't smile. But he *had* picked her and Cassidy up to go to the ceremony. It was a start. It was a very good start.

***

All across Chance, mothers hurried their children to cars, fathers checked their pockets for keys, and kids tugged at too snug shirt collars or dresses. Neighbors waved and dogs barked. It was just another day in suburbia.

Only, it wasn't just another day. It was one of goodbyes and new beginnings. It was and end of an era and the promise of a fresh start. Uncertainty and hope intertwined for some, while for others, sense of foreboding ruled. The mild spring winds carried with it the scent of cut grass, daffodils, and life's greatest inevitability…change.

To Be Continued…

Acknowledgements

Before I ever began writing Welcome to Chance as a series, I had an idea for a couple books. One about the Brightsiders and another about Feather Anne. Then Mae came to mind, followed by William. It wasn't until a fateful conversation with my dear friend Jen that I understood these weren't separate stories, but interwoven ones. So, my first debt of gratitude goes to Jen. I'm humbled by my support system in pursuing my writing goals. Namely by my husband, who more than tolerates my hours upon hours hovering over a keyboard, the long discussions about fictional people, and his keen ability to spot a plot hole I've missed. My friends and family who cheer me on, invaluable. My dad is a big Welcome to Chance fan, which is both adorable and appreciated. My mom and daughters are first to share on social media and shout to the world my latest book. To my beloved Colvins, the inspiration for the great love my Brightsiders share. Thank you for letting us into your world. I'd be remiss to not count my author tribe as an influence. What an amazing, talented, generous group. We cheer, commiserate, and encourage one another and I'm proud to be among you. Lastly, my thanks go to the places. My hometown of Rocky Hill instilled a deep love for that small-town life. Sweet towns like Wethersfield and East Hampton sneak their way into the story too. The New England coastline, oh how I love you.

About the Author

Elsa Kurt is a multi-genre author and speaker. She has written nine novels, several short stories and a book for aspiring and new authors called *You Wrote It, Now What?* When not writing or sharing her experiences in writing, publishing, and promoting, Elsa can be found gardening or spending quality time with her husband, daughters, and two dogs. To learn more about Elsa and her books, visit elsakurt.com or at @authorelsakurt across social media. Elsa loves to hear from her readers at authorelsakurt@gmail.com.

Social Media Links

Facebook:
https://facebook.com/authorelsakurt/

Instagram:
https://instagram.com/authorelsakurt/

Twitter:
https://twitter.com/authorelsakurt

Goodreads:
https://www.goodreads.com/author/show/15177316
.Elsa_Kurthttps://allauthor.com/profile/elsakurt/

Bookbub:
https://www.bookbub.com/authors/elsa-kurt

Pinterest:
https://www.pinterest.com/authorelsakurt/pins/

Join our Reader Group on Facebook and don't miss out on meeting our authors and entering epic giveaways!

Limitless Reading

Where reading a book
is your first step to becoming
limitless...

LIMITLESS PUBLISHING *Reader Group*

Join today! *"Where reading a book is your first step to becoming limitless..."*

https://www.facebook.com/groups/LimitlessReading/

57134113R00172

Made in the USA
Middletown, DE
27 July 2019